THE GUINEA STAMP

Alice Chetwynd Ley

SAPERE
BOOKS

THE GUINEA
STAMP

Published by Sapere Books.

11 Bank Chambers, Hornsey, London, N8 7NN,
United Kingdom

saperebooks.com

ISBN: 978-1-912546-89-3

To Richard and Graham,
who share my interest in the past

"The rank is but the guinea stamp
The man's the gold, for a' that."
ROBERT BURNS

Chapter I: Both Sides of the Channel

The day was bright for November, but a cold, blustering wind was blowing across the cliffs of Boulogne. A grenadier of His Imperial Majesty's guard suppressed a shiver as he monotonously paced out his allotted patrol along the high wooden fence which railed off the Imperial Baraque from the cliff top. It was just his luck, he reflected, to be posted on guard duty here, the coldest spot in the camp. He thought enviously of those others in less exposed situations and allowed his eyes to wander for a moment over towards the huge, pearl-grey building which had been erected as Napoleon's headquarters.

As he did so, he noticed a man standing over by the Signal Semaphor, that gibbet-like apparatus which had been installed to convey messages from one section to another of the Grande Armée. This stranger was no soldier, that was certain. He wore the high boots of a fisherman, a dark jersey and breeches, and his head was bare. He had paused irresolutely on his way to the Imperial Baraque, as if uncertain of his next movement.

The grenadier, too, hesitated for a split second on his pacing.

Had the visitor any right to be there? Ought he to be challenged? Even as the soldier's foot came down to continue his patrol, he knew the answer to these questions. His orders had been to guard the fence, not the territory surrounding the Emperor's headquarters. That was the responsibility of others. It was not for him to assume duties which had not been allotted to him. The army was no place for initiative, as every serving man knew well.

The stranger had not long to wait. An officer came forward almost at once, clicking his heels smartly. One never quite knew who people were up here; appearances could be deceptive. It was as well to pay the stranger as much deference as one would give to a superior officer — for the time being, at any rate.

"Your pass, Monsieur?"

It was courteously spoken. The stranger presented a document encased in oilskin. The officer scrutinized it carefully, taking his time.

"The Emperor expects to see me without delay," said the man.

His tone was quiet, but carried authority, his accent was that of the cultured Frenchman. The officer shot a keen glance at him.

"At once, Monsieur. Be pleased to follow me."

He led the way to the Baraque. From this grey building, Napoleon was able to survey his four principal camps, which stretched over an area of ten kilometres. The "Iron Coast", they called it, and not without reason; for from Étaples to Cap Gris-Nez it was bristling with guns, armoured forts, and picked troops which kept pouring in from all parts of France to swell the ranks of the Grande Armée which was to conquer England.

The fisherman was shown into the principal chamber of the Baraque, a large, lofty apartment hung with a silver grey paper and lighted by numerous long windows. Evidently he had not been here before, for his gaze briefly travelled round the room. There was only one chair that he could see, and that was drawn up to a long oval table covered by a green cloth. He approached, and made as if to sit down.

"*Sacré Nom!*"

The startled officer covered the distance between door and table in two strides and jerked the chair hurriedly from the visitor's grasp. The fisherman raised his eyebrows in mild surprise, but said nothing.

"Pardon, M'sieur! No one — but no one — may sit in this chair excepting only the Emperor! It is not permitted that any lesser person should sit at all in this apartment — even the Council must stand at meetings. It is understood, no?"

The visitor gave the slightest of shrugs, and turned away from the Imperial throne.

"*Soit*," he replied, docilely enough.

The officer eyed him keenly for a moment, then drew himself up and saluted.

"I will inform His Imperial Majesty of your arrival, M'sieur," he said, and quitted the room in good military order.

When the door had closed upon him, the visitor smiled somewhat enigmatically, and walked over to the seaward windows.

He was a young man of not more than middle height, slim, with good shoulders. His dark hair was ruffled by recent exposure to the keen wind, and his face and hands wore the brown, weather-beaten appearance of the man who spends his life in the open. There was nothing remarkable in his features, but the eyes were keen and alert, the expression one of intelligence. He carried himself well, as though poised for instant action, and his step was light in spite of the great boots he wore.

For a time he stood at the window looking thoughtfully across the Channel in the direction of England. It was impossible to discern the coastline with the naked eye, but he had heard that on fine days one could see the walls of Dover Castle from here with the aid of a telescope. Could it be that in a few weeks or months that fortress would yield, as London itself might yield, to the mighty conqueror who already had enslaved half Europe? With an abrupt gesture, he turned from the window to where an enormous map of the Channel and coasts hung on the grey tinted wall. He considered it for a few moments, brows knit in thought, then allowed his attention to wander to the painted ceiling of the room. Here a huge eagle was depicted moving through an azure sky dotted with golden clouds, directed by the Star of Bonaparte to discharge a thunderbolt at England. His brow cleared, and a slow smile twisted his lips.

He checked it as a footfall sounded from outside the room. With an expression of suitable gravity, he turned to face the door.

It opened, to admit a man of short stature, clad in a well-cut uniform of fine grey cloth. His black hair was brushed flat over a high forehead, and a pair of piercing dark eyes looked out from a sallow complexioned, though not unhandsome, face. At sight of him, the fisherman straightened, and bent his head deferentially.

"Majesty."

"Captain Jackson, I believe?" Napoleon's voice was curt and deep. "You have dispatches for me?"

The man called Captain Jackson produced a package from a concealed pocket, and handed it to the Emperor. Napoleon received it wordlessly, tore the seal, and glanced at the date.

"Eight days old! Too long, by God!"

"Tide and wind, Majesty, are at no one's bidding."

A sharp look from the dark eyes seemed to pierce into the fisherman's mind. It lasted only a second, then Napoleon moved over to the table, seated himself, and gave his full attention to the document before him. Captain Jackson waited, relaxing his stance a little.

"It is well," remarked the Emperor, at last, pushing the chair impatiently from the table arid standing upright. "As far as it goes, that is to say. Captain!"

Jackson jumped to attention.

"Majesty?"

"You have lately been in England for some time, I understand."

"That is so, sire."

"What have you to say of the situation there?" Captain Jackson answered without hesitation.

"Catastrophic, sire. Invasion is talked of everywhere, and hourly expected. Fieldworks have been thrown up on all the principal roads to London, and Martello towers are being built at frequent intervals round the coast. The lodging-house keepers of East Bourne in Sussex complain that the erection of a barracks on the beach quite ruined their trade this summer."

"Pah!" His Imperial Majesty snorted. "A nation of shopkeepers and farmers! Shall such a country be allowed to impede the destiny of mankind?"

"It would appear unlikely, certainly," replied Jackson, in a judicial tone.

"Impossible!" was the emphatic retort. "They want us to jump the ditch, and, by God! we shall jump it!"

"Assuredly," answered the fisherman, soothingly. "But it would be folly to allow oneself to imagine that England will be found unprepared. Already 340,000 men have come forward for service in the volunteer forces, and daily their numbers swell. Even the Prime Minister, Mr. Pitt himself, takes his part as Colonel of the Cinque Port Volunteers. Fashionable tailors are swamped with orders for showy uniforms, for each corps has its own particular dress."

"Pah! A nation of dandies, too!"

"As you say, Majesty. But do not be deceived; it is also a nation of sportsmen and even the dandy has usually learnt the art of self-defence."

Napoleon eyed him keenly.

"You I do not at all understand. You are an Englishman, no?"

Captain Jackson bowed slightly, but made no other reply.

"You are a man of education, I think, in spite of your so humble appearance. Your French is not the tongue of the *sansculotte*. Why, then, are you ranged against your countrymen? Why are you a smuggler and a spy?"

The captain shrugged, and spread his hands in a typically Gallic gesture.

"A man must live, sire. Under your gracious protection, free trade is a lucrative business. For the rest — I have my reasons."

"Which you do not mean to divulge? As you will. There are ways, however, of obtaining any information I may desire of you. I warn you, Captain, that those who seek to hoodwink Napoleon do not prosper."

"I am sure of it, Majesty. But this, you will allow, is a powerful incentive to any man to keep faith — or to break it."

He drew forth from his pocket a heavy canvas bag, and dropped it upon the table. The chink of coin instantly claimed His Imperial Majesty's attention.

"Gold?"

Captain Jackson nodded. "English guineas. There is more, if I can obtain wine of the right quality — at the right price."

Napoleon nodded, and began to stride about the room.

"You will be offered every facility. We must have gold! Gold to build fine ships and yet more ships — would to God I had some of the old sailors to man them, men of the calibre of the Grande Armée!"

"In England, the complaint is otherwise," stated Captain Jackson. "The condition of the vessels leaves much to be desired."

"Good! That is good! You would also say that the men —"

"The British Navy," replied Captain Jackson, gravely, "is still of the same quality as always."

Napoleon grunted. "Almost I trust you, for you do not bring me the account I wish to hear! You must learn the art of flattery, Captain, if you would prosper. But I can waste no more time with you. Go to Rochefort. I will give orders for your safe passage —"

A deafening burst of gunfire interrupted him. With an oath, he strode towards the seaward windows. Captain Jackson followed at a more leisurely pace.

All at once, the ground surrounding the Baraque was swarming with men. Grenadiers bustled hither and thither, officers shouted orders, their hoarse voices adding to the din of the guns. The Emperor threw up one of the windows and barked a question at the nearest group of officers. They came smartly to the salute.

"A British frigate, Majesty. They are firing on the Wooden Fort *again* —"

"*Nom d'un nom d'un nom*! Have we not a Navy? Have we not shore batteries? How is it that the enemy can approach unhindered thus closely to our coasts? Send for the Minister of Marine! Send for Admiral Bruix! Send for —"

Another loud burst of gunfire intervened. Four or five officers leapt as one man to do their Emperor's bidding.

Napoleon slammed the window shut, and took to pacing the room, his brows thunderous. Captain Jackson watched him in silence.

"We shall see!" Napoleon said, in intense tones. "We shall see! A favourable wind, and 36 hours — we shall be in London before the year is out!"

It was evident that he had completely forgotten the fisherman's presence. Captain Jackson waited patiently for a little longer, then ventured to break in upon the Imperial reverie.

"Have I your permission to retire now, Majesty?"

"*Comment?*"

Napoleon awoke unwillingly from his dream of entering London at the head of the victorious Grande Armée. He waved a hand wordlessly in dismissal.

Captain Jackson bowed low, and made his way from the Council Chamber to the reverberating echo of gunfire.

A light rain was falling monotonously. The river showed grey in the distance and patches of mist floated wraith-like over the sodden fields. The mud-splashed carriage drew to a standstill before reaching the crossroads and the coachman dismounted to consult his passenger.

"This be the village of Teignton, my lord."

The passenger poked his head from the window and surveyed without enthusiasm the deserted, rain-spattered road, the cottages of cob and thatch, which in summer would appear so picturesque under a riot of roses, and the moss-grown lychgate leading to the church. A poster was pinned to the gate; rain and wind had spoilt its pristine freshness but its impact was still strong. One word only appeared upon it, for words could have little meaning to a population that was for the most part illiterate. The word was printed in large letters of fiery red: INVASION. The picture underneath this caption left even the least imaginative of its viewers in no doubt as to the meaning of that single word.

Whether from sight of the poster or from contact with the chill November air, the passenger gave a slight shudder. The sudden movement brought a shower of raindrops down his neck, causing him to draw his head back again within the shelter of the carriage.

"The place we seek is a mile or so beyond the village itself," he said to the coachman. "We must go right at the crossroads, continuing along the road until we approach the Manor House. There is a turning hard by the house, which leads down to the river: it is this lane we must take. I am told that Teignton Manor is the only large house hereabouts, so there should be no difficulty in identifying it. I was also told that the lane is just passable for coach traffic, though it is narrow and rough. Let us hope I was not misinformed."

The coachman glanced at his horses, and echoed these sentiments, if not aloud. He remounted the box, and carefully negotiated the turning at the crossroads. A short journey brought them to the high stone wall which surrounded Teignton Manor. They at once perceived the lane which they were seeking. It was bounded on its one side by a wall of the Manor, and on its other side by a high bank.

The passenger reflected with satisfaction that, once in the lane, they would at least be secure from observation. The coachman studied the track with strong disfavour. It wound downhill to the river bank, and therefore was well drained; but its surface of rough, uneven stones would play the devil with his horses, and it was so narrow that there could be no passing even a pedestrian in safety. He turned the vehicle neatly enough into it, however, and proceeded cautiously along the many twists and bends. Once the nearside wheeler stumbled and almost lost its footing, but was set right again with practised skill. The decline eased off towards the bottom, and the lane widened, revealing ahead an open stretch of rough ground on which stood a cluster of poor cottages, a small farm and a modest tavern. Behind these buildings was the misty river, grey and rainswept. The scene was inexpressibly dreary.

The coach came to a halt outside the tavern and the passenger alighted. He glanced at the sign, swinging on rusty chains. It badly needed a coat of paint, but its lettering was clear enough: "The Waterman".

"This is the place," he said. "Find an ostler, and stable the vehicle immediately."

The coachman touched his cap, and wondered if such a place ran to a stable, much less an ostler. He held his peace, however, and drove his elegant, though mud-splashed equipage over in the direction where he supposed the stables to be situated.

Meanwhile, his passenger walked swiftly through the rain to the front door of the building. He found it fast shut, though it was barely four o'clock in the afternoon. He glanced at the small windows on either side of the door; they were unshuttered, but close curtained, and showed no light. He picked up the knocker and rapped gently, three times in quick succession. After a short pause, he rapped again, this time a single beat.

Nothing happened for a while, and he began to have misgivings. He stepped back a pace, and glanced at the upper windows. There was a faint light showing behind the curtains in one of these. He stooped, picked up a handful of loose stones, and flung them against the pane. Then he returned to the door, and repeated his performance upon the knocker exactly as before.

This time, he heard the sound of heavy footsteps descending the stairs. Presently the bolts were drawn noisily back and the door was opened cautiously an inch or two, and a round, rubicund face was revealed, topped by a shock of untidy red hair. A pair of bright blue eyes regarded the visitor suspiciously.

"Good afternoon," began the traveller. "You are the landlord of the Waterman Inn, I take it?"

"I be," growled a husky voice, reluctantly. "But if y'r honour be lookin' for a bed for the night, I don't take nobody in 'ere. 'The Three Fishers' in the village is the place for that, clean and comfortable, and the good wife a rare cook, so they say."

"I am obliged to you," replied the visitor dryly. "But I don't propose to entrust my person to a village inn, whatever its reputation. I am come here to meet an acquaintance of mine — and of yours, as I understand."

The landlord's glance sharpened, but his hold on the door did not relax.

"If that be so," he said, slowly, "'appen there'll be a word by which I may know y'r honour."

The gentleman nodded, and a shower of raindrops dripped from his hat.

"The word," he answered briefly in a low tone, "is Horatio."

The man's brow cleared. He opened the door wider to admit his visitor.

"If y'r honour'll 'ave the goodness to follow me," he invited.

The stranger stepped inside. The passage was gloomy in the fading November light, and exuded a smell compounded of stale liquor and cooking. He wrinkled his nose fastidiously. The burly red-headed man closed the door behind them and shot the bolts.

"You do not appear to do much trade," remarked his visitor.

"Nobbut a few villagers and sometimes a servant or so from the big house," replied mine host, casually. "I gen'ally opens up a bit later on, like."

"One wonders how you contrive to make a living," said the gentleman dryly.

"I manage," was the short reply, as the man turned to lead the way down the passage.

They passed an open door on the left hand side of the passage which revealed a dingy taproom with sawdust-strewn floor. On the right hand side were two doors, both of which were closed. The visitor guessed that the first of these would lead to a small coffee-room, perhaps seldom in use in this strange hostelry. At the second, the landlord paused, and tapped softly before entering.

"Come in," invited a low voice.

The landlord stood aside, to allow the visitor to precede him into the room.

"Good God! Peter!"

The man who had risen from his chair directed a warning glance at the speaker.

"Captain Jackson, at your service, m'lord."

His bow was short, curt, yet curiously graceful. The tones of his voice were overlaid by a faint Devon burr.

The older man returned his salutation with an apologetic smile.

"Of course. I beg your pardon. I trust I am not too tardy? The journey was rough and dirty."

"Be seated, sir."

Captain Jackson waved his hand towards a comfortable looking chair close to the cheerful log fire. In contrast to the rest of the inn, this room appeared sufficiently cosy. Its walls were panelled in dark oak, and it was simply but attractively furnished as a parlour. He turned to the red-headed landlord.

"A bottle of the best, Nobby — and no interruptions afterwards. Understand?"

"As you say, Cap'n," rumbled the landlord, and departed on his errand.

"'Pon my soul, you take me aback!" said the visitor, apologetically. "Every time I see you, it strikes me afresh. Good God, it's incredible!"

"Then I beg you will strive to conceal your amazement, sir. Up to a point, the good Nobby and myself work together; but I must warn you that he is not privy to all my secrets."

"In the name of Heaven, who is?" asked the other, drawing closer to the fire and spreading his numbed fingers to the blaze.

"Only one other besides yourself — at least, so I trust," was the wry answer.

"I doubt if even I am aware of the whole! You've come a long way since that day three years since — do you recall it?"

Captain Jackson came over and stood with his back to the fire. He stared reflectively ahead of him, his grey eyes less keen than was their wont.

"Perfectly," he answered, slowly.

"You were foxed, and it was only three o'clock in the afternoon," said the visitor reminiscently. "They said you had been half seas over in drink for days, and you only in your twenty-second year! Your parents —" He broke off, and considered the younger man. A shadow passed across the

Captain's usually alert face. "They were disturbed," finished the speaker.

Captain Jackson nodded.

"Too much leisure, and insufficient occupation. Well, you found me a cure for that, my lord."

The other man stirred uneasily in his seat.

"I had no notion of your going in so deep, Peter."

"It will be better if you forget that name, sir. I and my confederates do not deal in names," warned the younger man. "Yes, well, I had only half a notion of it myself. Would you believe it, during that first six months I used to be most abominably seasick?"

"You would not be the first sailor to suffer from that malady. Nelson himself, so they say —"

A discreet tap sounded on the door. Captain Jackson placed a warning finger upon his lips, and stepped softly to open it. On seeing no one but the landlord standing outside, his manner relaxed.

"I'll take that, Nobby. Do you leave this gentleman and myself undisturbed for a while." He relieved the landlord of the tray which he carried, and shut the door. "Now, sir. I think you'll find that what I have here is almost worth a journey from London."

The tray held a bottle of wine and two glasses. Captain Jackson set it down upon a small oak table, and uncorking the wine, poured it, and handed a glass to his guest.

"What shall be our toast, my lord?"

"Your health, my boy. It requires constant pledging. At all times you are in grave danger."

The other shrugged.

"There are worse evils. Let us rather drink to victory over our enemies."

My lord raised his glass.

"To victory, then — and to those, like yourself, who are helping to make it possible."

He drank, then thoughtfully surveyed the wine in his glass.

"You are right, P— Captain Jackson. This liquor is indeed something out of the common way. Is it —?"

"Some of my contraband? You have conjectured aright. This never paid duty at any port, my lord."

"Then do not tell me of it," remonstrated the other. "As a member of His Majesty's Government, I ought not to be drinking contraband."

Captain Jackson laughed. "By all means leave it, my lord, since you feel so strongly."

The other man registered his horror at such an unlikely course of action, and, for a few moments, the two drank in silence, savouring the excellence of the wine. At last, the Captain set down his glass with an air of finality.

"And now, sir, to business," he said. "I have something here which I fancy would interest the Prime Minister himself."

He produced what appeared to be a coin from a concealed pocket, and handed it to his guest. My lord took it, carefully scrutinizing the small object.

It was a medallion engraved on both sides, and bearing an inscription. On the one side was an image which the statesman managed at last to identify as that of the legendary Hercules crushing the sea giant Antaeus. The engraving on the obverse side was less difficult of identification: it was the Emperor Napoleon, victoriously laurel-crowned. What made my lord gasp with surprise, however, was the inscription which he translated, reading aloud in stunned accents: "'Invasion of England. Struck in London, 1804'."

He turned a puzzled face towards the Captain. "What can this mean?"

"Only that His Imperial Majesty believes in being beforehand with the world. This and others similar were struck in Paris, against the time when Napoleon should hand them out to his victorious armies in London."

"Madman!" exclaimed the statesman. "Opinion in highest naval circles is firm that he can never bring off this invasion with such craft as we know him to have designed for the purpose. What, then, can he intend? Has he some other card to play?"

"Many, from what I myself have observed. To begin with, there are 175,000 men encamped in the vicinity of Boulogne and a flotilla of at least 2,000 boats of various kinds ready and waiting."

"It must first evade the Navy," observed my lord.

Captain Jackson smiled grimly. "True. With Nelson standing off Toulon and Cornwallis off Brest, their chances of pushing their noses out into the Channel are small indeed. But if they should come —"

"We shall be ready." The statesman's mouth set in a grim line. "Our Volunteers will be waiting on the beaches."

"Armed with pitchforks," said the other, with a grimace.

My lord finished his wine, and placed the empty glass upon the table.

"I grant you that we have not nearly enough arms to go round. But the spirit of the Militia is splendid, and a pitchfork can be a fearsome weapon in the hands of a desperate man."

Captain Jackson nodded.

"On the whole, I agree with you, sir. But our most deadly enemy is not across the Channel, but within England."

The statesman raised his brows.

"You refer, of course, to the French agents who are working over here?"

Captain Jackson nodded. "That medallion which you are holding has another use than the one for which it was originally made. It is also the link between Napoleon's agents, the passport which one must show to another as a token of belonging to a common cause. God knows, sir, how many of these things are at present in the country!"

My lord looked thoughtful.

"Some of these agents have already been arrested," he said consolingly. "Others, like your friends in this area, are left alone in the hope that one day they may lead us to the more important members of their organization. You say that you are convinced there is a key man in this area from whom all the others take orders; without him, the rest would be of little account."

"I am certain of it. And yet, ever since I brought those French agents across the Channel by Napoleon's orders, my helpers have kept constant watch on their movements without once coming within reach of this man."

"You are certain that he exists?" asked my lord.

"Positive. We know that the others receive orders, for at times, these messages have been intercepted — just as I myself receive orders, without knowing whence they come."

The older man nodded.

"I understood you to say that these messages are left for you in the cove where you also go to pick up the dispatches for France. What arrangements have you for making these collections?"

"I go to the appointed place in the first week of every month. It is a tiny cove some few miles north of Torbay, inaccessible from the shore save by a steep and dangerous climb over the cliffs, and only accessible from the sea at low tide. There is a deep cave into which a man must crawl for a matter of ten yards or so; after that, its height increases so that he may stand upright. No one who did not know the place would venture in. The dispatches and messages are left for me in a plain wooden box — there's no clue there, sir — on a kind of recess high up on one side of the cave. The dispatches are sealed, of course; but you know how little that has prevented us from reading and making a copy of them."

My lord nodded again.

"And the messages? They are never written by hand?"

"No," Captain Jackson shook his head, regretfully. "They are made up of printed words cut from the pages of a book, and pasted on to a sheet of ordinary letter paper, such as may be readily purchased by anyone. It is some time, however, since I received one of them." He paused a moment, then added, slowly, "I have reason to think that I am no longer completely trusted."

"What makes you say so?" The older man's tone was sharp with anxiety.

The Captain shrugged. It was a very different gesture from that which he had made in the presence of the French Emperor: this time, it was restrained, casual, totally English.

"A combination of circumstances," he answered. "In the first place, I have undoubtedly been followed about on several occasions; although I have always, I trust, succeeded in evading my pursuers. Then, too, this long gap in the receiving of orders — that is unusual, particularly in view of the fact that I'm positive there is some important scheme afoot at the present time."

My lord let out a quick exclamation. "What exactly do you mean?"

"I'm not sure," replied the other, slowly. "I may be wrong. But for the first time, I'm being told to do something quite out of the common way. I have orders to deliver a number of kegs of brandy to the cove of which we've just been speaking, and to leave them there in the cave."

"But I thought you said you were no longer given these orders?"

"This was a shipping order, given me in Rochefort by Napoleon's agent," replied Captain Jackson. "What's more, the casks have been specially marked, so that there can be no mistake."

"And is this all?" asked my lord. "I see no positive signs of anything untoward in that."

"Perhaps not; but I've never before been given cargo for any destination but such as my own men had decided upon. It's unusual, sir, and in this game anything out of the common way merits attention. I mean to discuss it with Number One tonight, when you have left."

The older man leaned forward in his chair, an earnest, troubled expression on his usually urbane countenance.

"I beg of you, Peter, give up this mad game now! You have done enough. When I suggested, three years since, that you might relieve your boredom by pretending to turn smuggler, thus obtaining news from the French coast, I had no notion of your being so thorough about the business — much less of your pretending to spy for the French! That was a rash, unconsidered move, in my opinion."

"And yet necessary," replied Jackson. "You see, sir, I soon found that it would not do merely to act the part of a smuggler. The French authorities welcome English smugglers to their coasts just so long as they bring the precious gold guineas which are needed for building boats and manning them.

Without the gold, I would very soon have found myself gracing the interior of a French prison. That could serve neither my country nor myself. No, the smuggling had to be genuine — and from that one step, the rest followed inevitably."

"I suppose so," conceded the statesman, reluctantly. "But tell me, how did you set about becoming a genuine smuggler? I have never heard the whole."

Captain Jackson laughed softly.

"Inquiries made in one or two unconventional Quarters along the Devon coast soon put me in touch with a genuine band of freebooters, as they call themselves. They were a harmless enough group of men who looked on the business simply as a means of getting a livelihood — it may surprise you to know that they are patriots to a man, but they see no reason why a war with France should put an end to their trade. I was fortunate enough to be able to be of some service to the leader of the gang — he was on the run from a Preventive officer at the time!"

My lord tut-tutted. "It all sounds most improper. Perhaps I had much better know nothing of it."

Captain Jackson grinned. "As you will, my lord. The ostrich, I believe, works on the same principle."

The older man ignored this thrust. "How much do these people know of your own personal concerns?"

"Very little," replied Jackson. "Their leader — whom I can trust, as he owes me his liberty — knows I am an English agent. To the rest, I am simply a man who can obtain the best contraband out of France. Once it is landed in England, running and selling it is their affair provided that they sell only for gold. The guineas are paid over to me, when they have taken the profits, to procure more contraband. Thus English smuggler and French authorities both get what they want."

"So you are a guinea smuggler," said my lord, uneasily. "That in itself is a serious matter — an act of treason, in fact. Do you realize that the currency regulations —"

The Captain grimaced.

"Spare me your Civil Service jargon, by your leave, sir. I am fully aware of the precarious legal position in which I stand. But to keep faith with England, I must needs betray her. Only as a guinea smuggler could I gain the confidence of Napoleon."

"There was no need for you to aim so high! I had it in mind that you might bring us news from the Iron Coast; not that you might penetrate to Napoleon's very Council chamber."

"As I have explained, my lord, one thing led to another. Once I was known as an English smuggler, I was approached by the French — firstly to collect dispatches from this agent of theirs in Devon, secondly, to act as an agent for them myself. It would have been impossible to refuse, even had I entertained such a consideration. But how could I do so? What better way could a man find to serve his country, than to have a foot in the enemy's camp?"

"True, true: and we have learnt much from you, my boy. But you must end the affair now, before it is too late. You say that already they suspect you. Should you be arrested here, in England, it would be difficult to bring you off safely: and should you be taken in France —" He broke off and shook his head. "No," he resumed. "My conscience cannot acquit me of doing a serious injury to your parents by allowing you to continue in this way. It must end, my boy."

"My parents cannot feel what they are in ignorance of: nevertheless, I am inclined to agree with you, sir. For some time now, I have felt that I had reached the limit of my usefulness in this particular sphere. My work henceforward must lie with the Navy. But there is one last task I have to perform before I quit my free-trading for good."

The other man nodded. "You mean to expose this French agent? Have you any plan to that end?"

Captain Jackson frowned.

"There is all too little to go upon, at present. He must live somewhere in this area, for two reasons. One is that the dispatches have always been concerned with news and maps of this part of the coast: the other, that the agents who are known to us are all stationed in this area, and are of little value unless they can easily be reached. The only contact I have with him is the collection of orders and dispatches from the cove. It is not a locality which lends itself readily to snooping, and in any event, it is many months since I found any orders there when I have called. I must simply wait for something to turn up, I'm afraid."

"Then I can only wish you speedy success, my boy, and recommend you to be careful. But, from what I chanced to hear in Town, you have other problems —" He broke off, startled. A thunderous knocking had sounded on the door of the inn.

The two looked at each other in some perturbation.

"Now, who can this be?" said the Captain, softly. "Not, I believe, one of Nobby's regular customers."

Almost on the words an alarmed Nobby arrived hotfoot in the room. The knocking continued to grow in volume.

"'Tis a body of men outside, Cap'n," he said, in trembling tones. "I caught a glimpse from the upstair winder: too dark to say 'zackly who they be, but my guess is it's they Preventives! What'll I do? I'll 'ave to open up to 'em!"

Captain Jackson nodded.

"Naturally," he said, calmly. "But there's no need for alarm. Your secret cellar is safe enough from discovery, and we shall make ourselves scarce in yonder cupboard."

He nodded towards the wall which separated the parlour from the small coffee room beyond. My lord followed his glance, but could see no sign of any cupboard.

"Well, go on, then, man!" urged the Captain. "Best take that guilty look off your face, too!"

The big man nodded, and turned towards the door. Abruptly, the thunder of knocking ceased, and a loud shout rang through the inn.

"Open in the King's Name!"

Chapter II: The Eavesdropper

"That's our cue!" grinned the Captain and propelled the other man towards the wall which he had indicated a moment since.

His long, sensitive fingers groped for a second along the panelling. Suddenly, there was a sharp click, and a section swung inwards revealing behind it a large space in which they might easily stand upright. He was about to follow his companion into the cupboard, when he checked with an exclamation of impatience, and turned again into the room.

"I'd forgotten these," he muttered as he snatched up my lord's hat and gloves from the table. "And we may as well bring some refreshment along too!"

He thrust the articles hastily into the other man's hand, and returned for the tray which held their bottle of wine and glasses. This he proceeded to stow away on a shelf at one side of the cupboard.

"Have a care!" protested my lord in a whisper. "You'll ruin my topper, old fellow!"

"Damn your topper," was the cheery retort, delivered in an undertone. "Can't think why you brought it on a jaunt like this, anyway!"

"You could not possibly suppose —" began the statesman, but broke off as the Captain squeezed himself into the cupboard, and shut the door.

The resulting darkness was momentarily overpowering.

"How long do you think it will be necessary to remain here?" asked my lord, doubtfully.

"God knows. Depends how long it takes Nobby to get rid of the Preventives."

The older man groaned inwardly, and asked himself what exactly a respectable member of His Majesty's Government was doing in such an unlikely situation. To be crouching in a cupboard in the company of an acknowledged smuggler, hiding from those officers whom he himself had helped to appoint, was suited neither to his style nor his time of life! Then he thought of the man at his side. While he served his country in this particular way, Captain Jackson must always remain on the wrong side of the law. If he were to be taken by the Preventive Officers, not even his friends in high places could count on bringing him off safely. The thought brought beads of perspiration to my lord's forehead.

"Don't worry," the Captain was saying in his ear. "We may stay here indefinitely, for there's a ventilator in this cupboard. It also makes a useful peephole into the room beyond, and it's concealed from view in there. The only snag is that sound carries through it, so should anyone come into the coffee room —" He broke off, as a tiny ray of light pierced the gloom of the cupboard. The next moment, they heard voices in the room beyond. Evidently someone had indeed entered the room, and the light of a lamp was striking thinly through the ventilator.

The voices drew closer. Captain Jackson stood on tiptoe, and peered through the ventilator. He could see no one as yet, for the aperture afforded a view only of that section of the room which was nearest the fireplace. He could hear Nobby's voice, however, explaining the impossibility of something which his visitors were urging.

"Well, at least the men may have a drink, and warm themselves for a while by the fire in the taproom, I suppose," came the reply in irritable tones. "Send in a bottle of wine and a bite to eat for this officer and myself. It's damned cold in here — can't you offer us a fire?"

"I'll have the wench kindle one for your honour at once," said Nobby. "But I dunno about victuals —"

"Do so, and look sharp about it. The men must be better off in the tap than we are here," was the terse reply.

The listeners heard the shuffling of the big man's feet as he hastened to obey this command, and just then the visitors moved into Jackson's line of vision. He saw at once that they were not, as Nobby had feared, Customs men at all, but two officers of the local Volunteers, arrayed in a striking uniform of scarlet with dark blue facings. The younger of the two bore the insignia of a captain: he was a tall, handsome man with very blond hair curling over his head in the fashionable style known as a Brutus. His senior officer was short and stocky with iron grey hair. He carried himself erect, and spoke in short, clipped sentences. He awakened a chord of recollection in Captain Jackson's mind. He felt that he had certainly met the Colonel before; though where, he could not for the moment remember. It was this circumstance which caused him to remain a little longer at his peep hole.

The door opened again to admit a thin little serving maid in grey homespun, carrying materials for kindling a fire. She set about her task with the energy of a terrier worrying at a rat, and in a short time, the wood burst into flame.

"That's better!" remarked the Colonel flinging himself into a chair and extending his booted legs towards the blaze. "Give it another go with the bellows, girl!"

But the maid seemed not to attend. The Colonel, nettled, repeated his command in a military voice. She looked round, vaguely, then appeared to comprehend, for she applied the bellows vigorously.

"I think she's hard of hearing, sir," explained the captain, who had been watching her keenly. "Come to think of it, she must be, else she would have roused the landlord sooner when we were trying to get into the place."

"Very likely you're right," agreed the Colonel. "That'll do, girl — I say, that'll do! Off you go!"

She did not hear the first remark, but at the second, she gathered up her tools and scuttled away like a frightened grey mouse.

"Queer place this," said the Colonel in a casual tone. "Evidently don't welcome visitors — wonder how they make a living, stuck down in the river like this, away from trade?"

"I wouldn't be surprised to learn," remarked the younger man, with a slow smile, "that the really important part of the 'The Waterman's' business is not conducted in the taproom."

"Eh?"

The Colonel looked up sharply.

"Of course, you know the place, Masterman. You guided me here, after all, when we were hopelessly lost."

"I can claim but small knowledge of it, sir. I have merely noticed it in the distance on the few occasions when I've been staying at Teignton Manor. There is a fine view of this stretch of the river from the bedchambers situated at the back of the house."

"So they put you in a back room, these folk at Teignton Manor — what's their name? — Ah! yes. Lodge, that's it. Shabby, b'God, Masterman!"

A shadow crossed Captain Masterman's face.

"My sister and I are of small account in the world, sir, as you must know," he said, bitterly.

"Nonsense!" replied the other, hastily. "Miss Masterman's as handsome as she can stare. And you're not a bad-looking feller yourself, m'boy! Good family, too!"

"But no money," said Masterman, in a harsh tone.

"What's that signify?" asked the Colonel, gruff with embarrassment.

"My dear sir, need you ask? If a man cannot live in the style to which he was born, as far as Society's concerned he does not exist."

"Nonsense!" repeated the Colonel. "You're asked everywhere for twenty miles around Totnes. Tell you what, m'boy, you need a drink. Where is that damned rascal of a landlord all this time?"

Thankful to turn the subject, he rose from his chair and strode to the door, hailing the landlord in stentorian tones which carried all over the house.

"Beg pardon, y'r honour," panted Nobby, coming up the passage almost at a run. "I've brought y'r honour's wine, but there was a difficulty about the victuals. Will a cold meat pasty be to the liking o' you gennelmen? 'Tis all we can lay 'ands on at present."

"Then it will have to do, won't it?" was the impatient reply. "Very well, man, don't stand there dithering! Bring in that wine, and tell them to fetch the pasty at the double."

Nobby mumbled some reply which the eavesdropper could not catch, and heavily departed.

"Lunatics, the lot of 'em!" pronounced the Colonel.

He dropped into his chair again and extended his legs to the rapidly developing blaze, while he signalled to his junior officer to pour the wine. Captain Masterman complied, and presently handed a glass to his Colonel before taking a chair on the opposite side of the fireplace. His face was now in full view of the hidden watcher's eyes.

"Tell you what," said the Colonel, suddenly. "Not a bad idea if we asked these people Lodge for a bed for the night. No sense in going on to Totnes tonight — men tired, wet through, hungry — far better in the morning."

"But I thought the landlord said —" began Captain Masterman.

"So he did, but we can bed the men at that inn in the village he was talking of," was the reply. "What's its name — 'The Three Fishers', that's it. Know Lodge slightly, y'know, but only in the way that one's acquainted with most people who matter in the county. Still, enough to ask him for a shake-down for the night — matter of patriotism, anyway, ain't it? At the present time, I mean."

"I'm sure Sir George will be only too happy," replied Captain Masterman. "He and his lady are the soul of hospitality."

"Pretty little gal they've got, too," remarked the Colonel, thoughtfully. "Damned shame she's to marry a Frenchman!"

"Dorlais can scarcely be accounted a Frenchman nowadays," replied the junior officer. "He's been in England since he was a boy, and his sympathies and tastes are entirely English."

"Don't know that a Frog can ever change his spots — ha, ha, ha!" laughed the Colonel, overcome by his own wit.

The Captain laughed dutifully, but without conviction.

"Anyway, little Miss Kitty's wasted on him," went on his superior officer. "Pity it wasn't t'other one — her friend."

"You mean Miss Feniton?" asked Captain Masterman, in a guarded tone.

"I do, indeed! She's a stuck up piece of goods, if you like!" said the Colonel, with a snort.

"Miss Feniton is perhaps a trifle reserved," admitted the other man, reluctantly, "but I have never observed the least height in her manner."

"Reserved! Ice is warm in comparison. Give you my word! But I mustn't say too much — fancy you're a little taken in that quarter, yourself."

A trace of colour showed on Masterman's high cheekbones.

"Don't mean to poke my nose in," the Colonel assured him, soothingly. "None of my business, as I dare say you'll tell me."

The hidden watcher's mouth curved in amusement. It was quite evident that the junior officer knew his business better than to make any such remark.

"My fillies don't get on with the chit, that's all," finished the Colonel. "Easy going girls, too: defy anyone to quarrel with 'em."

Captain Masterman said all that was proper concerning the Colonel's young ladies. The senior officer looked gratified.

"No bamboozling me, though, my dear chap," he answered, with a shake of his head. "You prefer Miss Iceberg, I can see! Well, no hard feelings, though I don't think there's much hope for you, I'm bound to say. Got a suitor already lined up, by what I hear."

Captain Jackson saw Masterman's hand tighten on his glass, but the younger officer said nothing.

"That old fool Feniton's godson, Lord Cholcombe's son," continued the Colonel. "The dearest wish of Miss Joanna's dead parents, according to m'wife."

Masterman knew that his Colonel's wife was an inveterate gossip; there was no real harm in the lady, but she had a nose for news, and liked to be first with it.

"Lord Cholcombe," repeated Masterman, evenly; and Captain Jackson silently paid tribute to the man's self-control. "I don't think I am acquainted —"

"Mostly lives in London," explained the older man. "Haven't met him myself, but know him by repute, of course. Got a house in Exeter which the son uses from time to time. He's a rare dandy, by all accounts."

"Who, sir? Lord Cholcombe?"

"No, the boy. One of these fellers who considers the choosing of a waistcoat matter for a se'enight's debate — no use for 'em, myself. Like a man to look well turned out, but no sense in overdoing it!"

Masterman agreed, and offered to refill his superior officer's glass. The fire was by now blazing merrily. Warmth and the wine had mellowed the Colonel's mood, and combined to loosen his tongue a little.

"Queer upbringing that filly's had," he said reflectively, taking the fresh glass from Masterman's hand. "Parents died when she was in swaddling clothes, pretty near, and been under old Lady Feniton's influence ever since, except for a few years when she managed to escape to one of these ladies' seminaries. The old battle axe stuffs her head full of the pottiest notions, according to m'wife. Talks a deal about remembering her rank, and not marrying beneath her. You'd think Feniton was at least an earl, instead of only a baronet. Disappointed in not having a boy left to carry on the name, shouldn't wonder. Can sympathize — old family — damn shame Geoffrey being snuffed out suddenly like that, before he could get an heir."

"It was a coaching accident, wasn't it?" asked Masterman. "I remember my father speaking of it when I was a boy. In those days, as you know, we lived not far from Shalbeare House."

Kellaway nodded. "Sad business — both killed instantly. All for the best, though, perhaps, in a way. Old lady never liked the bride — what was her name? Forget now. Anyway, it don't signify. She always felt that Geoffrey had married beneath him."

"I believe I remember my father saying she was a clergyman's daughter."

"That's right. Genteel enough, but not the brilliant match Lady Feniton had hoped for. No doubt that's why the old lady's so set on the nobility for Miss Joanna."

"Perhaps it may happen that the young lady will have notions of her own on the subject," said Masterman, diffidently.

"Eh? Shouldn't think so: seems tractable enough, in her cold way. Anyway, take a brave girl to stand up to the old lady! She's one who knows what she wants, all right!"

Masterman agreed. It was evident to the unseen watcher that he did not like the conversation.

There was a tap on the door of the coffee room, and Nobby entered, escorted by the small serving wench. They bore the remnants of a large meat pasty, some cold ham and sliced bread, together with plates and cutlery. This they proceeded to set before the gentlemen with as much despatch as possible.

"Ah!" exclaimed the Colonel, with satisfaction, as the door closed behind them. "This is more like it! But we mustn't settle ourselves in too snugly, my boy — more important still, mustn't let the men do so! If we mean to seek shelter for them in the village, we must give the landlord there plenty of warning. Pity they couldn't have found a shake-down here, but never met a more unwilling host than this fellow — and, to own the truth, wouldn't bed a dog here that I was fond of. Wretched hovel!"

While he was talking, both men began to make a determined onslaught on the victuals which had been brought them; in a little while, conversation died away as they gave themselves up to the more important business of eating.

"Dare say they will have had dinner at Teignton Manor by the time we arrive there," remarked the Colonel, laying down his knife and fork. "Anyway, best to be prepared! Now if you've finished, Masterman, perhaps you'd be good enough to go and round up the men. Must get off without further delay."

From his vantage point in the cupboard, Captain Jackson watched Masterman rise and move out of sight in the direction of the door. He himself turned away, and silently released the catch which operated the hidden door of the cupboard. He stepped out, motioning to his friend to follow him. My lord obeyed, and Jackson moved the door across until it was almost, but not quite, shut.

"Volunteers, not Preventives, as you may have gathered from the conversation," he explained rapidly in an undertone. "But equally undesirable from our point of view, as neither of us wishes to be seen, more particularly not in each other's company. However, thanks to Nobby's inhospitable attitude, they are about to move off. It's highly unlikely that they'll attempt to enter this room, so you may remain here, if you like, while I keep watch from the cupboard."

"If you're certain that they are unlikely to burst in, it would certainly be more comfortable," replied the other, with a wistful glance at the easy chair. "Damn! Just look at the colour of my pantaloons!"

"Very eye-catching," commended his companion following his gaze. "You feel, perhaps, that they are a shade too bright?"

"I wasn't referring to their original colour," explained the statesman, with a shade of coolness in his manner, "but to the confounded dust which I have managed to collect in that damned cupboard."

"Often get dust in cupboards," replied the Captain, sympathetically. "I've noticed it myself. Don't bother — it will soon brush off. You wait here, then."

He darted back to the hidden door, and, silently moving it open, slipped inside. He was back at his vantage point in time to see Captain Masterman returning to his superior officer.

"The men are ready, sir," he reported, smartly. "All except Harris, who's drunk. They're putting him under the pump now."

The Colonel nodded.

"Form 'em up into marching order. I'll settle with this damned landlord meanwhile, and join you outside."

They moved out of Jackson's sight towards the door. He waited a moment, then joined his companion in the parlour.

"They're moving off," he said, briefly. "Nobby will give us the word when they're clear of the inn. Another glass of wine, in the meantime?"

My lord accepted gratefully. He felt the need of a restorative to his nerves.

It was not very long afterwards that the landlord appeared in the parlour, a look of strong relief on his ruddy countenance.

"They've gone, thank God!" he breathed. "Fair startled me out o' my wits, they did! I thought they was Preventives, for sure!"

"My guest is also leaving, Nobby," said Captain Jackson. "I gave orders for the gentleman's coach to be stabled at the farm, and the coachman entertained in the kitchen there. Nip over and desire the driver to bring the vehicle to the front of the inn as quickly as possible."

Nobby departed on this errand, and the Captain set down his glass.

"You must get away before they return," he said. "Fortunately you can avoid the village. When you reach the top of this lane, go in the opposite direction from that by which you came. Continue for a mile or so, until you come to a turning on the right. Follow this, which makes a detour of the village, bringing you out beyond it on to the main coaching road."

"Surely there can be no reason why they must not see my coach passing through the village?" demurred his lordship.

"Only that your crest is on its panels," retorted the Captain. "It may occur to one or both of those gallant officers to wonder just why a prominent member of the Government should be travelling this particular stretch of the road in winter. Such curiosities are apt to be noised abroad; that's the last thing either of us desires."

The older man nodded.

"Of course, of course: you cannot be too careful, my boy. Heaven forbid that I should add to the dangers that surround you. What do you mean to do when I am gone?"

"Seek a conference with Number One, if possible tonight. After that, I have affairs which must be wound up here before I move on. If anything urgent should arise I will communicate it to you in the usual way."

"I should like to have news of you even if there is nothing of an urgent nature to impart."

"Then I will send it — through His Majesty's mails. But do not look for any scholarly epistles, my lord!"

"It will be enough to hear that you are alive and well," replied the other, soberly. "When I think —" He broke off as the clatter of hoofs and wheels was plainly heard from outside the inn.

"Your coach!" exclaimed Jackson, with satisfaction. "Now, sir —"

He thrust my lord's hat and gloves upon him, and ushered him hastily from the room.

It was now pitch dark outside, though the rain had for the moment stopped. The lanterns which hung on either side of the carriage did little to dispel the gloom. My lord shivered as he stepped out into the cold, dank night air, and turned to extend a hand to his companion before entering the coach.

"This is goodbye, then, for the present," he said, in a low voice.

Captain Jackson took the hand, and gripped it for a moment in silence. Then he urged the other into the vehicle.

"I'll mount up behind until you reach the high road," he whispered. "Give your man the word to start."

The door was slammed, and the order given. Captain Jackson swung himself lightly up on to the footboards behind.

From beside the pump in the inn yard, a figure rose unsteadily to its feet, and staggered towards the front of the inn. The noise of the coach had wakened Harris from the drunken slumbers to which he had earlier been abandoned in despair by his comrades of the Volunteers.

Into his fuddled brain penetrated the idea that something was amiss, that something ought to be done. Reaching for his musket with clumsy fingers, he raised it unsteadily, and fired in the general direction of the winking lamps of the coach. The exertion exhausted his possibilities. He collapsed once more on to the ground, letting fall the gun.

The bullet, not surprisingly, went wide of its mark. Captain Jackson felt a sharp sting as it grazed his upraised arm in its passage.

"What the devil —?" asked my lord, poking his head through the window.

The coachman, thoroughly alarmed, made as if to rein in his horses.

"Drive on!" shouted Jackson.

The man obeyed, fear overcoming his natural caution as he rounded the bend and took the narrow lane at breakneck speed. Once on the high road, Jackson drummed on the roof for the driver to stop.

"What in thunder was all that?" asked the statesman, as the Captain poked his head in at the still open window.

"Lord knows!" was the undisturbed reply. "But Nobby will see to it, and I'll find out later. It may not be healthy down there at present. Farewell, my lord."

He waved his hand airily, and, not waiting for a reply, ran off towards the lane which they had just left. The darkness swallowed him up.

My lord opened his mouth to speak, saw the futility of it, and instead rapped on the front of the coach for the driver to proceed. The man, disliking the whole exercise, needed no second bidding.

As for Captain Jackson, having turned into the lane, he scrambled up the bank and over the stone wall which topped it.

He vaulted lightly down into the dark, deserted grounds of Teignton Manor, and was soon lost in the shadows.

Chapter III: Miss Feniton Holds a Conversation

Dinner was over at Teignton Manor, and the gentlemen were sitting over their wine. Mr. Dorlais had ridden over to dine with his betrothed; when the ladies rose to leave their menfolk, his dark eyes told her that he begrudged the customary period of separation before he might with propriety join her in the withdrawing room. Miss Lodge met his glance unresponsively, however. She thought it was time he was taught a lesson.

Miss Feniton noticed the silent interchange with amusement. Her dear Kitty was a romantic, and that was the cause of this temporary coolness between the lovers. It was Miss Lodge's romantic disposition which appealed so strongly to the other girl, whose chief characteristic was always said to be strong common sense. All the same, Kitty ought not to be allowed to toy with her happiness; Miss Feniton determined to give her a strong hint before the gentlemen came in, and then to contrive some means of leaving her and Guy undisturbed for a space. A reconciliation between two such ardent natures ought not to be too difficult to accomplish.

At first, however, Lady Feniton seemed set upon trying to wreck this amiable scheme of her granddaughter's. Having disposed of a pious hope entertained by Lady Lodge that it would not rain tomorrow, and given in a few short sentences her opinion as to what was wrong with Mr. Pitt's Government, she turned to Miss Feniton.

"I have been waiting an opportunity all day to tell you, my dear Joanna," she began, "that I have at last had the honour of a reply from Algernon."

"Indeed, ma'am?" replied Joanna, calmly, raising her green-flecked eyes to her grandmother's face. "You must show it to me presently."

"I will show it to you now," insisted Lady Feniton. "I have it here with me. No doubt Catherine will like to see it, too — and you, of course, Letitia. Not that it tells one a great deal — there are merely a few lines penned, I observe, by his secretary — too much trouble, I suppose, to put pen to paper himself. But there! All you young people are alike nowadays!"

"For my part," put in Miss Feniton, seizing this opportunity of promoting her benevolent scheme towards Kitty and Guy Dorlais, "I mean to escape that stricture, Grandmama, by devoting a small part of this evening towards the answering of some of my correspondence. I will agree that most of it is overdue."

Lady Feniton looked her disapproval. "The morning is the time of day for letter writing," she said, firmly. "However, here is Algernon's note."

She handed an expensive looking sheet of notepaper to Joanna, who took it and perused it silently.

"You'll no doubt notice particularly the sentence about his 'being happy to renew an acquaintance of such long standing and so many pleasurable memories'?" she asked, with a deep-throated chuckle. "I wonder if he includes under that head the many occasions when I was obliged to order corporal punishment for him?"

"He was only a boy when he stayed with you at Shalbeare House before, I recollect?" said Lady Lodge.

Her friend nodded. "He was here on two occasions: the first when he was only ten years old, the second — let me see, Joanna would have been rising nine that time, if I remember

— yes, he would have been about fourteen, I suppose. A handful, but I knew how to school him, you may depend!"

Lady Lodge could have no doubts whatever on this score, and said as much.

"There was some nonsense about his name, I recall," continued Lady Feniton, reminiscently.

"Yes, I remember that, too," interposed Joanna, having read the letter, and passed it on to Lady Lodge. "You would call him Algernon, ma'am, although he insisted that he was never called so at home. He became quite heated on the subject, and it ended by —" her voice tailed off.

"By my having the gardener thrash him soundly," concluded her grandmother. "Algernon he was baptised by that foolish mother of his, and Algernon he remains, as far as I am concerned!"

Miss Feniton fell silent. She was recalling how she had concealed a portion of game pie in the pocket of her apron so that it might be smuggled in by a sympathetic nurse to the defiant, dry-eyed small boy. The incident must have made a strong impact upon her, she thought with surprise, for at that time she had been only five years old herself.

"It is a vastly polite letter," said Kitty, having received it from her Mama. "Can you recollect what he was like, Jo?"

Miss Feniton was obliged to shake her head. In spite of the sharpness of that one memory, her other recollections of Lord Cholcombe's heir were faint and confused.

"My dear Kit, all small boys are much alike," she said, with a light laugh. "They are all noisy, boisterous, and slightly contemptuous of the opposite sex. I make no doubt that he was just the same as the rest of his species."

"But what were his looks, I mean?" persisted Kitty. "Would you say he was a handsome child? Was he fair, for instance — or dark?"

This question produced some conflicting replies. Miss Feniton settled for fair hair, while Lady Feniton was positive that it had been brown.

"It was not a face you remember," finished the dowager. "Not like Geoffrey's, for instance, which made an indelible impression wherever he went. Still, one can't have everything: his father is a Viscount, and may any day succeed to the Earldom. Such a prospect could atone for any want of looks in Joanna's future husband."

"There is quite a firm understanding, then?" asked Lady Lodge.

"Firm as the Bank of England! Geoffrey wished it from the moment that Joanna was born, and Cholcombe was just as decided. They were great friends, as you most likely know, before Geoffrey's marriage. He used to spend a vast deal of time in Town in those days. We quite expected — but never mind that, now!"

Miss Feniton knew the meaning of this veiled remark. At one time, it had been supposed that her father would marry Lord Cholcombe's sister. It was another instance of the many half uttered slights upon her mother's memory. They had little real meaning for her, as she could not remember her parents: but they were not without a certain effect of which she was not completely conscious. If the mother had been such a disappointment, might not the child be so, too?

"It is a very pretty-spoken letter," approved Lady Lodge. "When is Mr. Cholcombe expected at Shalbeare House?"

"In rather less than a fortnight from now," answered Lady Feniton. "I have been thinking, Letitia — why do you not all come back with us when we return? Feniton is poor company for anyone, as who should know better than myself! Besides, it will look less particular if we have a party staying when Algernon makes his visit. I will ask Mr. Dorlais, too, Catherine, so you need not look so downcast," she added, glancing at Kitty's tell-tale face. "He should make a most suitable companion for Algernon, being much about the same age."

"Oh, thank you, Lady Feniton!" exclaimed Kitty, in delight. "Indeed, I feared it would be so dull when you are all gone home! You will say yes, won't you, Mama?"

Lady Lodge, who was a very different calibre from her guest, assented at once, though with the proviso that "we must ask Papa, of course".

"Oh, he will agree, I feel sure!" said Kitty, secure in her power over both her parents. She smoothed the chestnut Titus crop which gave her such an elfin appearance, and turned her dark blue eyes solemnly upon Miss Feniton as a sudden thought struck her. "But perhaps Guy will not come," she said, doubtfully.

"If he does not, it will be your own fault," murmured Joanna, significantly, in her ear.

Kitty raised her brows. "Why, whatever can you mean?" she whispered back.

"Conversation after dinner should be general," reproved Lady Feniton, sharply. "I feel quite sure that you two girls have had time enough in solitude today to enable you to unburden yourselves of all your little confidences! But why do you suppose, Catherine, that Mr. Dorlais —" she gave the words light emphasis, for she disapproved of Kitty's use of her betrothed's Christian name, and wondered that Letitia could allow it — "should not accept my invitation?"

Kitty blushed. "He — it is possible, ma'am, that he may have another engagement," she stuttered, nervously.

Lady Feniton smiled acidly, "When you are so charmingly in looks, Catherine? I do not think it likely! I must say, Letitia, that though in general, I do not approve of those dreadful shorn locks, they do suit your daughter's style. Not that I mean you to copy, Joanna," she warned. "Yours is quite another kind of beauty, and Carver knows to an inch just what best becomes you."

Miss Feniton made no reply, but racked her brains feverishly to discover a way of diverting her grandmother's attention long enough to enable her to have a private conversation with Kitty Lodge. If the worst came to the worst, she thought desperately, she would have to postpone it until they retired to their bedchambers for the night. Meanwhile, she could at least try to leave her friend alone with Mr. Dorlais for a space. If she braved her grandmother's displeasure, and withdrew to the morning room, ostensibly to write letters, she knew she could rely upon Sir George Lodge, at any rate, to distract Lady Feniton's attention from the engaged couple. Upon her grandfather, she could place no such reliance. Outside his library, he was a broken reed, drifting hither and thither at her ladyship's whim. Which was probably why, reflected Joanna, he rarely left the library when he was in his own house.

Her opportunity did not come, and in a little while, the gentlemen joined them. Guy Dorlais went at once to Kitty, placing a chair at her other side.

"Now I am supplanted," remarked Miss Feniton, with a smile. "I must tell you that you are about to have a signal honour paid you, Mr. Dorlais!"

"What is that?" he asked, with a humorous flash of his dark eyes.

"You are to be invited to make a stay at Shalbeare House," said Joanna, solemnly. "Kitty fears, however, that you may have a previous engagement."

"What is all this, sweetheart?" he asked, trying to take Kitty's hand.

She snatched it hurriedly away, saying in muffled accents, "Take care! Lady Feniton is watching us!"

"What do I care for —" he was beginning, when Lady Feniton cut into the conversation.

"Sir Walter and myself are thinking of making up a small house party when we return home, Mr. Dorlais. May we hope to count you among our guests? Sir George and Lady Lodge are to come — and Catherine, of course. As to the other members, I am not yet quite decided, except for one gentleman Lord Cholcombe's son. Are you at all acquainted with him, sir?"

"You make me very happy, ma'am," replied Guy Dorlais, with a bow. "I shall be delighted to accept. Yes, I have some little acquaintance with Cholcombe — I fancy that on one occasion, we took part together in some private theatricals at the house of a mutual friend, and I have run across him from time to time at the Exeter Assemblies. I understand that he has a house in Exeter, though he is more frequently in London."

"Oh, so you know this Mr. Cholcombe!" exclaimed Kitty, eagerly. "Pray tell us what he is like, Guy, do!"

Dorlais hesitated. "Well, it's not so simple, Kit, to describe a fellow one's met so seldom. What do you wish to know about him?"

"Everything!" said Kitty, without hesitation. "His colouring, height, whether or not he is handsome, his tastes and interests — oh, anything at all you can think of!"

"A tall order," he said, smiling, "but I'll do my best." He screwed up his eyes in an effort of recollection. "His colouring is fair — no, perhaps not exactly. Let us say medium colouring. As to height, he's neither tall nor short; as far as I recollect, just medium height, you know. I wouldn't call him exactly handsome, but then, I don't know what your standards are." He smiled down at her. "He's certainly not plain, however," he finished. "I suppose one might fairly say —"

"Medium!" concluded Kitty, in disgust. "I ask you, Jo, are not gentlemen hopeless when it comes to anything that really matters?"

"But why does it matter?" asked Dorlais, quickly. "Why is this Mr. Cholcombe so very important to you, all at once?"

"He's not important to me," laughed Kitty, "but to Joanna."

"To Miss Feniton?"

"Yes, he —"

"I think," said Joanna, rising from her seat hurriedly, "that I had best go and write those letters of mine now." She glanced at Lady Lodge. "Will you please to excuse me, ma'am?"

Lady Lodge opened her mouth to give a gracious assent, but it was stillborn. Lady Feniton broke in upon her.

"I suppose you may have an hour, if you insist upon it, Joanna. But I am sure that there can be nothing which may not very well wait until tomorrow. Do not stay longer, or I shall be obliged to send for you."

Guy Dorlais had risen with Joanna, and now moved forward to open the door for her, his back towards the group of which Lady Feniton was the centre. He made an expressive little grimace at Joanna as she passed him: she permitted herself an answering, half rueful smile.

She made her way unhurriedly to the morning parlour, a room which was situated at that side of the house which overlooked the shrubbery. It was a pleasant room in summer, with its long glass doors giving on to three stone steps which led down to the garden. At present, these doors were shielded by heavy damask curtains of blue and gold, and a bright fire glowed on the hearth. Her letter writing had, of course, been an excuse: nevertheless, she thought, as she closed the door behind her, she might as well employ her hour of enforced solitude in that way as in any other. There were a few letters which ought to be answered.

The writing desk was situated away from the fireplace, on the wall adjacent to the glass doors: it would be no hardship to be sitting away from the fire, for the room was very warm. She crossed over, and made herself comfortable at the desk, drawing the materials for her task from their various pigeon holes.

She saw at once that the quill required mending, and searched for a penknife. Having found one, she began patiently to shape the nib.

It seemed very quiet in the room. The scraping of the knife and the gentle tick of a clock upon the mantel shelf were the only sounds to break the silence. Possibly that was why it was so easy for her to detect the faint noise of a footfall on the path outside the doors — or had she imagined the sound, after all?

She remained perfectly still for a moment, her long white fingers poised above the pen on which she was working.

No, she had not imagined it, for now there was another sound, an unmistakable thud, as of some heavy object falling to the ground. She started to her feet, her heart beating a shade faster than usual.

No doubt some young ladies might have called for the servants, gone into a fit of hysterics, or even swooned. Joanna

Feniton had not been reared by her grandmother in this tradition.

She boldly approached the French windows. Then, in one swift movement, she drew aside the curtains, unfastened the door, and threw it open. A rush of cold, damp air swept into the cosy room.

"Who is there?" she demanded, in admirably level tones, stepping a little way out of the door.

Then she noticed the man who was just picking himself up from the ground. Evidently he had been walking close to the house, and in the dark had failed to notice the steps, stumbling over them.

Captain Jackson stood erect when she spoke and faced her. There seemed nothing else to do, but he cursed his luck inwardly. Everything seemed doomed to go awry on this contrary night. To make a run for it now would only bring the whole house about his ears. There was a faint hope that he might be able to fob off this young woman with some plausible story, if he stood his ground. He must think fast, though.

She surveyed him curiously in the light which escaped from the open door, and decided that she had never seen him before.

"I observe that you are not one of the servants," she said, after a long scrutiny. "Who are you, and what do you want here?"

Her voice was clear and cold, the voice of one accustomed to asking questions, and to being supplied with satisfactory answers. No doubt under other circumstances, it could be a pleasant voice, and he noticed automatically that it would certainly carry well. This latter observation urged him to caution in his dealings with the lady.

"Beggin' y'r pardon for disturbin' ye, ma'am," he began, in rich Devon tones, "but I do've lost my way in the dark, the servants' entrance I be seekin'."

"Indeed?" The temperature of the voice dropped a degree or two. "May I ask by what gate you entered the Manor?"

"Why, the back gate, ma'am. You see —"

"What I fail to see," she interrupted, acidly, "is how you managed to arrive at this point, if you did indeed enter at the back gate. There is a well-defined path from there which leads straight through the orchard and kitchen gardens to the servants' door."

"'Twas the dark, ma'am — can't barely see a 'and afore ye. If ye'll but 'ave the goodness, ma'am, to direct me — beggin' y'r pardon for the trouble, I'm sure I'll be —"

"You are about to say, no doubt, that you would be vastly obliged to me if I should do so. The prospect of giving so much pleasure tempts me, I must confess, but I shall contrive to resist it. In short, my man, I find your story singularly unconvincing. So, I am certain, will Sir George."

The man came a step nearer, then checked as he saw her fall back a little.

"I swear to you, ma'am, that I mean no harm here," he said, in a low, earnest voice. "I came but to seek work, if I can find it — I'm an honest man, not such as you need be afeared on —"

Miss Feniton studied him again. His face, though tanned and healthy, did not seem to accord with his manner of speech. There was intelligence, almost sensitivity, in the features: but his voice was rough, his words those of the slow-thinking yokel. She was intrigued: here might be matter for passing an otherwise dull hour.

"Very well. Before handing you over to the owner of the house, I myself will hear what you have to say. However, it is too cold out here for conversation. We will go indoors."

She gestured towards the open window. The man stood still, obviously waiting for her to precede him into the room. She shook her head, smiling ironically.

"Oh, no! On this occasion, you will go first — and no tricks, mind! I may be only a female, but I am not entirely without resources, as you may find to your cost if you should attempt anything rash."

He shook his head wordlessly, and walked slowly up the steps, and into the room. She stood aside so that he might enter. His mind was racing furiously. Here was the devil of a tangle, and no mistake! What tale could he possibly tell that would prevent this girl from handing him over to Sir George Lodge, whom he knew to be a magistrate? Nothing sentimental would serve, that much was evident: she was by far too calm and collected a young woman to be taken in by any hard luck story. She seemed to have a devilish dry sense of humour, though. Could he perchance make any capital of that?

She followed him into the room, taking up a stance by the writing desk.

"Close the door," she ordered, sharply.

He turned to obey. The thought crossed his mind that now he might perhaps make a run for it, slamming the door shut against her. There would be a short interval before she could summon aid, during which he might possibly win clear of the Manor grounds. The recollection of the mysterious shot outside "The Waterman" gave him pause, however. He could not afford to be the quarry of two sets of hunters in so small an area. Besides, he had other reasons for wishing to avoid a hue and cry here.

He closed the windows, and pulled the curtains into place, as she had bidden him. Then he turned to face his captor.

He saw a slender young lady in a dress of white muslin, fashioned in the prevailing classical style, with high waist and flowing skirt. Her black hair was dressed *a la Psyche*, in a tapering cone bound with pink ribbons; a cluster of loose ringlets fell to the nape of her neck. In the glitter of the candlelight, her hair showed unexpected auburn tints. He thought that her eyes were her finest features, hazel, deep and luminous. At present, their expression was cold and withdrawn.

"So you came here to seek work?" she asked him, in a tone of amused incredulity. "Do you generally interview prospective employers after dark?"

This was a tricky question, and he feared that it was only the beginning. From her expression, she was evidently shrewd and intelligent. He would have need, he thought wryly, of all that spontaneity for which he was noted.

"I've but just arrived in the parish, ma'am," he protested. "'Twas impossible to come here earlier."

She nodded, considering him with a calculating eye. "From the sea, I should imagine, judging by your dress," she said. "Are you a fisherman?"

"I have been, ma'am." He kept his face expressionless.

She surveyed him again for a moment, a slow smile playing about her mouth.

"I have always understood that a man, once trained to the sea, cannot give it up. It would seem that you are an exception, then?"

He broke off as she drew a quick breath, her eyes widening in horror. Automatically, he followed the direction of her gaze: it was fixed upon his left hand. Then he noticed that blood was oozing from the graze on his arm, soaking into the sleeve of his jersey, and running down his fingers in slow drips on to the carpet.

"Why — you are injured!"

He shrugged. "It is nothing — a scratch."

He rolled back his sleeve, revealing a forearm smeared in blood. He drew a handkerchief from his pocket, and tried to cleanse the stain.

"You must have that seen to," she said, in a firm voice. "I will ring —"

"No!"

He dropped the handkerchief, and strode towards her, grabbing her wrist with his right, uninjured arm. Her chin went up, and her eyes narrowed. Now their expression was as hard as flint.

"Release me at once!"

He shook his head. "Only if you undertake not to ring that bell."

"I shall do no such thing! Your attitude makes evident what I suspected from the first — that you have been telling me a pack of lies. Unhand me at once, I say!"

"Let me explain," he pleaded, relaxing his grip a little. "There are reasons — urgent reasons — why I must be seen by no one at present. I swear that I mean you no harm —"

"I observe," she said, disdainfully, "that your hand is still upon my arm."

"I beg your pardon."

He released her, and stood back a little, poised for instant action, should she decide to make any move to betray him.

There was a moment's pause, while each weighed the other.

"Take this," she said, at last, handing him a flimsy scarf of pink muslin which hung over the chair on which she had been sitting. "Bind up that wound."

He hesitated, shrugged, then took the scarf and made a clumsy attempt to deal with the bandaging. She watched his efforts for a moment without speaking, then moved towards him.

"Here, let me do it."

She wound the scarf about his arm with deft fingers. Then she stooped and picked up the fallen handkerchief.

"I believe that may suffice to stay the flow. It is, as you say, only a surface graze. Perhaps you had best attempt to cleanse your arm with this, since you will not allow me to procure a basin of water for your use."

"Thank you," he said, gravely, taking the handkerchief from her outstretched hand.

He made some attempt to wipe the blood from the arm, but gave it up at last, and pulled his sleeve down over the bandage. Then he stooped, trying to remove the bloodstains from the carpet with the aid of the handkerchief. She stopped him with a gesture.

"That is useless. I myself will attend to it later." He gave her a curious look.

"Allow me to say that your coolness has my admiration, madam. I notice that you do not faint at the sight of blood."

"I have not the trick of fainting," she replied, contemptuously. "But I am waiting: you may remember that you promised me an explanation of all this."

He took a pace or two about the room without speaking. At his first movement, she surreptitiously lifted the penknife from the table, and held it in her hand against the skirt of her gown, so that it was partly concealed by the folds of cloth.

Suddenly, he stood still, and swung round upon her. He found himself confronted by the weapon, held menacingly in a steady, white hand. He lifted an eyebrow, and laughed softly.

"So you believe in taking precautions? Well, I don't blame you for that. For all you can tell, you could be in danger of your life." He paused, to study the effect of his words. The firm line of her chin did not alter, her expression was still one of cold disdain. He gave a little crooked smile: "You must allow me to say that you are a remarkable young lady, Miss Lodge."

The fine brows drew together, and the hazel eyes were shrewd.

"So you know my name?"

"I know that Sir George Lodge is the owner of Teignton Manor; I imagine that you must be his daughter? You could not be his wife!"

She ignored this remark. "Imagination is an invaluable possession. You seem to be particularly gifted in that respect."

"Then I am wrong — you are not Miss Lodge?"

"I did not say so. Furthermore, I cannot conceive how my identity can possibly concern you."

"No." He shrugged, ruefully. "No, of course not."

"I am still waiting," she said, pointedly, "for that explanation."

He hesitated a second or two longer.

"You shall have it." He spoke impetuously. "I believe I can trust you."

"I am honoured." She inclined her head ironically. "Do you know I was labouring under a total misapprehension? I had the notion — you will laugh at it, I feel sure — that I was the one who was showing a certain amount of trust in you?"

"Yes, you are," he agreed, cordially. "Why is that, I wonder?"

She appraised him thoughtfully, her expression still cold and disdainful.

"You see," she answered, with a frosty smile, "I like oddities. And — you must forgive my plain speaking — I find you most odd."

"Your speaking is the only plain thing about you, Miss Lodge — if you will permit me to say so. But tell me, why do you find me odd?"

"I do not like flattery at any time," she replied coldly. "From one in your position, it is ludicrous. You might say that was one of many things which I find odd about you."

He grimaced. "The compliment was sincerely meant. If I have offended, I ask pardon. What are the other things?"

She sat down upon the chair which stood by the writing desk. He noticed that she placed the penknife close by her hand upon the open leaf of the desk.

"They are too numerous to relate," she said, dryly. "But let us begin with the fact that I observe you to have two forms of address."

He raised his brows.

"When you first spoke to me," she continued, watching his expression closely, "it was in the manner of a country yokel. Now your voice has altered slightly: the accents are very nearly those of a gentleman."

He bowed, smiling ironically. "I always endeavour to conform to my company, madam."

"I can believe that. Delightful as it is to converse with one of your undoubted powers, Mr. —" She paused, and looked inquiringly at him. "I'm afraid you have the advantage of me in the matter of names."

"Call me Captain Jackson," he answered, carelessly.

"That is your name?"

"Is Miss Lodge yours?"

"Check!" she agreed, with a frosty smile. "As I was saying, Captain Jackson —" she gave the name a faint emphasis — "much as I enjoy your conversation, I feel that it is time to come to the point. Why were you lurking outside this window? And do not try to tell me again that you were seeking work, for I shall not believe you!"

"That is a pity," he said, mockingly. "But I wish you will employ some other word than 'lurking'. It imparts a sinister quality to my actions which I promise you is unjust. Very well —" as she showed signs of impatience at this preamble — "I am coming to the point, I assure you. If you must know, I entered the grounds of this house in order to escape the unwelcome attention of someone who appeared unduly anxious to meet me."

"The parish constable, no doubt?"

He smiled, showing strong white teeth. "Not on this occasion."

"Who, then?"

The smile faded, and a look of regret came over his face.

"There you have me, ma'am."

"Is that all?" she asked scornfully. "You cannot suppose that such a trumpery explanation will satisfy me! Sir George Lodge is a magistrate — as I make no doubt you already know! and I feel sure that he will be able to extract a more convincing story from you."

He regarded her thoughtfully for what seemed a long time.

"Well?" she demanded at last, impatiently. "What have you to say? It must be to the purpose, mind!"

"I can only ask you — beg you — not to disclose me to Sir George. This is not entirely for my own sake."

"Then for whose? I suppose you will now tell me that you have a wife and six starving children?"

"I'm sorry to disappoint you: I am not married. In all seriousness, though — if you betray me, the harm you do will not be to myself alone, but to your country."

"To my —" She broke off, astounded. Then she laughed mirthlessly. "Oh, now you surpass your previous efforts! Very well, then, I am ready to be entertained — what is your latest story?"

"I cannot blame you for being so incredulous, in view of the fact that, so far, I've been obliged to tell you a certain amount of untruths. But, if you reflect a little, you must see that I dare not trust anyone on so short an acquaintance. More particularly —" He broke off, knitting his brows. There was something about this proud, cold young lady which attracted him, and the attraction went deeper than her obvious good looks. There was an appeal of the spirit: he felt that, making allowance for their differences in situation, they were the same kind of people. For one unguarded moment, he was tempted to unburden himself to her. He realized at once the danger of such a course, and attempted a compromise.

"More particularly —?" she queried, with a sideways mocking glance from her fine, expressive eyes.

"Look here, the fact is that I dare not tell you the whole truth," he admitted, candidly. "There are issues involved —" He broke off. "It would be too dangerous," he finished, lamely.

"That I can well believe!" she mocked. "No doubt it would serve to put you behind bars!"

He made an impatient gesture. "My fate is of no account," he said, speaking rapidly, "except in the bearing which it has on the fate of England. You cannot but be aware of the deadly peril in which the country stands at present."

"With beacons piled high on every hill, ready to be lit, and feverish plans for retreat should the enemy invade our shores, it is scarcely possible to be unaware of it," she agreed, laconically. "All the more reason, Mr. — er, Captain Jackson? — for my viewing your present activities with suspicion. You admit that you are anxious to evade Sir George — in fact, anyone in authority. Then, too, you have sustained what looks very like a bullet wound, and admit that you are running away from someone. For all I know, you could very well be — let us say — an enemy spy. One hears stories —"

"And if I were, do you suppose I should stay to parley with you in this way? To overpower you should not prove an impossible task, I believe."

"Upon my word," she said, impatiently, "you must think me a simpleton! You admit that you are already being pursued by one party. Is it likely that you would take action which might involve you with others? No, I can see perfectly that your only possible course is to persuade me to silence by telling some plausible tale that will take me in."

"Then I am lost indeed!" he answered, with a wry smile and an expressive spreading of his hands. "I can easily see that yours is far from being a credulous disposition."

"Quite so," she answered. "Then perhaps I might now have the truth?"

He thought rapidly for a moment. The truth, even if he dared to tell it, would sound like an even more fantastic lie than any he had yet uttered. Yet this young woman must be won over in some way: how much dared he say?

"You would not believe me —" He broke off suddenly. A knock had sounded on the door.

The two occupants of the room exchanged glances. The man's was questioning, the girl's faintly surprised. Her expression changed quickly, and she motioned silently to the curtains which concealed the long French windows. In a trice, he had slipped silently behind the sheltering folds of damask.

Miss Feniton remained where she was, but picked up a book which was lying close at hand.

"Come in," she invited, in even tones.

A ruddy-cheeked abigail obeyed the summons. Miss Feniton looked up from her book abstractedly.

"M'lady's compliments, ma'am, and would you be so very obliging as to slip up to the withdrawing room for a few moments, if you please?"

Miss Feniton nodded. "Thank you; I will follow you presently," she said, in dismissal.

The girl withdrew. Miss Feniton waited a while, to be certain that she was out of earshot, then crossed to the window and moved the curtain aside. The man made as if to step out, but she shook her head.

"No doubt you heard what passed," she said, in a rapid undertone. "I am called away, but will return here as soon as possible. Meanwhile, you would be well advised to wait where you are, I am quite determined to hear your story: should it satisfy me, it may be that I shall consent to remain silent about your activities of this evening. Should I find you gone when I return, I shall know what to think — and how to act."

With this veiled threat, she was about to turn away, but he stayed her with a gesture of his unbandaged arm.

"One moment, only!" he whispered. "Tell me something, in your turn — what is your real name?"

She gave him a quizzical look. "May I remind you that I don't yet know yours? Still, since you will have it, I see no harm in giving you the information. I am a friend of Miss Lodge's — Joanna Feniton. And now I must go!"

She turned hurriedly away, thus missing the expression which crossed the man's face — a look compounded of surprise, consternation and amusement.

When the door had closed behind her, he emitted a low whistle.

"Good God!" he muttered.

He thought rapidly for a moment, then pushed aside the curtain and went to the writing desk. He picked up the quill which Miss Feniton had been mending, and, dipping it in the standish, wrote a few lines rapidly on the paper which she had set out for her own use: he wrote in a curious, backhand scrawl, but it was evident that writing was no unfamiliar accomplishment with him.

When he had finished, he hesitated for a moment. There was a certain risk in leaving a note here, in full view of anyone who should chance to come into this room. No ready alternative occurred to him, however, and the wording of the note could convey little to anyone other than the person for whom it was intended. He shrugged, folded the letter, and directed it in clear, block capitals to Miss Feniton. He placed it in a prominent position on the writing desk.

Then he went over to the window, and softly opened one of the long glass doors. He stepped outside, and, leaning forward, arranged the curtains carefully across the window. This done to his satisfaction, he closed the door, though he was unable from his present position to latch it. He stepped out into the night.

The darkness soon hid him from view.

Chapter IV: Miss Feniton Takes Sides

When Miss Feniton reached the drawing room, she found two gentlemen in regimentals seated beside her host. They came to their feet as she entered the room. She recognized them instantly.

"How do you do, Colonel Kellaway? I trust your family is well?"

Captain Masterman watched while she greeted his senior officer. It was so easy to see why people judged Miss Feniton to be cold and proud: her calm manner was in marked contrast to the unrestrained warmth with which Miss Lodge had welcomed them a few moments since.

She next took Masterman's hand, and asked him how he did. His feelings were somewhat disturbed, for Colonel Kellaway had hit upon the truth when he had remarked on his junior officer's admiration of Miss Feniton, but he managed a polite reply to her formal inquiries after his sister.

She showed no disposition to linger in conversation with either of the officers, but looked questioningly at her hostess.

"I believe you sent for me, ma'am?"

"Oh, no!" protested Lady Lodge, hurriedly. "That is to say —"

"I sent for you," explained Lady Feniton, firmly. "You will naturally not wish to be writing letters when there is company in the house."

Joanna felt a pang of dismay, but managed to conceal it. "Of course not, Grandmama. Perhaps, however, I may be excused for a space while I tidy away the litter I have left in the parlour downstairs? It is not the kind of thing that I should wish the housemaids to deal with, being my private correspondence."

She began to cross the room. Captain Masterman was at the door immediately, waiting to open it for her.

"Nonsense, child!" objected her grandmother. "It can wait until later. I particularly wish you to hear what these gentlemen have to tell us of the state of our National defences. It is a subject which must be of interest to every one of us."

Miss Feniton saw that she could not make her escape for the moment without drawing down more attention upon herself than she altogether liked. She subsided, therefore, awaiting a suitable opportunity to find another excuse for quitting the room later on.

Colonel Kellaway was answering the dowager. "As to that, ma'am, you need be in no alarm. Devon is not thought to be a very likely spot for a landing. Give 'em a warm reception, though, if they should chance this way, eh, Masterman?"

"I think it unlikely," said Lady Feniton, coldly, "that you will ever find *me* in a state of alarm, Colonel."

"Just so, m'lady," he answered, hastily. "Of course not, wouldn't think it for a moment! Simply a manner of speaking, y'know!"

"But indeed, Augusta," protested Lady Lodge. "I am sure the Colonel may be excused for supposing you to be alarmed — I am very sure that I am! Why, I hear that they have a great fleet of boats waiting to cross the Channel — "

Guy Dorlais broke into a laugh. The other men glanced at him with an answering smile.

"Have you forgotten our Navy, ma'am?" he asked. "They squat like cats at a mousehole, only waiting a chance to pounce!"

"But — they sometimes leave their posts, do they not? Augusta, you have told me how they frequently lie up in Torbay, when the weather is bad in the Channel, or they have occasion to put in to port for some little thing or other," finished Lady Lodge, uncertainly.

Lady Feniton nodded. "We have several times entertained the ship's officers at Shalbeare House," she said. "And the village of Tor Quay is as full as it can hold with their wives and families."

"That's so," agreed the Colonel. "Of late years, the Fleet's taken to lying up in Torbay in preference to Plymouth. The Sound's a dangerous anchorage in bad weather — Torbay's more sheltered."

"I can vouch for that," said Lady Feniton, pleased. "Shalbeare House is at all times and seasons sheltered from the worst of the winds; and I doubt if our climate can be excelled in the whole of England."

"Though by some it is thought to be too relaxing," murmured her husband.

He so rarely spoke, that everyone gave him full attention when he did so. Looking nervously around, he saw that he was the focus of every pair of eyes in the room. He fidgeted uneasily in his chair, coughed, and fingered his somewhat crumpled cravat. His wife eyed him severely.

"How should you know, Feniton, when you are seldom outside that library of yours?" she asked, scathingly. "What kind of judge of air can you set yourself up to be, I should like to know? If I do not find the air of Torbay relaxing, I am sure you could not!"

He made an apologetic murmur, and subsided.

"Grandpapa was not expressing his own views, however, but those of others," interposed Joanna, quietly.

"I do not require you to tell me, Miss, what your grandfather means! I suppose he is very well able to explain himself, should he choose to do so. But we are interrupting your account, sir —" turning to Colonel Kellaway — "You do not believe, then, that there is any real danger of a landing being made hereabouts?"

"Hardly likely, milady. London must always be the main objective, and Devon is too far removed from the capital. Ireland is our real heel of Achilles in the West."

"The last venture there could scarce encourage them to try again in that quarter," interpolated Sir George.

"But what of this tunnel that they are said to be building under the Channel?" asked Lady Lodge, apprehensively. "Only the other evening, at the Winterbournes', I heard a rumour that the French have engaged a mining expert on the venture, and that it should be completed by Christmas!"

Lady Feniton threw her friend a look of contempt. "Fiddlesticks, Letitia! It's a mercy that everyone is not as credulous as you! Pray, how do you suppose that the workmen should manage to breathe under water, to begin with? You'll be suggesting that men might fly, next, I suppose!"

This remark served to draw Sir Walter out of the abstraction which usually claimed him in his wife's company.

"There is no saying to what limits man's ingenuity may reach, Augusta. You appear very confident that men may not breathe under water: have you never chanced to hear of the Nautilus?"

Lady Feniton repeated the name, for once at a loss.

"It is a special kind of vessel, invented by an American," explained Sir Walter, patiently. "It is capable of underwater travel, and men have been known to stay shut up in its interior while it was submerged for several hours without any ill effects."

"Oh, yes!" exclaimed the Colonel. "Fulton — Robert Fulton — that's the chap's name! Bit of a gimcrack, though, ain't he? Had it from a Naval officer of my acquaintance that they carried out some trials of another invention of his — sometime in September, if my memory serves me — whole thing was a wretched fiasco! Thought he could blow up half the French flotilla, seemingly; but his wretched 'infernals', as the Navy calls 'em, just refused to go off."

"I have heard nothing of this," said Sir George, with interest.

"No, well, dare say it wasn't noised abroad. This fellow Fulton sometimes works for the French, as well — he was granted a French passport three years ago to enable him to make experiments along the coast over there. Being a neutral, money's the only thing that interests him — typical of these Yankees, I must say."

"What exactly are these infernals, as you call them?" asked Lady Feniton, interestedly.

Joanna stirred uneasily in her seat. Her interest in the conversation was as great as her grandmother's but she could not forget the man she had left in hiding. Her eyes wandered to Kitty and Guy. They, too, were listening intently, without making any comment. She found this odd in Mr. Dorlais, who would generally take an active part in any conversation of note. English by adoption though he was, she reflected, perhaps at times he might find a certain confusion of loyalties when the war with France was under discussion. She wondered anxiously what possible excuse she could contrive for quitting the room: she must go soon. It was too dangerous to leave the man Jackson concealed there for much longer. Someone might go in, and surprise him. Yet she did not wish to miss any of this most interesting conversation.

Colonel Kellaway was answering her grandmother's question.

"I can best describe them as a sort of log of mahogany, ma'am, with wedge shaped ends. They contain enough ballast to keep their upper decks afloat, and are filled with gunpowder. A clockwork device is fitted to the gunpowder, and when a peg is removed on the outside of the machine, the whole thing explodes, five to ten minutes later."

"Merciful Heavens!" exclaimed Lady Lodge, with a little gasp, "They must be almost as dangerous to those who use them as to the enemy, I imagine!"

"Something in that, ma'am," acknowledged the Colonel. "I recollect that my friend did say they weren't sorry to return the unused machines to Naval stores when the exercise was over. A broadside from the French while those things were aboard —" He nodded significantly, leaving the sentence unfinished.

Lady Lodge turned pale; she was easily alarmed. Her husband looked at her, smiled reassuringly, and said. "Would you not like a little music, gentlemen? You must find it tedious to be talking of such matters after a day spent in military exercises."

Colonel Kellaway voted himself very willing for the change; and as Captain Masterman's chief concern seemed to be to fall in with his superior officer's wishes, no objection was raised by him.

Miss Feniton was invited first to the pianoforte, as was only civil, considering that she was a guest in the house; but she declined in favour of Kitty.

"I will take my turn later," she said. "I have left my scarf downstairs, and feel the need of it."

Before her grandmother could intervene, she rose, and quickly left the room.

She almost ran down the staircase towards the parlour. Captain Jackson's story should soon be in her possession now,

71

or she would know the reason why! He had seemed to be on the point of confiding in her at last when they had been so unfortunately interrupted — though of course, she told herself, it was only too probable that what he had to confide would turn out to be the most complete fabrication, after all. But her curiosity was now thoroughly aroused, and she must hear what he had to say: judgment could come afterwards.

She reached the parlour, breathing quickly, and entered, closing the door firmly behind her.

"You may come out now," she said, softly.

There was no answer: the curtains hung limp and lifeless.

With a startled exclamation, she darted across the room, and swept them aside.

No one was there. The man had vanished.

She pushed her hand against the glass doors: they gave at her touch, opening outwards.

She stood still for a moment, gazing out into the darkness of the shrubbery. Of course, she told herself impatiently, she ought to have expected this. Why should he wait there for her return? He had gained a start of her, even if she had raised the alarm almost immediately after he had left. No doubt by now he was far enough away for safety.

She felt an odd sense of disappointment, that was not all unsatisfied curiosity. Something about the man himself had attracted her interest: she would have liked to know him better.

Slowly, she turned away from the windows, and stood by the writing desk, deep in thought.

It was then that she saw the folded note.

At first, she did not take in the superscription, although it was written plainly, in large lettering. A second glance revealed her name. Eagerly, she snatched it from the table, and opened it with fingers which trembled slightly.

It bore only a few lines of writing, without any formal opening words.

I fear I can add nothing to the little I have already told. Perhaps someday I may be able to disclose the whole to you. Until that time, trust me if you can — keep my secret, if you do. Your devoted servant, madam, J.

She was reading this cryptic message for the third time, when she was startled by hearing the doorknob turning in someone's grasp. Quickly, she swung round, the paper clutched in her hand.

Mr. Dorlais and Captain Masterman stood hesitantly on the threshold.

"May we come in?" called Guy Dorlais, cheerily, then, altering his tone as he saw her startled expression — "'Pon my word, Miss Feniton, is anything wrong? You look as though you'd seen a ghost!"

"I —" She stopped, struggling for composure. "By all means come in," she continued, after a barely perceptible pause. "I was just about to return to the drawing room, in any event."

"Your grandmother dispatched us to help you find your scarf," explained Guy, with a grin. "We didn't dare refuse, eh, Masterman?"

The other man made no reply. His eyes were fixed upon Miss Feniton in a puzzled stare. His gaze switched from her face to the open curtains: he strode towards them.

"Why, these doors are unfastened!" he exclaimed, in surprise. "Did you find them like this, ma'am?"

"No," replied Joanna, carefully folding the note which she held, and so avoiding his eye. "I opened them myself. I — felt a little faint, and wished for some air."

Both gentlemen expressed concern at this statement, and Guy Dorlais offered to fetch Miss Lodge.

"There is no need, thank you," said Joanna, hurriedly. "I am now quite myself again. It was nothing — the heat of the room, no doubt."

She placed the letter carefully in her reticule, while both men watched her in silence. Then Captain Masterman closed the doors, secured them firmly, and pulled the curtains back into place before them.

As he stepped back into the room, his sleeve caught at the penknife which lay on the desk, sweeping it on to the floor. He stooped to retrieve it, then paused. Following the direction of his gaze, she noticed with misgiving that it was fixed upon that portion of the carpet which was stained with Captain Jackson's blood. The stains were not visible from where she stood: but surely at such close quarters, he could not miss them?

"Anything up, Masterman?" asked Dorlais curiously, seeing the other man's hesitation.

"Nothing," replied the captain, straightening himself, and laying the penknife down upon the table. He turned to Joanna. "I trust you found your scarf, Miss Feniton?"

Joanna felt the beginnings of a blush rising to her cheek. She turned and set about tidying away the writing materials from the desk, in order to conceal it.

"I must have left it in my room, after all," she replied, as carelessly as she was able. "It's of no account. I am warm again now. Shall we return to the withdrawing room, gentlemen?"

Captain Masterman nodded, and opened the door for her to pass through. She started towards it, then turned back to see why it was that Guy Dorlais was not keeping pace with her.

She saw that he was bending earnestly over the spot where the penknife had fallen.

Chapter V: Conference at "The Waterman"

It had begun to rain again, and a gusty wind caught at the bare branches of the trees, making them creak and groan. The night was black, with the impenetrable darkness of November, the time a little after midnight. A man trod catlike across the yard of "The Waterman," and softly raised the cellar trap. It opened on well-oiled hinges and he entered, closing the trap carefully behind him and noiselessly shooting the bolt.

A lamp suspended from the ceiling showed a small dark chamber, thickly covered with cobwebs, and having a very uneven stone floor on which stood a few empty barrels. One of these was upended, and the landlord was perched upon it, patiently waiting. At first sight of the other man, he started to his feet, frowning.

"So you're still alive, then," he stated without emotion.

Captain Jackson grinned. "And kicking," he said. "Did you give all that venison pasty to the good Colonel, Nobby?"

Nobby briefly described the Colonel in other, more colourful terms, before volunteering that he might perhaps find a portion of the pasty in the larder, if he looked hard enough.

"But there's someone waiting to see you upstairs." He gestured with his head at the ceiling. "That makes the second caller today — danged if I ever knowed such goings on! Ye'll mak' this place too 'ot to 'old us."

"Who is it?" asked Jackson.

"Same feller as gen'lly comes — 'im as ye calls Number One," explained Nobby, briefly.

The Captain nodded.

"I'll go to him at once. But first tell me what happened earlier this evening — d'you know who fired that shot?"

The landlord snorted. "One o' they Militiamen — drunk as a lord, 'e was. They 'ad to leave 'im be'ind when they went off to the village. The noise o' the coach must 'a roused 'im. The poor fool jumps up an' takes a pot shot at it, then falls down agin, dead to the world. I rushed out when I 'eard it, an' found 'im lyin' there. 'Twas too dark to see proper, though I 'eard the coach goin' on up the lane as though the devil was after it. I couldn't be sure whether you was in it or no, much less whether you'd been 'it, but I guessed as I should see ye soon enough if ye'd been wounded, an' if not, that ye'd keep clear for a bit, to see 'ow matters stood, like."

"What's happened to the fellow now?" asked Jackson with a frown.

"Don't ask me! I threw a bucket o' water over 'un, an' that soon sobered 'im up. Started 'ollerin' that Boney'd come, so I let 'im 'ave another for good measure. Then 'e says where are 'is mates, an' I says they'm over to the village. 'E asks me the way, an' off 'e goes, soakin' wet as 'e is. Whether 'e ever gets there or no, I can't say, an' don't rightly care."

The captain pondered this information for a moment in silence, then shrugged his broad shoulders.

"Not much he can tell, after all," he said, ruminatively. "And no one will attach much importance to the story of a drunkard, anyway."

Nobby used a descriptive word for the unfortunate soldier.

"We can forget him," said Jackson, walking towards the door of the cellar. "Bring me that pasty and a mug of ale upstairs, there's a good chap. Better make it two mugs," he added, remembering his visitor.

Nobby acquiesced, and the Captain made his way to the parlour where he had earlier entertained a prominent member of His Majesty's Government.

The man who was standing before the fire when Jackson entered the room was not nearly so distinguished looking as the former visitor. Like Jackson, he was wearing fisherman's attire: a dark woollen cap was pulled down at an angle over one eyebrow, and his face was almost concealed by a thick black beard. In spite of the beard, it was evident that he was of no very advanced age.

They nodded a casual greeting, and fell to exchanging information. Nobby appeared presently, bearing a tray which held the refreshment earlier bespoken by the Captain. Having dismissed the landlord, Jackson fell to with a will, but the other man showed little interest in the food.

"I ate a good dinner earlier," he said by way of explanation.

"Lucky fellow!" said his friend, with a rueful grin. "At least your life is not quite so topsy turvy as mine is."

"It's bad enough," replied the other. "I don't mind telling you, Captain, that at present I feel almost like throwing in my hand!"

Jackson raised an eyebrow. "Woman trouble?" he hazarded, shrewdly.

"The same! You may thank Heaven, my dear chap, that you are heart whole and fancy free."

"Mm," replied Jackson, thoughtfully, and fell into a momentary reverie.

He roused himself after a moment, and drained his mug.

"You say that all the local French agents have unaccountably moved their quarters, and are being watched by ours," he said, frowning. "And so far you have heard nothing concerning their new hideout? Or is there anything fresh to report?"

"Yes, there is," replied Number One. "Four got word to me yesterday. Two of them have been traced — to a farm situated about a mile from Kerswell Cove. There is no news yet of the others."

Captain Jackson whistled.

"The Cove!" he said, and it was evident that the information startled him. "Do they mean to make a run for it, think you? If so, that is proof positive that I am no longer trusted by the other side."

"Lord knows! What makes you think that they don't trust you, anyway? Have you anything definite to go on?"

"I've been followed on a few occasions," said Jackson, slowly. "But that might possibly be a matter of common precaution with all agents who are not of French extraction. No, what I mislike particularly is the fact that for some time past, I've had no orders from them — no printed orders, that is to say. Also I've been told nothing of what's afoot at the present moment — and there's obviously something very important in the wind when they whistle all their watchdogs from their holes in this way. There's that business of the brandy, too — I don't like that." He broke off, frowning. "D'you know, Number One," he said, suddenly, "I think it might be no very bad idea to take a closer look at those kegs which are destined for the Cove? I've suddenly had a notion — fantastic, I grant you, but then the whole business is deuced odd."

"What exactly have you in mind?" asked Number One, rising.

"It's scarce likely that they should run brandy out of France for the pleasure of taking it back into the country again, is it?" asked Jackson. "Yet why else should it be left in Kerswell

Cove? The place is nothing but a post office for Boney and his agents."

"It might be destined for the farm nearby, which appears to be their new headquarters," suggested Number One.

"That's exactly what I have in mind."

"Nothing extraordinary in that, then, is there?" asked the other, puzzled.

"You don't find it out of the way that Boney's agents should be supplied with large quantities of best brandy, presumably for their own consumption?" asked Jackson, derisively. "*Vive L'Empereur!*"

The other man frowned. "Yes, I see what you mean. They've got more important concerns than running contraband, too, so that isn't the answer — anyway, your gang handles that side of the business skilfully enough. No need for any outside help. What do you suggest, then, Captain?"

"That we find out exactly why these kegs are so very important that they can't be handled in the usual way," replied Jackson, and started for the door, snatching up a candle from the table as he passed by.

The two men made their way to the kitchen quarters of the inn. At this time of night, these were deserted. The only sign of life was the smouldering fire, damped down to last until morning.

Jackson lifted a lantern from an iron hook beside the fireplace.

"We'll need this," he said, sliding back the horn shutter and lighting the candle within. "Best shield it, though. By rights, there should be no one about at this time of night, but one can't afford to take a chance."

His companion took the lantern, and together they made their way to the back door, which Jackson softly unfastened. It gave on to a yard which overlooked the river, and which was bounded by a stone wall. Blackness enfolded them as they stepped outside the door, and, crossing the yard, moved along in the shelter of the wall. The rain blew softly into their faces, and their nostrils were assailed by the dank river smell. They came at last to a strip of rough, miry ground which separated "The Waterman" from the small farm. This they traversed as quickly as possible, their boots squelching into the sodden earth, which was crossed and recrossed by the tracks of a farm cart.

"Must remember to tell Dick Stokes to throw some shingle down," muttered Jackson. "Getting beyond anything just here!"

Presently they arrived at some roughly constructed outbuildings. In the largest of these, my lord's coach had reposed earlier in the evening. The two men were not bound for this, however, but turned instead into an open barn. One half of it was piled high with sweet-smelling hay; across the other half was set an old, rusty, broken down wagon, almost blocking the entrance. With some difficulty, they squeezed behind the wreck, uttering a few muffled oaths.

"My cursed breeches!" muttered Number One, feelingly. "I've ripped the damned things!"

"Small clothes appear to be in the wars, tonight," returned the Captain, with a grin that was lost in the darkness. "Never mind your confounded breeches, man, but lend me a hand here!"

He seized a hayfork from its place against the wall, and began shifting the pile of hay which lay behind the old wagon. He had soon revealed an iron ring set into the stone floor of the barn. Number One set down the lantern, and tugged at the ring. A square of the flooring rose up, revealing underneath a short flight of stone steps. The two men climbed into the aperture, bearing their lantern.

"We'd better close it, I think?" asked Number One. The other man assented, and took the lantern while his companion carefully lowered the heavy slab. "Phew!" he said, expressively, as he followed Jackson to the bottom of the steps.

Captain Jackson did not trouble to reply, but removed the cover from the lantern, so that they would have more light. He then reached upwards, and hung the lantern upon a hook which depended from the low ceiling.

The light fell upon a large cellar. Apart from a small space near the foot of the steps down which they had just come, the whole place was stacked to capacity with barrels and cases. Narrow lanes between the merchandise allowed a man to edge his way from point to point amongst it.

Number One laughed. "Your contraband appears to be a flourishing concern — pity you don't reap any of the profits yourself!"

The other agreed wryly. "More particularly as I must pay the penalty if they nab me," he said, carelessly. "However, a man can't expect adventure and security to go hand in hand."

"Reckless devil, ain't you?" asked Number One. "Won't even take the trouble to adopt a reasonable disguise."

The Captain surveyed his friend's black beard with an amused eye.

"Are you suggesting, my dear chap, that I should enshroud my features in fungus similar to that which you wear?" he asked, derisively. "Heaven forbid! My art must be sufficient disguise."

"It is, too," admitted the other, with grudging admiration. "All the same, have a care, Captain."

The warning was uttered seriously, in the tones of one who had Captain Jackson's welfare very much at heart. Jackson smiled.

"Don't worry, I will. As you know I must go aground shortly for a while we must make fresh arrangements for that."

"As to that, there is a slight complication on my side," admitted Number One, and told him briefly what it was.

"Damnable luck!" exclaimed the Captain, when he had heard his companion out. "But I suppose it was only to be expected. That puts us both out of the running, and at what I suspect to be a time of emergency, too! Is there nothing to be done?"

"Not on my side, at any rate," said Number One, firmly. "As much as my life's worth to default, give you my word! The fact is, I'm hamstrung, my dear boy! Don't know about you," he added, hopefully. "Is there any chance that you could —"

Jackson pondered deeply for a moment or two.

"I could do it, of course," he said, reluctantly. "But, truth to tell, I'm not sure that I wish to."

"Your own affair, naturally, my dear chap. But it isn't as if the lady means anything to you."

"Isn't it?" asked Jackson, cryptically. "I'm not sure."

"What do you mean?" asked the other, his curiosity thoroughly aroused.

Jackson shrugged. "I'll tell you at some other time. At present I don't think we need concern ourselves unduly, for I fancy I see a way whereby we may very well handle the affair as matters stand. The farm where these French agents are hiding is only a mile or so from Kerswell Cove, you say."

The other nodded.

"And Kerswell Cove, Number One, is about the same distance from Shalbeare House, the residence of Sir Walter Feniton, is it not?"

"True. So you think —"

"Lady Feniton is hospitable, and entertains widely," remarked the Captain. "It is one of her few virtues. You must surely have been at Shalbeare House at some time or other in your chequered career, Number One?"

His companion nodded.

"Then you will doubtless recall a small marble temple situated by an ornamental lake in that part of the grounds which slopes down towards the sea?" asked Jackson.

"I'm not sure," replied Number One, screwing up his face in an effort of recollection. "The place is a landscape gardener's nightmare, after all — any amount of pseudo-Greek temples and the like!"

"But only one ornamental lake, if you recall," persisted Jackson. "The temple should make a very safe rendezvous, don't you agree? Who, my dear chap, will wish to sit on a marble bench in mid-winter, admiring the prospect of a frozen lake? Only, I feel, the very eccentric."

Number One professed himself to be in complete agreement with this point of view.

"That's settled, then," said Jackson. "And now let's examine the drinking supply of Boney's agents, for the night progresses, as no doubt you've noticed, and I have many calls on my time."

"How if we were to try poisoning the stuff?" asked Number One, with a grin.

"Unless, if what I suspect proves to be true," was the reply. "But follow me, and we'll soon find out."

He led the way through the maze of contraband until he arrived at a section where all the kegs were marked with a bright slash of red paint encircling their widest part. Here he paused.

"This is the cargo for which I shall receive no payment," he said, frowning. "Well, every captain is entitled to know what cargo he carries, eh, my friend?"

He produced an implement, and proceeded to tackle the cork which was driven into the bunghole of the cask. After a short tussle, he succeeded in extracting it. He laid it aside, and pushed two exploratory fingers into the bunghole.

"Well?" asked Number One, expectantly.

Captain Jackson carefully withdrew the fingers, and silently displayed them to his companion after he had first made a brief scrutiny himself. The light was far from good in the cellar, but both men could plainly discern upon the fingers traces of a grey powder.

"What the devil —?" began Number One, puzzled.

The Captain carefully drove home the cork before replying. When he did, his face was grave.

"It's as I feared," he said. "These kegs do not contain brandy at all, but gunpowder. And I am not to be trusted with the secret. The question is — what's in the wind?"

Chapter VI: The Cottage by the River

Somewhere in the distance, a cock crowed. Miss Feniton awoke from a troubled sleep and sat up in bed. Some matter weighed uneasily upon her mind, but for the moment, she could not determine exactly what it was. Perhaps her conversation with Kitty last night had been the cause of her present sense of uneasiness. She had managed to slip into her friend's room unobserved by Lady Feniton, and they had talked earnestly for almost an hour.

She had taxed Kitty with coldness towards her betrothed.

"Oh, it's so difficult, Jo! You do not understand!" Miss Feniton had said that she was only too anxious to try, if given the opportunity.

Kitty hedged a little, and finally burst out with the words: "There are times when I could wish that Guy were not a Frenchman!"

Joanna stared. "Frenchman? When he has been educated at an English public school, and even plays cricket at White's Conduit Club — what can you mean?"

"I — I — oh, I don't know! Only sometimes I wonder if his sympathies are not on the other side of the Channel," said Kitty, in a low voice.

"This is a deal of nonsense, my dear! How much sympathy do you suppose he could possibly feel for the people who sent his parents to the guillotine, and brought him a refugee to his uncle's home in Devon when he was still only a boy?"

"Then why," asked Kitty, defiantly, "does he not join the Volunteers? When I see other gentlemen, such as Captain

Masterman for instance, in their regimentals, I tell you, Jo, I feel downright ashamed!"

"Have you asked him his reason for this?"

"Oh, yes! But he always turns the subject off, without giving a direct answer."

Joanna pondered this for a moment in silence.

"Perhaps he does not find the time, as he is so occupied with schemes for his uncle's farming," she offered, tentatively, at last.

"Farming!" retorted Kitty, her voice charged with scorn.

"Not romantic, perhaps, I grant you," said Joanna, laughing. "But very necessary to the country in time of war, nevertheless."

"It is not altogether that, either," replied Kitty, slowly; and now Miss Feniton gained the impression that they were about to come to the hub of the matter. "It is surely strange that — oh, why is it that so far he has shown no anxiety to fix upon a date for our wedding? There is no impediment on either side that I can think of, and we have now been betrothed a full three months!"

This certainly had been difficult to explain: indeed, Joanna herself could think of no reason for such cautious behaviour on the part of one whom she would have judged to be an impetuous character. She had done her best, however, and eventually left her friend feeling perhaps easier on the subject than she herself could be.

Having gone over all this in her mind again, she slipped down between the sheets once more, and tried to doze. She did not know what time it was, but certainly it must be too early to think yet awhile of rising.

To her annoyance, she found herself quite unable to relax. She sat up in bed again, and, after a moment's hesitation, leapt out and drew the curtains back from the window.

She looked out on a grey, windswept sky. A few last shrivelled leaves lingered on the gaunt trees, and the gardens were wet and desolate. She glanced at the clock on the mantelshelf. It was only half past five. She shivered as the cold air of the room struck through her thin nightgown. It was no use; she was too wide awake now to think of returning to her bed. She decided to dress.

She crossed to the other side of the room, and, picking up an ewer, poured some cold water into a basin. Hot water was to be had only by summoning one of the maids, and she had no wish to disturb the whole house. As she set down the ewer again, an unwelcome thought suddenly assailed her, bringing a wave of panic.

She had forgotten to clean the blood-stained carpet in the parlour downstairs.

So many things had conspired together yesterday evening to make her forget. She had been considerably flustered by the discovery that Jackson had gone, and by the reading of his letter. Scarcely had she recovered from the shock, than Guy Dorlais and Captain Masterman had entered the room, and it had become necessary to attempt some kind of explanation of what they had found there. She had accompanied them back to the withdrawing room without being able to think of anything except Jackson's letter, and what it could mean. Later, when she had recovered a little, she had found herself caught up in Kitty's doubts and fears. The result had been that here it was morning, and the carpet still as it was last night.

She must attend to it at once. She dared not leave it to the housemaids. Already, the stains had been noticed by two members of the household; she did not want anyone else to know. If the affair should reach her grandmother's ears, she knew that Lady Feniton would never rest until she had found an explanation of it.

She completed her cold wash, and dressed quickly, doing up her hair with fingers that trembled with excitement and apprehension. Would the servants be astir yet, she wondered? She must find a pail and scrubbing brush, but it would cause a sensation if she were to ask them for such articles. All would be well if there should prove to be no one in the kitchen quarters of the house. She must hurry.

She finished at last, and, creeping from her bedchamber, stealthily descended the stairs. There was no one in the hall, as yet. She walked noiselessly along the many passages which led to the domestic quarters.

Again she encountered none of the staff. Well pleased, she turned a corner, and found herself confronted by the very thing she required, a pail of water with soap and a scrubbing brush laid ready beside it.

She felt her spirits rise at such a piece of good fortune. Then she heard voices coming through the partly opened door of the kitchens nearby. It was obviously two women indulging in a gossip before starting work. Perhaps at any moment one of them would come out, and seize upon the pail, exclaiming at seeing Miss Feniton standing there. It was now or never, she decided. She noiselessly lifted the pail, scooped up the other articles, and hastily bore them off by the way she had come.

She had barely rounded the corner out of sight of anyone issuing from the kitchen, when she heard a muted shriek from that direction.

"Well, I'm danged!" exclaimed a puzzled female voice, "Where can I'v' bin an' gone an' put that pail, then? I'd 'a sworn I'd left 'un 'ere!"

Miss Feniton hastened her steps, doing her best to avoid spilling the water in the pail. It seemed a very long way to the parlour where she had yesterday evening talked with Captain Jackson, but at last she reached it. She set her burdens down, and thankfully closed the door, locking it as a precaution against being disturbed in her work. The curtains were still drawn; she pulled them back, and unfastened the French window, hoping that the gusty air would help to dry the carpet when she should have finished her task.

She rolled up the sleeves of her pin-tucked white gown, reflecting wryly that such attire had obviously never been intended for work. Then she went down on her knees, and once more examined the stains.

They were not, she decided, so very conspicuous, after all. Possibly the two gentlemen who peered so intently at this spot last night could not really have determined exactly what the marks were. No direct question had been asked, at any rate. If she cleared them away now, that might be the end of the matter.

She attacked her task with an energy which might well have been envied by the most robust of Lady Lodge's housemaids. Her efforts were rewarded. When she finally paused, leaning back to rest on her ankles and dropping brush and soap into the water, there remained no trace of a bloodstain on the carpet. Instead, there was only a large wet patch close to the writing desk. She trusted to the air coming in from the open door to dry this out quickly.

She rose from her knees, drying her hands upon a kerchief which she had brought with her for the purpose. Then she moved away from the desk and stood with her back to the window, pulling down her sleeves.

A step sounded on the gravel walk outside. She swung round quickly, one sleeve still rolled up above her elbow.

"Good morning, Miss Feniton."

It was Captain Masterman standing there.

"I — oh, good morning, sir," she stammered.

"I trust you slept well?" he inquired, stepping over the threshold into the room. "It is an unexpected pleasure to see you astir so early."

She began to pull down her sleeve, giving a great deal of attention to fastening the tiny buttons at the cuff.

"As a matter of fact, I slept but indifferently," she answered, as carelessly as she was able. "I hope you were more fortunate, Captain Masterman?"

He inclined his head gravely. "You will no doubt recall that the Colonel and I are obliged to make an early start back to Totnes. That is why we took our formal leave of the family last night. But I am sorry to learn that you did not sleep well. I trust nothing occurred to discompose you yesterday evening?"

His glance travelled from the pail to the wet patch upon the carpet as he spoke. She gave a little forced laugh.

"Why, no! Nothing in the world! Why do you ask?"

He frowned. "No reason, of course. That is to —" He broke off, studying her sleeves with evident interest. She became aware that there was a wet patch upon one of them, and a faint colour came into her cheeks. He lowered his gaze at once.

"One of our men told a strange tale last night," he went on, abruptly. "He would have it that he saw a coach down at the inn on the river, and called upon it to halt. Its driver ignored the summons, so our man fired upon the vehicle."

"The inn on the river?" asked Joanna vaguely, with some idea of gaining time to think.

He nodded. "The place where we called to try and obtain shelter for the night 'The Waterman'."

Joanna frowned. "But what is so strange about that, sir? Surely a coach may call at an inn without question?"

"Not this inn, Miss Feniton. The place is nothing but a wretched hedge tavern, and no coach can have been near it for years! No, our man was right to challenge it — that is, if any reliance can be placed on his word, for I regret to say that he was the worse for drink at the time, and had been left behind when the rest went to the village, on that account. Anyone there on legitimate business would have halted, and given a reasonable account of himself to a soldier of the Volunteer corps."

"Legitimate business?" faltered Joanna.

"Well, ma'am, I have heard it rumoured that the landlord of 'The Waterman' is hand in glove with a gang of smugglers."

She drew in her breath sharply. He raised his eyes once more to her face, studying her expression keenly. Her colour had ebbed away now, leaving her face strained and tired. She had herself well in hand, however.

"But surely Sir George would know of it, if there were any truth in that?" she asked.

"Not necessarily. In such cases, often whole villages are concerned in the business, and they all keep together. Besides, as long as everything is conducted quietly, without any acts of violence, there is no occasion for a magistrate to interfere."

"What do you mean to do about it?" she said, hardly daring to look into his face.

He shrugged. "What is there to do? I cannot be sure that my man has not conjured up these fancies in his drunken mind. Of course, if I were to be presented with any corroborative evidence —"

"But that is not likely, I take it," said Miss Feniton, in a firm voice.

"No," he replied, meeting her gaze.

Their glances held for a moment, then Captain Masterman turned away.

"I must not keep the Colonel waiting," he said. "I believe he will be ready now." He extended his hand. "I shall look forward to the pleasure of seeing you again when I and my sister join the party at Shalbeare House. It was good of Lady Feniton to invite us. Until then, Miss Feniton, I must bid you farewell. Your most devoted, ma'am."

He bowed stiffly over the still damp hand which she reluctantly offered him. Then, with one last glance at the wet patch on the carpet, he stepped out on the path. He turned for a moment to smile at her, raised his hand in salute, and was gone.

He left her in a state of considerable mental stress.

How much did he suspect? It was impossible to judge from his manner: all that could be said with any certainty was that he must have seen that all was not quite as usual. It was out of the question that he should not have realized what she had been doing in the room before he came upon her, but did he understand the significance of her action? Had he been merely making conversation when he had recounted the story of the drunken Militiaman? Or had he been inviting her confidence, knowing that she was in some way involved in that affair?

Her thoughts flew uneasily to Captain Jackson. He had been wounded slightly last night, and now she had heard an explanation which fitted that fact. Could this mean, then, that Jackson was an associate of smugglers — was this the secret which he must guard so zealously, which was too incredible to be believed, and too dangerous to be confided? From what little he had let drop, she had begun to suspect that he was concerned in something of quite a different character something of which he need not be ashamed. Evidently, she reflected with a wry little smile, she had allowed herself to become infected with Kitty Lodge's romanticism.

She thought of the note which he had left for her, and wondered how it would read now, by the cold, disillusioning light of early morning. She could soon put it to the test: it was still reposing in the reticule which she had been using last night.

She unlocked the door of the parlour, picked up the pail, and placed it outside the passage. She would have preferred to carry it back to the kitchen, but dared not, for fear of encountering any of the domestic staff on her way. This done, she returned to her room.

The reticule was still lying on her dressing table. She picked it up, and pulling back the drawstrings which held it fast, thrust her hand inside. A puzzled expression came over her face.

Yesterday evening when she had been interrupted in the parlour, she had pushed the letter hastily into the top of her reticule. She had not opened the bag since then, therefore there could be no reason why the paper should not be the first thing which came to hand. But it was not.

Impatiently, she emptied all the contents out on to the table.

At any other time, she might have been amused by the objects which she had managed to collect. A small toilet box, a hinged ivory fan and a pocket handkerchief with her initials embroidered in one corner she might have expected to see: but how had she acquired a piece of court plaster, a length of blue ribbon and a pink rosette off a shoe? There was, however, no piece of paper.

Captain Jackson's note had gone.

She sat down to consider this disconcerting discovery. It was obviously out of the question that the paper had fallen out of her bag. The drawstrings were too tight for that. No, the only possible theory was that someone had deliberately taken it.

Who would do such a thing, and for what purpose?

After a second's reflection, she dismissed the notion that it had been one of the servants. Most of them were country girls, who could not read, and the note could have no meaning for them. Besides, even if there should happen to be one among them who was dishonest, she would surely look for something of more value than a letter.

Try as she might, she could fix upon no one except Captain Jackson himself who could possibly have any interest in taking the note. It was not impossible to think of reasons why he might wish to recover it. He could not be sure that she would not show the paper to Sir George, and it was always possible to identify handwriting. Yesterday evening, he had seemed extremely anxious to avoid a meeting with Miss Feniton's host. Perhaps he was already known to the magistrate?

How exactly he would have found the means to take the letter from her reticule, she could not determine. The bag had been on her arm most of the evening after he had so abruptly left the parlour, although it had lain on the dressing table while she had talked with Kitty after everyone else in the house had retired. It had also remained there while she had been downstairs this morning. Was it possible that Jackson had contrived to re-enter the house during one of these short periods? There was no saying.

Wearied of mystery, she stood up, debating what to do. There must be some way of finding out more about the man Jackson, but what? Would it be of any use to poke about in the vicinity of "The Waterman"?

She seized upon the idea eagerly. She remembered having been told in the past that there were some cottages and a small farm situated down there on the river, beside "The Waterman". At this time of day, the cottagers' wives would most likely be found out of doors, drawing water from the well, or feeding their handful of livestock. It should not prove beyond her powers to enter into a trivial conversation with one of them. If there had indeed been mysterious doings at the inn last night, she ought to be able to glean some gossip concerning the affair. She might even learn something more of Captain Jackson.

She went to the wardrobe, and took from it a warm pelisse and red velvet bonnet and a pair of fur lined half boots. She donned these garments hastily, then opened a drawer and found her gloves. She glanced at the clock. It was just turned six.

As she was walking downstairs, she decided to leave the house by the French window in the parlour. She must first, however, ascertain that the officers had departed on their journey. It would never do to give Captain Masterman further reason to suspect her of furtive behaviour. This time, he might feel impelled to take more positive action.

Outside the parlour door, she came upon one of the housemaids: The girl was staring thunderstruck at the pail which still stood there. She started violently at Miss Feniton's somewhat stealthy approach.

"Lawks, ma'am!"

"I'm sorry if I startled you, Polly. Can you tell me if the gentlemen have already left the house?"

The girl paused to collect her wits before replying.

"'Tis a queer ol' mornin', ma'am, an' no mistake, what wi' pails gettin' up an' walkin' on their own, an' —" She broke off, evidently realizing that she had not answered Miss Feniton's question. "Yes, ma'am, they went not five minutes agone — did you want to speak wi' them, ma'am?"

"No, it's of no consequence," replied Joanna. "I wonder, Polly, could you possibly procure me a cup of hot chocolate? I am minded to take a stroll before breakfast."

The girl looked at her doubtfully. Evidently she considered that one more odd event had been added to the morning's score.

"You'll pardon me, I'm sure, ma'am, but bain't 'ardly the weather," she said. "Where shall I bring you the chocolate?"

Joanna indicated that the parlour would suit her very well, and Polly departed, wondering what other freaks of fate awaited her during the course of the morning.

Hardly more than ten minutes later, Joanna was making her way through the kitchen gardens to a gate which opened on to the lane running down to the river.

There was a high wind blowing, but she was sheltered from it in the lane by reason of the high banks set on either side. She made her way downhill carefully; the track was rough and stony, and she had no wish to end her adventure with a ricked ankle. At last she reached the end of the lane, and came out to the plot on which stood the buildings. The inn was nearest, and she surveyed it carefully.

It appeared to be deserted, although a wisp of smoke was coming from its chimney. She walked on past it, until she came to the farm. Here, too, was no sign of life. On its other side, were two cottages which she could see at a glance were derelict. Disappointed, she turned her attention once more to the farm.

It was surely strange that there should be no one about? At this hour of day, the countryside was usually full of activity. It had simply never occurred to her that she would not meet some worker, male or female, down here. She was momentarily at a loss. She had no wish to knock at the door of either place and ask questions, and for the life of her she could think of no good excuse for rousing these people. Such an action would cause comment, and give rise to gossip which might reach the ears of the family at the big house. Her questions, when put, must be casual-seeming, certainly not anything in the nature of an interrogation.

At one side of the farm was a slipway giving access to the river beach. If she walked along the strip of shingle at the river's edge, she should be able to see into the yards at the back of the buildings, and might perchance spy someone working there. A civil good morning ought to pave the way for her questions, carefully put. She could think of nothing better to do, and took her way down to the river.

As she stepped out on to the beach, she again became exposed to the full force of the wind. A sudden unruly gust tugged at her bonnet, blowing it on to the back of her head, and considerably disordering her dark curls. She put up her hands to right it; but a second, more violent gust tore at the fluttering ribbons before she could reach them. In a moment, that expensive creation of an exclusive Exeter milliner went whirling through the air.

Miss Feniton made a grab for it. It eluded her, landing flat on the water, and skimming neatly along on the surface like a child's toy boat. It was only a few feet from the edge: she looked about her for something with which to recapture it, and saw close at hand the fallen branch of a tree. She seized this with an involuntary exclamation of satisfaction, and at once began to fish for her property, the light of the sportsman in her eye. Several times, she almost had it, but a shift of wind would carry it out of reach again. Becoming more determined as her efforts proved unavailing, she also became less cautious in her movements. A final desperate lunge with the stick succeeded in impaling the bonnet, but brought its owner stumbling forward into the water.

With difficulty, she managed to keep her balance, and so avoid measuring her length in the river; but her half boots, stockings and the lower part of her pelisse and gown were soaked. At first, she disregarded this, grabbing the bonnet with a little cry of triumph, and casting the stick away from her into the river. Then realization of her plight came swiftly, causing her to grimace in dismay. Carrying the sodden, useless bonnet in one hand, while with the other she raised her dripping skirts, she moved back on to the dry shingle, her boots squelching unpleasantly at every step.

She paused irresolutely, and looked about her. She could see into the farmyard, but the place was deserted, save for some scrawny hens scratching disconsolately in the mire. She sat down upon the stones, and, drawing off her boots, proceeded to empty the water out of them. While she was donning them again, she paused to consider what her next move should be. She had no desire to return to Teignton Manor in this plight, quite apart from the discomfort of the lengthy walk back in wet stockings and footgear.

Obviously, she must apply at the farmhouse for the means of drying her garments. There was sure to be a woman about the place somewhere, and she now had the perfect excuse for knocking, and demanding to see a female. Her small accident might yet prove the best means to achieve her ends.

Heartened by this thought, she made her way with difficulty up the slipway, and to the door of the farmhouse. She knocked loudly.

There was no reply. After what she considered a reasonable pause, she knocked again. She shivered as she waited, for the wind was whipping her wet garments about her legs, and her head was bare. When she still obtained no reply, she seized the knocker once more and beat out a veritable tattoo upon the door.

At last, she was certain that there was no one there. The house wore an aura of emptiness, difficult to define, but plainly perceptible. She was wasting her time in knocking.

Disappointed and by now chilled through, she turned away, and walked down with slow steps to the gate. It was then that she noticed a tumbledown cottage standing quite isolated in the far corner of a meadow opposite the farm. She looked more closely: at first, she judged it to be derelict, but she soon noticed a trail of thin smoke issuing from its chimney. Evidently it was inhabited. Should she try there for help, or at the inn, which was nearer?

A second's reflection provided the answer. She recalled what had been said by the two officers of their reception at the inn, and decided that the landlord would scarcely be more welcoming to an unaccompanied female than he had been to the Volunteer forces. It would take a little while to reach the cottage, but surely there she could hope to find a homely body who would make her welcome to a seat by the fire until her clothes were dry?

She at once set out for her objective. Her steps were necessarily slow, owing to the weight of water in her boots and garments, and to add to this, she soon discovered that the meadow was marshy. Her feet sank frequently into deep mud, having to be withdrawn again by considerable effort. She did her best to select the drier patches, but soon gave this up, as it involved making a considerable detour, thus placing the cottage at an ever increasing distance.

With grim determination, she plodded her difficult way along, until she had approached to within thirty or forty yards of the place. She stopped for a moment, then, surveying it critically. She was obliged to ask herself how anyone could ever live there. Most of the windows were boarded up, through lack of glass: one only, like a small eye in a large head, reflected light from a watery sun. The roof required rethatching, while the walls seemed to sag around a battered door that was a stranger to paint.

There could be no doubt about the smoking chimney, however. Someone did indeed live in the place, for a fire burned; and although she had noticed similar signs of life at both the inn and the farm, surely not all the inhabitants of this particular area could be abroad on business of one kind or another this morning?

She hurried forward. The ground was firmer here, and she was able to cover the remaining distance quickly. Breathing somewhat rapidly, she knocked upon the door in an imperative manner.

There was no immediate reply, but she had a distinct feeling of being overlooked. She glanced sharply at the one unboarded window. Somewhat to her surprise, it was closely curtained in a piece of dimity of noticeable cleanliness. The discovery pleased her, for she fancied that here she detected a woman's touch.

She moved nearer, trying to peer into the room. Her view was effectively screened by the curtain, but she thought she could make out a shadow which moved behind it. She scarcely paused before knocking again, this time impatiently. By now, she was unable to control her shivering, for her feet and legs were almost numb with cold. It flashed through her mind, even in the midst of such discomfort, that she must look more than a little dishevelled.

At last, the door was partially opened. A man's voice spoke from behind its shelter.

"Who's there?"

"Is there by any chance a woman about the place?" asked Miss Feniton, in a voice made faltering by cold and breathlessness. "I have had the misfortune to fall into the river, and am wet through. If I might be permitted to dry myself by your fire for a little —"

The door was opened fully.

Miss Feniton hesitated. She still could not see the man, who remained hidden behind the door, but the view now afforded her of the room showed that it certainly held no other occupant. It was a small, dim apartment, even in the extra light afforded by the open door; but her appraising glance discovered a bright fire blazing on the hearth, and a comfortable looking chair drawn up beside it. This was just what she needed.

"Is your wife within?" she repeated.

"I have told you before this that I have no wife, Miss Feniton," was the unexpected reply. "But for all that, you need not scruple to enter."

Chapter VII: Captain Jackson's Story

She drew in her breath sharply in surprise. "You!" she said and hesitated for a moment. Then she walked in. He closed the door firmly behind her.

He turned, surveying her in one comprehensive glance. Her black curls were blown in disorder about her face, which was pinched with cold. In one hand she still unthinkingly carried the sodden bonnet, while her muddied skirts and footgear told their own story.

"You *are* in a pickle!" he said, with a brief smile, and indicated the armchair with a graceful motion of his hand. "You'd best get out of those wet things without delay, if you would avoid a chill."

"Thank you," replied Miss Feniton, coldly, "that will not be necessary. A few moments before the fire should suffice to dry out most of the moisture, and enable me to be on my way again."

"Nonsense!" he said, briskly, moving towards the door in one corner of the fireplace wall. "I'll lend you a dressing robe."

He opened the door, and proceeded to clatter up a short flight of obviously uncarpeted stairs. Her fruitless protests followed him, but he paid no heed, returning presently with a dressing gown which he flung over the arm chair.

"There you are! I apologize for the masculinity of the attire, but no female garment is to hand. Now, if I remove myself for a space to the upper room, you may get out of those wet garments, and into this. Pray call me when you are ready."

"Do you imagine," asked Miss Feniton, in amazement, "that I shall do any such thing?"

He raised his eyebrows. "Why ever not? Surely you are not —" his voice quivered with amusement for a second — "missish? I had not expected that: it doesn't seem in character."

"So you have been reading my character, have you?" Miss Feniton retorted, moving over towards the fire and stretching out her hands to the welcome blaze.

"It is a trick on which my safety often depends," he answered soberly.

"I see. And may I ask what you made of me?"

He gestured towards the dressing gown. "By all means — when you have divested yourself of that wet clothing."

"I fear, then, that I must forgo the pleasure of ever knowing," she answered, dryly. "May I sit down?"

"But of course!" he said, promptly. "Miss Feniton, you must see that this is absurd! Do you positively wish to catch a chill?"

She made no reply. After one brief look at her face, he went quickly to the cupboard in the corner, and took something from one of the shelves. He returned to her side, laying a small pistol on the arm of her chair.

"Do you know how to use this?" he asked.

She nodded, too startled for speech.

"If you should find anything to complain of in my conduct towards you, do not hesitate to do so. And now, if I remove myself upstairs for a space, will you consent to make use of the robe? I will remain aloft if you wish, until you are ready to be on your way again. Otherwise, you may summon me to talk with you; it shall be exactly as you desire."

He quitted the room without more ado, leaving Miss Feniton looking after him with mixed feelings. Common sense prevailed, however, and, with a shrug, she began to draw off her boots and muddied stockings. She spread these before the fire to dry, and then removed her wet pelisse.

This done, she hesitated. At last, she unfastened the girdle which bound her gown about her waist, and, after a moment's struggle with the buttons of her sleeves, drew the gown over her head.

She picked up the dressing gown. Owing to the smallness of the closely curtained window, the light in the room was poor; but the leaping flame of the fire caught the glint of a richly tinted brocade. It seemed a strangely luxurious garment for a mere fisherman to possess. She donned it thoughtfully, fastening it securely about her, then turned to spread the hems of her clothing before the fire.

She stood pensively looking down into the flame for a while. At length, she went to the door which gave to the stairs, but her steps were slow. Hesitantly, she opened the door a little.

"You may come down now," she called, in a low voice.

She returned much more quickly to the fire. Presently, she heard the man's feet on the staircase. He entered, and came towards her.

She looked up. It was not easy to read his expression, for the light of the room gave her only a hazy impression of his features. His eyes seemed to be considering her, though, for a long time. Truth to tell, he was seeing quite a different young lady from the one who had interviewed him yesterday evening. Her soft black hair was falling about her face, giving it a gentler expression, and in the firelight her lovely eyes looked fuller and deeper. Cold followed by warmth had imparted a glowing tone to her skin, and the deep red dressing gown set off admirably her dark beauty.

"I trust you will know me if we should chance to meet again," she said, tartly.

"I beg your pardon," he said, starting from his reverie. "It was impertinent of me to stare you out of countenance — but I find you so changed."

"It is certainly not very gallant to remind me that I am not looking my best," she remarked, reproachfully, but with a twinkle in her eye which he could not see.

"On the contrary — I have never seen you looking to better advantage."

"But then," she reminded him, "you have seen me only once before this, after all."

"True. On that occasion, I was the one to be at a disadvantage. But will you not be seated? What can I offer you? I don't imagine you would care to partake of a glass of wine, and I have no ratafia here. You should have a warm drink, though — a cup of tea or coffee, perhaps?"

Miss Feniton was about to decline either beverage, but again common sense prevailed. She had indeed felt thoroughly chilled until this very minute, and had no wish to suffer for her adventure by being kept to her bed for a day or two. She therefore accepted the offer of a cup of tea, with calm gratitude; and then sat down, eyeing the pistol as she did so.

There was a kettle standing on the hob; the man reached over, placing it on the fire.

"I must apologize for the limitations of my hospitality," he said, with a smile. "One fire must do the job of both cooking and heating in this establishment. However, though primitive, I think you will find everything clean — we are even so fortunate as to be in possession of one uncracked cup, I find."

"Is this your home?" she asked, curiously.

He shook his head. "Merely a *pied a terre*. I am never in one place for long."

"I had already noticed that," she answered, dryly.

"You received my note last night?" he queried, watching her face, which was illuminated and softened by the light of the fire.

She nodded. "Yes, I did; but I lost it again, I fear."

"Lost it?" His voice was sharp.

"I believe that someone must have removed it from my reticule either yesterday evening or this morning," she said, looking at him questioningly.

He was silent for a moment or two. The kettle began to sing, and he fetched a battered teapot from the cupboard.

"Who do you suppose it was?" he asked, bending over the fire.

"That depends. It could have been, for instance, yourself."

He turned a surprised look upon her. "I? Why on earth should you suppose I would do a thing like that?"

She shrugged, and a dark curl fell forward on to her face.

"It is not impossible to think of reasons. Since you appear to be so anxious to conceal your identity, it may be that you would not risk leaving a specimen of your handwriting in my possession."

"What makes you suppose that I have any other identity than my acknowledged one?" he asked, busying himself with making the pot of tea, and carrying it to the plain, well-scrubbed deal table in the middle of the small room.

She turned to face him.

"Come, it is time that we ceased fencing, Captain Jackson. You are no ordinary fisherman. Though I have no certain information about your real identity, there is much that I suspect concerning your affairs."

She paused. He raised his brows, expectantly. She decided upon bold tactics.

"I suspect, for example, that you are a smuggler."

"You do?" he seemed amused. "Why, may I ask?"

She told him briefly the circumstances on which her suspicions were founded. He heard her out in silence, a slight frown between his brows. When she had finished, he laughed softly.

"You may be right. But are you sure that you know of no one else who could have taken that letter? It might be important."

"It was not you, then?"

"Good Lord, no! Although I must admit that it would have been wiser in me never to have written it: you might have carried it straight to Sir George Lodge."

"And he would have been able to identify you by the handwriting?" she asked, shrewdly.

He shook his head, "You are astute, Miss Feniton, but I am not inexperienced in matters of this kind. The handwriting was disguised, in any event."

"But it was that of a gentleman, nevertheless," she parried.

He fell silent, and poured out the tea. He handed her a cup, which she took with a quick word of thanks.

"Then you can think of no one who might have taken it?" he persisted.

"Not unless Mr. Dorlais or Captain Masterman could have done so," she answered, in a tone of irony. "They came into that room after you had gone, and found me reading the note. They also saw me place it in my reticule."

"But they could not have seen the wording?"

"Of course not," she said, with a trace of indignation.

"Then they could have no reason to be interested in it, unless —" He paused, frowning.

"Do you really have the impudence to suggest," asked Miss Feniton, with some heat, "that two gentlemen whom I have known for many years would stoop to petty theft? You must not judge everyone by yourself, you know!"

He disregarded this remark. "Did either of them by any mischance observe the bloodstains on the carpet, do you know?"

"I'm afraid they did." Her voice changed, became almost apologetic. "Captain Masterman remarked on the open window, went over to shut it, and in so doing knocked a penknife on to the floor. Naturally, he bent to pick it up, and I am certain that he noticed then, although he made no remark. Afterwards, Mr. Dorlais went over to that spot also, and seemed to be examining it."

"And neither made any comment?"

"Only something concerning the open window. I felt obliged to offer some explanation of that."

She looked away, a little confused.

"What did you say?" he asked, curiously. "Did you —?"

She shook her head, so that the firelight caught the warm tints in her dark hair.

"You lied to them?" he asked, incredulously. "You made up some tale to save me from discovery?"

"Do not flatter yourself," she answered, coldly. "If I lied, it was with the far less philanthropic intention of saving myself. I had previously told no one of your presence in the house; it was a trifle difficult to do so then, was it not?"

"Why did you say nothing?" he asked, quietly. "Was it in response to my appeal, I wonder? Did you indeed believe me when I said that I meant no harm by my presence in the grounds of the Manor?"

"I did not know what to believe," she answered candidly. "But I did know —" She stopped suddenly.

"Yes?" he prompted.

"That I meant to find out more about you — for myself," she finished, the light of battle in her eye. "I am quite determined to hear the whole truth from you, sir, on this occasion."

He came towards her, relieving her of the now empty cup.

"Are you indeed? And supposing that I don't choose to tell you? What then?" he asked, mockingly.

"Then I shall force you — with this," said Miss Feniton, suddenly taking up the pistol and levelling it at his chest. "Now will you speak, Captain Jackson? Or don't you value your life?"

He laughed softly.

"I assure you that I am in deadly earnest," she warned him.

The hand which held the pistol was as steady as a rock, the forefinger curved ready on the trigger. A pair of hazel eyes met and held his glance coolly.

"I make no doubt of it," he replied, lightly. "But are you confident that you have sufficiently considered the difficulties of your present situation?"

"What do you mean?" she asked, suspiciously.

"Why, simply this have you ever been alone with a corpse, Miss Feniton?"

She swallowed, but her hand did not quiver on the trigger.

"There is always a first time for everything. I was reared in a somewhat Spartan tradition."

"Last night," he said, reminiscently, "you bound my arm — the merest scratch! with all the tenderness of which a woman is capable when her compassion is aroused. Today, you propose to shoot me in cold blood for no better reason than that I will not gratify your curiosity! It has been truly said that females are strange creatures!"

The pistol wavered. "I suppose it may appear that curiosity is my only motive," said Miss Feniton, consideringly. "And yet —" She stopped.

He regarded her questioningly.

"I have a right to know!" she finished, in a decisive tone. "I — I in some sort shielded you from the law! You owe it to me to explain yourself."

He nodded gravely, "I, too, feel the force of that argument. And yet you must believe me when I say that the secret of my doings is not wholly mine to divulge."

"If you mean," she said, contemptuously, "that you are indeed a smuggler, and that you hesitate to betray your gang, I understand you very well! I have heard that there is honour among thieves, but have never credited it until this moment!"

"If only that were all," he said, ruefully, "I might confide in you straightaway, and take the consequences! But far more hangs on this than a brush with the Preventive men —" He broke off, and brooded for a space.

"So you said before," she reminded him, and quietly putting down the pistol, bent over the garments which she had spread before the fire.

"These are almost dry," she said. "I shall not need to trespass upon your hospitality for much longer."

He stepped back. "If that is so, I could almost wish that you had fallen bodily into the river!" he exclaimed, with a smile.

She threw him a quelling glance. "Gallantry is not to my taste, sir. I believe that I have mentioned this before."

"You are very hard, Miss Feniton. Have you no compassion, I wonder?" he asked, jestingly.

"That is for you to judge. You told me that you had read my character."

"Did I so? That was presumptuous in me."

"Probably: but I should be interested to hear your findings."

He studied her for a moment before replying. A tentative smile lingered on her warm lips; the firelight caught at the auburn tints in her glossy dark hair.

"'Sweetest nut hath sourest rind, such a nut is Rosalind'," he quoted, softly.

She started, and flushed angrily.

"Insolent! How dare you!" she exclaimed. Then her sense of humour immediately gained the upper hand, and she relaxed in her chair, laughing quietly. "Well, at any rate, it is certain that you have received the education of a gentleman," she said, accusingly. "Shakespeare in the mouth of a fisherman, indeed! That is very likely!"

"Only this morning, you would have said that it was not more likely that you should be sitting here, in a fisherman's cottage," he reminded her. "Nothing is certain."

"Yet here I am, and here are you," she agreed. "Why? Will you not tell me your history?"

The invitation was given in a gentler tone than any that he had yet heard from her. He gazed into her face, and was struck again by the luminosity of those grey-green eyes. He turned away, fighting a desire to tell her all, to risk his safety on the whim of a spoilt, arrogant girl who would most likely never set eyes on Captain Jackson again.

"I am just a man who found a task to do — and did it," he answered, gruffly.

"And what was this task?"

He shrugged. "Something which called for the kind of talents I possess."

She considered him. His face was turned away from her, but his whole carriage was alert, watchful, ready for any emergency.

"You have known danger," she said, spontaneously.

He nodded. "I find it exhilarating," he confessed.

"That is why you do — what you do?"

"Partly — yes, mostly, if I am to be honest. But also, someone must undertake my work."

"Tell me truly," she said, speaking very quietly, "do you — are you — it has crossed my mind that you might be a spy: is it possible?"

Again he nodded.

"For your own country, or —" she swallowed — "or for France?"

"For both," he answered, recklessly.

She drew a quick breath, and for a second her face reflected all the horror she felt.

"But — you surely cannot be so dead to all feelings of patriotism —"

"Acquit me. What I do is done in the service of my country."

She sighed. "I do not understand —"

"How should you? It is difficult enough."

He brought a wooden chair from beside the table, and placed it close to hers, seating himself.

"Now that you know so much, I may as well tell you what I can of the rest. The Government wanted news out of France. To obtain it, a link had to be found between the enemy and ourselves. Even in time of war, the smuggler provides such a link: Boney, in particular, has made great use of English smugglers. These Devon men with whom I work, however, have taken part in no spying activities — their interest lies only in the free trade, which they regard as a legitimate livelihood, in spite of Customs laws."

He paused, and watched to see how she took this. She nodded.

"That I understand. But you, yourself —"

"Smuggling is a cover, spying for the enemy is a cover, to my real activities," he went on, rapidly. "Both enabled me to find out what the enemy is planning."

"But that puts you in a situation of the utmost danger!"

"Do you care?" he asked, unexpectedly.

The animation died out of her face, and was replaced by her usual reserved expression.

"Why should I? It seems strange, however, that you should choose to place yourself in such a position."

"Someone must do so, Miss Feniton. Increasingly, wars are being fought not only by active combatants, but by those who supply them with the information they require. Besides, I've already told you that to me danger is a challenge to be met."

"I wonder if I can believe this strange story?" she asked, musingly.

"That must be as you choose. There is one point, however, on which you have no choice."

She raised her brows. "And that is —"

"I must have your promise that you will respect my confidence."

She drew herself erect in her chair. "Must, sir?"

"Must, Miss Feniton," he repeated. "I will beg it, if you wish, but I have the feeling that you might despise a beggar."

"I hope I am possessed of as much Christian charity as the next woman," she retorted, with a frosty smile. "But I must admit that you are right: I do not care for my equals to come begging to me."

"You admit me as an equal, then?" he asked, curiously.

"It is evident that you have the right. Will you not tell me who you really are, since you have honoured me with so much of your confidence?"

A shadow passed over his face. "You haven't yet given me the promise for which I asked," he reminded her, gravely.

She paused a moment, evidently considering the matter.

"Why do you hesitate?" he asked. "You go against your own instincts, you know. You have shown already that you trust me."

"You are insufferable!" she said, stung by his assurance.

"Perhaps you are right: of late, I've been too little in female society to have remembered the art of making myself agreeable. Nevertheless, what I said was true, wasn't it? You have already given me your confidence?"

Miss Feniton had her fair share of faults, but a lack of honesty was not among them. She nodded.

"That is true, though I cannot account for it. It is against all reason."

"It is said that females have a reasoning all their own," he answered, smiling.

"A great deal too much nonsense is talked of females!" she said, with a snap. "We are as rational creatures as you!"

"No doubt," he agreed, gravely. "We will argue that on some other occasion. But the promise?"

"Since you make such a point of it, I give it — but conditionally only. That kind of promise can sometimes defeat its own object. If I should ever feel that your safety — or the safety of others — depended upon my divulging what I know, I should be obliged to break my word to you. You may be sure that it would not be lightly done."

He was silent for a while. "I see that you consider everything," he said, at last. "But I am satisfied. You must realize that I would not have the temerity to demand such a promise for my own sake alone. Somewhere in this area of Devon, Miss Feniton, there are genuine French agents at work

— one man in particular, the leader of this band, represents a deadly threat to England while he is at large, and his identity unknown. It is my purpose to uncover him; should he realize that I am not what I appear to be, my chances of doing this would be gone."

Her face changed, and she caught her breath sharply. "Do you know this man, then — does he know you? I do not quite understand —"

"Neither. I collect his dispatches, and carry them to France. But I have never set eyes on him — nor he on me, as far as I know."

"You do that?" The lovely eyes widened in dismay. "But —"

"Don't worry. The letters are opened, and copies sent to London before they are delivered to Boney."

She clasped her hands tightly in her lap.

"It — it is an appalling risk," she said, falteringly. "But if you never meet, how do you obtain these dispatches?"

"They are left for me to collect in a place that we both know of," he answered.

"I see," she said, slowly. "And how is it that you are certain that this man is to be found in our part of Devon?"

"One thing that suggests it is the situation of our unofficial post office; another, the dispatches themselves. They contain maps and information such as would be known only to an inhabitant of the area."

"Does the handwriting offer no clue to his identity?" asked Miss Feniton, thoughtfully.

He shook his head. "The dispatches are printed. I do receive orders from the same source, too, but these are made up of printed words pasted on to a blank sheet of paper — I suppose, because the orders are usually of a more impromptu nature than the dispatches, and there is not the time to have them printed. The words are most likely cut from magazines or other books of no permanent value. It's a clever idea, as it leaves no possible clue to the identity of the sender."

"I wonder?" she said, frowning. "It would be a Frenchman, of course — and living hereabouts. There are a few émigrés, but —"

"This man need not be a Frenchman at all," he pointed out. "Most gentlefolk are sufficiently acquainted with the language."

"But surely an Englishman could never do this?" she asked in horror.

He shook his head. "Who is to say what men will do, and why?" he asked, quietly. "Money, love of power, fear — these are powerful incentives to a man to break faith."

She rose and stood before the fire, deep in thought.

"I must go," she said, at last, rousing herself. "Already I have been absent for more than an hour, and although no one is likely to have noticed it yet, I must not try my luck too far. In any case, these garments are quite dry now."

"Shall I leave you for a few moments, then? You will wish to change."

"If you please. Perhaps it will be as well to take leave of each other now, and then I need not again disturb you. Unless," she added, as an afterthought, "you will wish to secure the door after me."

"But I mean to accompany you to Teignton Manor," he said recklessly.

"No." She shook her head, decisively. "After what you have just told me, I certainly shall not permit you to take such a risk. Excepting for my mishap, I came here in perfect safety, and there can be no reason why I should not return alone."

"At least I must show you an easier way to reach the lane," he protested. "I watched you making your way through mud and dirt by the longest route to the cottage."

"For that I should be grateful — but only if you can show me from the door of your cottage," she replied, smiling.

"I can, of course, but —"

"No objections," she said, firmly. "Allow me ten minutes down here alone, and I shall be ready to depart. I suppose you do not possess a looking glass? I have not one with me."

"A — oh, to be sure! One moment!"

He raced upstairs, returning at once with a small round mirror, which he propped up on the table against a teacup.

"Madam's dressing table," he said, with a courtly bow. "I regret the absence of the abigail — you have a comb, I trust? Ah, splendid!"

She gurgled with laughter. "You are absurd! Very well, then — ten minutes."

He vanished through the door which led to the stairs.

She stood in thought for a moment. This time, his story had carried complete conviction, even though it was more fantastic than any he had so far produced. He has a strange man, this Captain Jackson, evidently a man of many parts: and she did not yet know who he really was.

She shook off her reverie, and began to dress. Then she sat down with a smile at her improvised dressing table, and did what she could to make her hair tidy. When she had finished, she picked up the battered bonnet which had been the cause of all the trouble. Never again, she thought, with a fastidious wrinkling of her nose, could she wear such a poor wreck as it had become. She let it drop, rose, and went to the door at the foot of the stairs

He came at once when she called him, and stood for a moment looking down at her.

"You are Miss Feniton, now," he said, involuntarily.

"And pray who was I before?" she asked, with a smile.

"You looked like a child — a small girl, uncertain of herself. But Miss Feniton is always assured, always mistress of the situation."

"It's well that she is," retorted the lady. "For when you are concerned in it, the situation is apt to become a little out of hand!"

He laughed. "On that note, we part. Will you come with me, and I will put you on your way home? That is, if you are quite determined that I shall not accompany you?"

"We have already settled all that," she said, firmly, and followed him into the back of the cottage.

He opened the door, and indicated in a few words how she could find her way by a path across the meadow to a stile which led into the lane.

"You should meet with no one," he said, hesitantly. "But it goes against my instincts to let you go unaccompanied. Will you not change your mind?"

"Captain Jackson, you are a most persistent person!" she said. "But I am equally firm, you know!"

She looked up at him as she spoke. He drew back a little, within the shadow of the door, as though reluctant to allow her to see his face by the light of day. She could not fail to understand his action, and felt a fleeting chagrin that he should still not be prepared to trust her completely.

"I thank you for your timely hospitality," she said, holding out her hand in farewell.

He took it in a firm grasp, and retained it for a moment, once more searching her expression.

"*Au revoir*, Miss Feniton. Perchance we shall meet again."

She shook her head. "I do not think it likely. I shall shortly be leaving the Manor for my own home."

"Shalbeare House?"

She looked at him curiously. "How do you know? But I forget — you told me once that it is your business to know such things."

"It is, indeed. I, too, shall shortly be leaving this place. It has become a trifle warm of late, and with you gone, can have few attractions."

She withdrew her hand from his grasp. "I must again remind you, sir, that I do not care for flattery."

"I do not flatter, madam."

"Then that is worse!" she retorted. "You must see that it is not proper for me to accept a compliment from a gentleman with whom I am not even acquainted!"

"Not — oh, I take your meaning. Of course, we have never been formally presented."

"Precisely. I might waive some of the formality, however —" here she looked menacingly at him — "if I did but know your real name."

There was silence for a long moment. At last, reluctantly, the man answered her.

"I must not tell you now; forgive me. Someday, I promise, you shall know — meanwhile —"

"Meanwhile, I am to know you only as Captain Jackson," she stated, disappointment in her tone.

He bowed gracefully. "And as your devoted servant, Miss Feniton."

She smiled, and inclined her dark head, then turned quickly to follow the path he had indicated.

The man stood at the door and watched until she was out of sight.

Chapter VIII: Miss Feniton is Introduced to a Poet

A little more than a week later, Miss Feniton left Teignton Manor for her own home. She was accompanied not only by her grandparents, but also by the Lodge family and their personal servants, the resultant cavalcade reminding Kitty (or so she said) of a Royal procession.

During the interval, Miss Feniton had made no more excursions to "The Waterman" and its environs, neither had she confided her adventures to Kitty. There was a quality about those events which rendered them unlike any others of her life, and which made her a little shamefaced when she considered them in retrospect. Had she been foolish, gullible, lacking in common sense? Or had her instincts guided her aright in thinking that she could trust the man Jackson?

No solution had offered itself to the disappearance of her letter. It remained missing: Miss Feniton's abigail, when questioned cautiously, denied any knowledge of it with an artlessness that enforced belief. One incident only served to remind Joanna of the events of that fateful evening. This was the delivery of a parcel to her one morning by one of the maids who lived in the village.

The girl had come into Miss Feniton's bedchamber with the usual morning cup of chocolate. She placed it on the table at the side of Joanna's bed, and then handed her the package.

"For me?" asked Joanna, surprised. "I was not expecting anything."

The girl made no reply, but went over to see to the fire. Miss Feniton tore the wrappings from the package with impatient fingers, and disclosed a pink muslin scarf, counterpart of the one which she had used to bind about the arm of a certain fisherman a few nights since.

She gazed at it in astonishment for a moment, then quickly began to search among the wrappings for a note of any kind. She soon saw that there was nothing enclosed.

"Where did you get this?" she asked the girl.

"'Twas brought to our door by Ned Stokes, ma'am — 'im that lives in the farm down by the river."

"Was there any message?" asked Joanna.

The girl shook her head. "Only to deliver it into your own 'ands, ma'am, when there was no one else by."

"Thank you," replied Miss Feniton, with a nod of dismissal. "Oh — you do not need to mention this to anyone else, Sukey."

"I should think not, ma'am!" said the girl, emphatically. "Ned Stokes told me that, most particlar, an' it don't do to go agin' 'im!"

Miss Feniton nodded again, and the maid left the room.

Joanna sat staring for some time at the scarf, before finally pushing it to one side, and taking up her now almost cold cup of chocolate.

Shalbeare House was situated on the north shores of Torbay, quite close to the village of Tor Quay. The house had been built originally in the seventeenth century, but it had been extended and improved upon until it now presented a typical Georgian appearance with its stuccoed facing and pillared portico. Inside, however, traces of its origin still lingered; one or two of the rooms, notably the library, had some fine oak panelling. The staircase was Jacobean, and a magnificent example of the work of that period.

As soon as Lady Feniton had seen her guests established in their respective rooms and interviewed her butler and housekeeper, she went to her granddaughter. Miss Lodge and her Mama were busy superintending their unpacking, so that for the moment, Joanna had no duties to perform. She was sitting in the Chinese drawing room when Lady Feniton came upon her.

"I have just been opening the post, Joanna," she began. "There is a positive assurance here from Algernon Cholcombe that he will be with us on Friday."

"And Mr. Dorlais is to come tomorrow, while Captain and Miss Masterman arrive on the following day," said Joanna, apparently unmoved by this information. "Our party will be complete by the end of the week, therefore."

"It is perhaps a pity that Colonel Kellaway was unable to accept my invitation," remarked Lady Feniton, thoughtfully. "I don't know that I would have asked Masterman and his sister, had I not thought that the Kellaways would come, too. That Masterman girl is very pert and forward, though there can be no objection to the brother — he is everything that is agreeable and gentlemanlike. It would be a fine thing for him if he were to make a match of it with one of the Colonel's girls — though I declare they set my teeth on edge!"

"They are very good-natured," replied Joanna. "One cannot be surprised that the Colonel is too busy at present for visiting."

"I thought it very good in him to allow young Masterman leave of absence — with the proviso, of course, that he should be available if necessary."

Miss Feniton assented to this absently.

"However," said her grandmother, suddenly. "That was not altogether what I wished to speak to you about."

Joanna looked up inquiringly into Lady Feniton's face. For once, the older woman showed signs of uncertainty.

"It is understood, of course," she began, after a pause, "that young Cholcombe comes here in order to make you an offer. Nothing definite has been said on Lord Cholcombe's side; but in a recent letter to your grandfather, he expressed a strong desire to see his heir settled, and mentioned the early understanding with our family. Algernon's acceptance of my invitation seems to me to clinch the matter. Had his interest been fixed in any other quarter, you may depend that he would have sent a polite refusal."

She paused, and regarded her granddaughter searchingly.

"I need not tell you how much I desire this match," she continued. "Everything is as it should be — rank, fortune and age. I would not wish to see you married to a man much older than yourself — I have myself had sufficient opportunity to observe the adverse effects of a great disparity in age upon happiness in matrimony. However, we won't go into that at present. Your *birth* is equal to his, if not your rank; the first Feniton came over with the Conqueror. You are the last of an ancient line, Joanna: the name dies when you wed. It behoves you to fuse it with one which may not disgrace your children. Such a one is the name of Cholcombe. In time, you will be a Countess; it is some recompense for ceasing to be a Feniton."

Joanna stared thoughtfully into the fire. "And if Mr. Cholcombe does not find me to his liking?" she asked, slowly.

"You must make every endeavour to fix his interest. He comes looking to be pleased. You must be a great deal plainer than you are, or a great deal stupider, for him to take you in dislike. There is one thing I feel I ought to mention —" She paused again, evidently uncertain how to proceed. Joanna looked at her questioningly. "I have sometimes thought that —

it occasionally appears —" She floundered a little, then took a firm grip upon herself.

"Your address is sometimes a thought stiff," she said, firmly. "That is only proper in most situations, considering who you are. But young men are more often caught by a lively girl — unless, of course, she should happen to be a positive beauty, in which case she may be as stupid as she chooses! Now you, my dear child, are very well-looking, as I dare say you cannot help knowing; but you cannot claim to be a second Helen of Troy."

Joanna laughed. "Indeed, no, ma'am! Nor could I wish for a face which had the powers of destruction of that young woman!"

"Just so," replied her grandmother, repressively. She knew very little of the history of Troy, and had no particular wish to be better informed. "You will therefore appreciate that it is all the more necessary to display to the full the charm of your character."

"Do I understand you aright, ma'am?" asked Joanna, with a touch of height in her manner. "Are you suggesting that I should attempt to *lead on* Mr. Cholcombe?"

"Nothing of the sort!" protested Lady Feniton, hastily. "But a girl must meet a man half way. It don't do at all to be too mumchance and correct!"

"If that is so," said Joanna, her nose now alarmingly in the air, "then I scarce think it worth the trouble of changing my name at all. I shall remain Joanna Feniton, the last of an honourable line, and may be at liberty to conduct myself as I choose!"

Lady Feniton's face and neck were suddenly suffused with a scarlet flush of anger. For a moment, it appeared as if she were about to fall into an apoplexy. Joanna steadily opposed her choleric glare with a cold, haughty gaze from her green flecked eyes. Woman and girl sat staring directly at each other for what seemed a long time. Gradually, the older woman's eyes dropped, and her flush subsided.

"It seems you are my granddaughter, after all," she said, forcing a laugh. "I have thought sometimes that there was too much of your mother about you for my taste. It appears I was mistaken, and that you are very well able to hold your own. I am heartily glad to see it! However, we shall not quarrel, I think, over what is a misunderstanding on your part. Possibly it was wrong in me to attempt to dictate your future conduct towards Algernon Cholcombe. You must blame my anxiety to see you affianced to him, and think no more of it. I undertake to leave the affair in your hands from now on. Let us say no more on that head."

Joanna found it difficult to conceal her amazement. In all her life, she never remembered having heard her grandmother admit to being in the wrong. She was not completely mollified, however, and this showed in her face.

"I need detain you no longer," said Lady Feniton, in tones of dismissal. "You will no doubt be wishing to see if Catherine has all she requires. Perhaps you will step into the library on your way, and desire your grandfather to attend me here. Remind him that he has duties to perform as a host — he is all too apt to forget everything once he sets foot in that sanctum of his."

Joanna, with some stiffness still in her manner, undertook to execute this commission. She found her grandfather seated at his leather-topped, mahogany desk, poring over a handsomely tooled volume of Virgil. He looked up briefly on her entrance, then, seeing who it was, let his eyes drop to the book once more.

She sat down in a chair at the other side of the desk, and for a moment, there was a companionable silence. She fixed her eyes upon a painting which hung on one section of the wall which happened not to be completely covered by books. It was a seascape, depicting a small cove burnished by the rays of the setting sun. Red Devon cliffs met red-gold sand in a glory of translucent colour; the green-blue sea caught the tawny glow of the sunset, and threw its colours back reflected in white edged waves which reared and fell against the golden beach. Involuntarily, Joanna caught her breath as she gazed at the scene.

"You are looking at my picture," said Sir Walter, putting a forefinger into his book, and glancing up at her.

She nodded. "It is — wonderful! So full of light: as if —" she paused, trying to find the words which could do justice to her sensations — "as if the artist had tried to contain the whole power and splendour of the sun on that one small canvas! When did you acquire it, grandfather? I have not noticed it before."

He shook his head. "No: I had put it away, and forgotten it. I had it of Price Turner, the saddler, when I was last in Exeter. His nephew is a Royal Academician, you know, but the uncle seemed to have little regard for this particular work, for he was very willing to sell it to me. I am pleased that you should approve it."

"Is it a local scene?" she asked, considering the picture carefully again.

"I believe so, though I myself do not know the place. But there must be many such small coves around this coast. If only one had the painter's eyes, to see them all like this! What glory lies around us, my dear child, if we could but see it!"

"Grandpapa," she said, softly, "you are very right. But my errand is to bring you back to earth, not to encourage such flights of fancy."

"Oh." He sighed deeply, removed his forefinger from the book, and gave her his full attention. "What must I do now?" he asked, in a tone of resignation.

"Grandmother wishes to remind you that you have duties to perform, and requires you to attend her in the Chinese withdrawing room."

"*Me miserum*," he said, with a mock groan. "But your grandmother is right, of course," he added, in a brisker tone. "I fear I am an indifferent host." His faded blue eyes smiled into hers, then sharpened as they rested on her face. "You appear to be somewhat put out, child," he remarked, gently. "What's amiss? Have you, too, been hauled over the coals?"

She nodded, laughing ruefully. "Grandmama has been reminding me that I have not the beauty of Helen."

He raised an eyebrow, then nodded, relapsing into his former abstractedness.

"Hers is a legendary beauty — the loveliness of all women of all time embodied in one ideal woman who cannot be resisted. But you are a real woman, my dear, and therefore possessed of only a fraction of that loveliness — and of that power for evil." He broke off, becoming more practical. "But why should your grandmother say any such thing? I am amazed that she should know anything of Helen of Troy; it shows that marriage to me has not been quite without its uses, after all."

"She was telling me," explained Joanna, slowly, "that as I am not possessed of an irresistible beauty, I must make use of such other charms as I possess to ensure that — that Mr. Cholcombe shall make me an offer."

"So!" The old man watched her with a gentle expression in his eyes. "And that is why you were put out — not at the comparison with Helen?"

She nodded thoughtfully. "Do you, too, so very much desire this match, sir?"

"Do not you?" he countered, swiftly.

He was studying her now with the eyes of a scholar, giving her all the alert attention which was usually devoted only to his beloved books. She coloured faintly under the searching scrutiny.

"I believe so," she said, striving to be completely honest with him. There was too deep an understanding between these two for any pretence. "After all, I must marry someone; and this is, as Grandmama says, a highly suitable match. Of course, I am not yet acquainted with the gentleman, but I can hardly suppose that I shall take him in violent dislike."

"What exactly do you mean by the word 'suitable'?"

"Oh, that his rank and fortune are such as you must both — we must all — approve, I suppose," she answered.

"As to rank, my dear, I am perfectly indifferent," he replied.

"But —" she began, surprised — "but do you not share grandmother's views, then — do you not feel that as I am the last of our line, it is my duty to link the name with one of equal antiquity, and greater rank?"

He shook his head. "When you marry, Joanna, I would wish you to choose —" he accented the last word faintly — "a man who may be worthy of you. To the rest of the world, perchance, he may even appear a paltry fellow: so long as you are content, that is all that signifies. I wonder if you are at all acquainted with the work of the Scottish poet, Robert Burns?"

Joanna shook her head. She thought that her grandfather was going off at a tangent again, as he was only too apt to do, and wondered if it would be too unkind to mention once again that Lady Feniton was expecting to see him at once.

"He died some few years since," went on Sir Walter. "His work is perhaps somewhat difficult to follow, for much of it is in the dialect of the Lowlands, but it is well worth the effort involved in unravelling his meaning. I have one particular poem of his in mind which is very much to the purpose of this discussion: it concerns poverty. Some of his conclusions may perhaps appear to be arrived at a thought hastily: but I believe that no one will challenge him when he states that: 'The rank is but the guinea stamp, The man's the gold, for a' that.' Be guided by him in this, child, and fix your thoughts upon the man himself, and not his rank."

"That's all very well," objected Joanna, with a smile. "But I don't know the man, sir. He may or may not be worthy, but it will certainly take time to discover. I must say," she added, quizzically, "that I do hope he is not *too* worthy. There is something about that word —"

He gave an answering chuckle. "Which conjures up a dried old stick of a fellow? I am completely of your mind. By all means, let young Cholcombe be just a little unworthy!"

"I notice," said Joanna, still smiling, "that you make no objection to my choosing him on the grounds of his fortune?"

"Did I not? Well, no. You see, my dear, one is forced to be practical, after all. Up to the present, you have been reared as a young lady of fortune: you cannot therefore expect to feel completely content with less than you have become accustomed to. I do not mean to say that one cannot be very happy without money: I only insist that it is more difficult, especially when one has been reared to an adequate competence. You have had the wrong training for austerities, my child, therefore must try to fall in love with a man who has sufficient for the requirements of you both."

"I thank you for your advice," replied Joanna, with mock demureness, "but I do not aim as high as to fall in love, as you put it."

He considered her for a moment, all his raillery gone.

"Do you not?" He shook his head. "You make a sad mistake there, my dear."

She felt shaken by this reply, but tried not to let him see it.

"Grandmama!" she exclaimed, in horrified accents. "She will be beyond anything vexed! You must go to her at once, sir!"

He made a comical face of dismay, and rose to put away his book. With his hand on the place in the shelf, he turned.

"Had your grandmother aimed so high, she would not now be conducting her own personal 'Reign of Terror'," he said, half in jest, half in earnest. "I, too, you know, was once considered a good match."

Chapter IX: Suspicion

The next day brought Guy Dorlais to Shalbeare House, though not until the late afternoon. Ever since an early hour of the morning, Kitty had been straining her eyes for a sight of his curricle coming up the drive; so that when he finally arrived, she was at first in a fervour of excitement. This cooled, however, before he had fairly had time to step over the threshold, and she was noticeably offhand in her greeting.

"What's amiss, my love?" he whispered, when, general civilities being over, he was able to take his place beside her upon the gold and red striped satin sofa in the drawing room. "Have I done anything to vex you?"

Kitty turned a face full of polite incredulity towards him. "Vex me, sir? Pray, what should make you imagine that I am vexed?"

"You can't bamboozle me, my own, though you act very prettily," he replied, with a smile. "Come, confess: there is something."

Kitty tossed her head. "I have never been in better spirits," she lied, glibly. "If you find me cross, it is perhaps in contrast to whatever company you may have been keeping during the earlier part of the day!"

"So that's it!" he exclaimed, with a chuckle. "You dear, silly creature! To be sure, you cannot compete in charm and conversation with Noakes and Stoddart. I was obliged to spend the greater part of the morning in consultation with them. We have a plan to drain Five Oaks acre, you know, and turn it to pasturage. The vegetation would be lush, and —"

But Kitty was of no mind to talk farming, neither did she relish having her tantrums treated as though they were of little consequence.

"Indeed!" she answered, tartly. "So that is what kept you from my side! It is as well that I know who my rivals are!"

A frown marred the dark, handsome face. "What nonsense is this, Kit? Surely you cannot be in earnest? You must realize that I have responsibilities."

"What are servants for?" she asked, pettishly. "Do you not pay Noakes and Stoddart to free you from these duties? At least, your uncle does."

The frown deepened. "But I've no wish to be freed from them," he said, without weighing his words. Such an admission was not what Miss Lodge wished to hear in her present frame of mind, and a moment's reflection must have told him so. "You know that I am extremely interested in farming, and I fancy that already I have made some difference in my uncle's land. Why, only the other day, he —"

"I suppose it is because you are really a Frenchman that you must play so hard at being the English Squire," said Kitty, remorselessly.

Joanna could not help overhearing the words. She was sitting close by, sustaining an erratic, uninteresting conversation with Lady Lodge. She saw Dorlais stiffen, watched him abruptly leave her friend's side and go over to have a word with his host and Sir George, who were chatting together on the opposite side of the hearth.

She longed to intervene, say a word of warning to her friend, but one look at Kitty's face persuaded her that it would be ill-judged to do so at present. There was something else, too: the words which Kitty had made use of had started an uneasy train of thought in her own head. There was little opportunity at present for following it up, however. Lady Feniton had been absent from the room for a few moments, but she now returned, full of schemes for the entertainment of her guests. Sir Walter was restrained from creeping back to his beloved library, and made to take a hand of cards, a thing he detested. Joanna and Kitty, offered a choice between backgammon and their embroidery frames, found themselves unable to agree. Miss Feniton was for backgammon; but Miss Lodge, her powers of concentration completely dissipated, considered that there would be more opportunity for feminine chatter over the embroidery. Joanna yielded, as was proper since Kitty was a guest, and a servant was dispatched to fetch the work. To Kitty's disgust, however, Lady Feniton completely destroyed any hope of a *tête-à-tête* between the two young ladies, by placing herself between them, and directing the conversation in her usual efficient manner. Thus the evening passed away without opportunity for a reconciliation between the lovers, or for any intervention on Joanna's part.

The following morning, Captain Masterman and his sister arrived. Miss Masterman was not generally well-liked: she was the kind of a young lady who believed in exploiting her femininity to the full, and did not scruple to belittle others if it aided her purpose. She was possessed of an extremely good figure, and the prevailing fashion of light, flimsy materials enabled her to set it off to advantage. She was pretty in a hard, competent way that was very different from Miss Feniton's cold reserve. Like her brother, she was fair, with blue eyes; she wore her flaxen hair dressed in a chignon and ringlets, with a curled fringe on the forehead. Kitty avowedly detested her: Joanna, who was calmer in her judgments, could not altogether like the girl.

When the newcomers were fairly settled in, Lady Feniton strongly recommended a walk in the grounds. She pointed out that the day, though chilly, was bright; and the gravel walks, at least, would be dry underfoot.

Objections melted away under her forceful persuasion, and presently the five younger members of the party set out.

The grounds of Shalbeare House extended over several acres, and had been laid out early in the eighteenth century with all the extravagances of landscape gardening peculiar to that period. Nothing had been omitted: there were temples and grottoes, artificial ponds and streams, rustic bridges and even a hermitage. It had been considered at the time a masterly touch of the Gothic to pave this with sheep's marrow bones; and one enterprising Feniton of the last century had gone so far as to insert an advertisement in one of the journals for a genuine hermit to take up occupation of the building.

"And did he find one?" asked Miss Masterman, when Joanna had told this story.

"I do not know; but I dare say my grandfather will be able to tell you."

"It is dreadfully Gothic, and vastly disagreeable inside," said Miss Masterman, peering in at the entrance and giving a theatrical little shudder. "I do not envy your hermit, if hermit there was. It's not the kind of place for a rendezvous, either," she added, evidently pursuing some new train of thought.

"It seems that there is no romance in your soul, Miss Masterman," said Dorlais, in a tone of raillery. "Aren't you stirred by the stark simplicity of this retreat? Don't you find here more than a dash of Mrs. Radcliffe?"

"You are quizzing me, sir!" she answered, with a coy, upward glance from under her long, silky lashes. "You must know that

I am not at all clever, like Miss Feniton and Miss Lodge: I fear I can lay no claims to being bookish."

The slight emphasis on the last words left her hearers in no doubt as to Miss Masterman's opinion of young ladies who could lay such claims. Kitty reddened slightly, began to speak, then thought better of it, and bit her lip.

"One scarcely needs to be a scholar to have read *The Mysteries of Udolpho*, however," said Joanna, quietly.

"Oh, I fear even that is beyond me!" exclaimed Miss Masterman, glancing at Guy for understanding. "The only reading that I can at all comprehend is in the Lady's Magazine — or perhaps The Monthly Museum, at a pinch! I find long works tedious — but I am accounted rather a volatile creature, so that may explain it."

"Shall we walk farther, or turn back now?" asked Joanna, seeing from Kitty's expression that it would be wiser to change the conversation before Miss Lodge enlivened it with one of her disconcerting bursts of candour. "The sun has gone, and I for one am none too warm."

"By all means, ma'am, let us turn back," said Captain Masterman, instantly. "If you are feeling the cold, I am sure no one can wish to be keeping you out of doors. Perhaps we may walk a little more sharply on our return journey."

He offered Miss Feniton his arm, and after a second's hesitation, she accepted it. He then turned to Kitty. Guy Dorlais had hung back a little, answering something which Miss Masterman had said. After an indignant glance in their direction, Kitty accepted the other arm, and the Captain set off at a smart pace along the path, between the two friends.

Dorlais and Miss Masterman were left standing outside the hermitage.

"I do hope," said Georgina Masterman, gazing after the others with an expression of exaggerated anxiety, "that Miss Lodge is not — vexed — with me?"

"I beg your pardon?" he asked, puzzled.

"I rather fancy," said Miss Masterman, gazing up at him with wide blue eyes, "that Miss Lodge did not care for you to be talking so much to me. You two are engaged, are you not, and sometimes such a situation makes a girl very possessive. I quite understand how she feels, of course."

"Oh, fustian!" he said, in some embarrassment. "I beg your pardon," he added, hastily, feeling that perhaps this had been less than civil, "but I'm sure you're mistaken. Kitty felt the cold, that is all I'm sure that you must, too, for it is deuced chilly, standing here. Shall we follow the others?"

He started forward without waiting for her; then, recollecting himself, checked, and offered her his arm. So it was that Kitty Lodge observed them, when she turned her head for a brief glance, coming arm in arm down the path.

This incident did not help in healing the breach between Kitty and her betrothed. For the remainder of the day, Joanna was concerned chiefly in trying to conceal from the rest of the party the coolness which existed between two of its members. After everyone had said good night, and the bedroom candles been taken, she watched her opportunity to slip into Kitty's room.

She found her friend face down on the bed in a flood of tears. Joanna's lovely eyes softened, and she raised the other girl in her arms.

"Kitten!" she expostulated, softly. "You little goose!"

"H-How can I be a kitten and a-a g-goose at the same time?" stammered Kitty, between laughing and crying.

"Because you are unusually gifted at being two things at once," said Joanna, reproachfully. "Now dry your eyes, and tell me the whole."

This caused a fresh outburst from Kitty, and it was some time before she could be sufficiently soothed for coherent conversation. When she was once more able to express herself freely, she launched into a violent diatribe against Miss Masterman. Joanna heard her out in silent sympathy, until she appeared to have exhausted her flood of words.

"I agree that she is a tiresome female," said Joanna. "The determined man-hunter invariably is. But I think you judge her too harshly, Kitty, in deeming her responsible for the coolness existing between you and Mr. Dorlais. That began before she arrived here — almost as soon as he came in fact; I do not altogether understand why."

Kitty sat up, and dried her eyes fiercely. "He — he was so much occupied with his schemes for the farm, that he could delay coming to me for more than half a day," she complained, bitterly. "While I was counting every minute, impatient to set eyes on him, thinking of nothing else! How can he possibly love me, if I am always to take second place in his affections?"

"Always?" queried Joanna, with a little smile. "Is that quite just?"

"I tell you that I am so tired of this way of going on, that I am minded to break our contract!" said Kitty, a set expression on her usually lively face.

"You cannot mean that, Kitty!" exclaimed Joanna, in dismay. "Only think — think of the gossip, for one thing: the stir made in the county by such a step would bid fair to rival the invasion rumours, I imagine!"

"Everyone is welcome to discuss my affairs, if it gives them pleasure to do so," replied Kitty, loftily, but with eyes full of tears. "I do not mind!"

"But you would mind very much if you were not to wed Mr. Dorlais," said her friend, quietly. "And it's no use to pretend that you would not, Kitty, for I shan't believe you!"

"What is the use in our being married, if we are always to be at cross purposes?" asked Kitty, despairingly. "It may be hard to break off our engagement — indeed, you cannot know how hard, Jo, for you were never in love! — but I feel it is better to do so now, than to endure a lifetime of disillusionment!"

Joanna was hard put to it not to smile at this pronouncement, made with an air of high tragedy.

"If only you had not such a fatal penchant for the dramatic," she expostulated, ruefully. "Let's try and consider your case calmly. To say that you and Mr. Dorlais are always at cross purposes is as absurd as your statement that you are always to hold second place in his affections. The truth of the matter is — I'm afraid you must face it, Kitty — your notions are altogether too romantic. No one who has seen you together can possibly doubt the strength of Mr. Dorlais's attachment to you; but a man of principle is not likely to forget every duty, every interest, in his feelings for the woman he loves. If she's wise, she will recognize this fact early in their association, and not seek to be too possessive. For her part, she can —"

Kitty leaned forward suddenly, and placed her hand over her friend's mouth. "Not another word, Jo, of how you feel a woman in love should act! I won't allow you to be a judge! When you have succumbed to the passion yourself, then perhaps I may listen to you!"

Miss Feniton shook her dark head. "I had much rather not succumb to it. I am a deal more comfortable as I am, judging from your situation!"

"Oh, but this is not all of it, my dear! There are moments — transports such as one never knows in any other connection — in short, to be out of love is to be only half alive!"

"But to be wholly sane," replied Joanna, with a twinkle.

Kitty sighed. "I wish I could be more like you," she said, ruefully. "You always seem to know just how to act, and what to think!"

Joanna laughed softly. "You make me sound odious, Kit! What an impossible creature I must be, if this were true!"

"Isn't it?"

Joanna shook her head. "There have been occasions when — I have acted most unwisely," she said, slowly, "when I have certainly not followed the dictates of good sense."

"I am delighted to hear it!" said the irrepressible Kitty. "I should never have guessed such a thing was possible! But when, my dear Jo, and where? Do, pray, tell me the whole!"

"Not now — it's too late," said Joanna, quickly. "In any case, there's little to relate. But you know, Kitty," she went on, ingeniously, "I could wish that I knew just how to think and act on the morrow! You may not realize it, my love, but the thought of Mr. Cholcombe's arrival puts me in a certain flutter of spirits!"

"Of course," said Kitty, with ready sympathy. "I am a brute! I have been so full of my own troubles, that I was forgetting what an ordeal that meeting must be for you. Do you suppose that he will make a formal offer at once?"

"I trust not," said Joanna, alarmed at this suggestion of unseemly haste. "I had imagined that he would allow a little time to elapse: it would certainly be more proper."

Kitty nodded thoughtfully. "Don't worry, dearest Jo," she said, at last. "I dare say that, as usual, you will know just how to act — but, if not, you may count on me!"

Joanna might be pardoned for reflecting that she could expect little help from one so palpably unable to manage her own affairs successfully: but she merely thanked Kitty affectionately, begged her not to tease Mr. Dorlais on the morrow, and bade her good night. She retired to her own room, taking a feeling of unease as a bedfellow.

Chapter X: Arrival of Mr. Cholcombe

The party at Shalbeare House was sitting in a salon on the ground floor on the following afternoon, trying to decide whether it was worth leaving the leaping fire on the hearth for the attractions of a windy walk among the dead leaves in the shrubbery. It was one of those cold, grey days for which November is justly famed, when even to the enthusiast, the out of doors can hold little appeal. While the opposing merits were being debated with as much animation as could be expected after an excellent luncheon, the sound of a carriage approaching the house drew everyone present to the window.

A vehicle was observed coming up the drive, and presently four handsome bay horses swept round the bend before the entrance, bringing to a standstill the elegant carriage to which they were harnessed. Scarcely had the coachman drawn rein, before a second vehicle arrived, this one piled high with luggage.

A servant jumped down from the first carriage, and opened the door with its crested panels. The figure of a gentleman emerged, wearing a curly brimmed beaver, a dark blue riding coat ornamented with exactly the right number of capes, and a pair of shining, tasselled Hessians. With one gloved hand, he anchored the beaver firmly on to his head as he stepped from the coach, and, pausing only for a brief word with the man who had now emerged from the second vehicle, mounted the steps to the door of the house.

Miss Feniton quickly withdrew from the window, her heart beating a trifle faster than usual. Kitty threw her a sympathetic look, and edged near enough to squeeze her hand surreptitiously.

"This will be Algernon Cholcombe!" exclaimed Lady Feniton. "Did ever you see so many traps? I am aware that he has a certain reputation as a dandy, but surely he must be persuaded that he is to be staying with us for no less than six months!"

"I only wish he will stay long enough for his man to confide to mine the secret of that blacking," muttered Guy Dorlais, ruefully.

"I think nothing of dandies, for my part!" cried Miss Masterman, with a toss of her golden head. "I am always telling my brother that nothing so much becomes a man as military uniform; and there is nothing dandified in that, you know," she added, looking coyly at Guy.

Miss Lodge glanced quickly at her betrothed, half mocking, half serious: unwittingly, Georgina Masterman had said quite the wrong thing to please that gentleman.

"My dear Miss Masterman, I am sure we are all delighted to have your opinion," said Lady Feniton, in her most repressive voice. "However, it may not be quite the last word on the subject."

Miss Masterman subsided, and in response to a glance from her brother, said humbly that she was very sorry if she had given offence to anyone present.

"Not at all," replied her hostess. "No one here, I hope, is so foolish as to take umbrage at idle chatter."

By this time, Joanna was almost beginning to feel sorry for Georgina, and would have intervened with some softly spoken word: but at that precise moment, a footman announced the Honourable Algernon Cholcombe.

Mr. Cholcombe came forward into the room, and made a graceful, finicking bow to the assembled company. He offered his hand to Lady Feniton.

"How d'ye do, ma'am? It is many years since I had this pleasure."

His voice was pleasant, thought Joanna, clear and mellow, with just the right amount of fashionable drawl. She took note of his attire, and approved the well-cut coat of dark green superfine and the waistcoat of quilted white Marcella, but she was uncertain whether the pantaloons of yellow kerseymere were in quite such good taste. Mr. Dorlais and Captain Masterman could have assured her, however, that these were all the crack in Town. The latter gentleman was also admiring the fall of Mr. Cholcombe's spotless cravat: he had a particular reason for closely observing the newcomer. Evidently this man favoured the tasteful, elegant style of Beau Brummel, rather than the colourful eccentricities of the more ostentatious dandy. It was a point in his favour, Masterman grudgingly admitted.

The man himself was in no way remarkable, the Captain went on to reflect. True, Mr. Cholcombe's light brown hair was cut in the prevailing Roman style, and his features were pleasing; but no one could truthfully assert that he was an Adonis. His only claim to notice lay in his superb tailoring, and possibly in the natural grace of his movements. He was bowing to Miss Feniton at that moment, and his bow, thought Captain Masterman bitterly, was a triumph of the art of courtesy.

The confusion of Joanna's feelings may be readily imagined. It caused her manner to become even more stiff than usual. After one quick glance into his face, she had lowered her eyes, and they remained steadfastly fixed upon the carpet during the very short time when she and the new guest were in conversation together. He had soon turned away to be introduced by his hostess to the other members of the party. On seeing Guy Dorlais, he exclaimed in delight.

"Ah, Dorlais! How splendid to meet you again! Do you recollect the theatricals at Trelawney's place? 'Pon my word, you made an excellent Benjamin Backbite — I declare we all felt uncommon nervous of you, afterwards!"

Joanna, watching Guy's expression closely for some reason that she could not quite define, noticed a guard come over it.

"You are very good," he replied. "But I fear we were all outshone by your own performance on that occasion! Have you seen Trelawney lately, by the by? I believe I owe him a letter."

She paid scant attention to the reply. The worst moment — that of meeting Mr. Cholcombe — was now over, and she could let matters take their course. She manoeuvred into position beside Kitty on the sofa.

"What do you think of him?" Kitty whispered.

"How can I possibly say as yet?" replied Joanna, with one eye on her grandmother.

"You do not mind if I say this, Jo," whispered back Kitty, in an apologetic tone, "but I do not consider him as handsome as Guy!"

"Perhaps not." Joanna considered Algernon Cholcombe dispassionately. He was at present chatting to Sir Walter, an animated expression on his mobile face. "It is a pleasant countenance, however; I fancy there is good humour and sensitivity in it. He carries himself well, and his address is good: so far, there is nothing to complain of."

"Oh, Jo!" exclaimed her friend, in deep disappointment. "It does not sound as though you are become a victim to love at first sight!"

145

Joanna shook her head, laughing, and, in response to a signal from her grandmother, moved away to another part of the room to join in the conversation there.

Her first opportunity to become better acquainted with Mr. Cholcombe came over dinner. He had the place of honour, next to Lady Feniton and Joanna was seated upon his other side. He soon proved himself an entertaining companion: she had not been wrong in detecting a sense of humour in his face. Lady Feniton had done full justice to the appetites of her guests. An excellent turtle soup was followed by turbot with lobster sauce; when this was removed, boiled fowls, a saddle of mutton and an enormous game pie were carried in by the footmen.

"I am irresistibly reminded," said Mr. Cholcombe in a low tone to Joanna, "of another occasion when I was regaled with game pie at Shalbeare House."

"You mean —" she asked, uncertainly.

His eyes smiled down into hers. "You cannot have forgotten — although perhaps you might, for you were very young at the time — scarcely more than a babe in arms!"

"If you mean the occasion when I carried a piece of pie from the table, requiring Nurse to take it to you, when you were in disgrace," she said, "I was all of five years old, let me tell you!"

"Were you so?" He pretended to be impressed, twinkling at her. "I had thought you the merest babe, and rated your exploit the more highly on that account."

"It was a little daring of me," said Joanna, reminiscently. "But then, I felt your punishment to be totally undeserved!"

"Do you know," he said, laughing. "I've quite forgotten the fault for which I was punished? At this distance in time, I can only remember my indignation and your compassion — and how good that pie tasted, after a long fast!"

"It was about your name," explained Joanna. "My grandmother —"

"Oh, yes, I recollect now!" he interposed, swiftly. "She insisted upon dubbing me Algernon — I see it still sticks!"

"Yes," said Joanna, doubtfully. "It is not your name, then?"

"On the contrary. It is one of the many names which my parents saw fit to bestow upon me. Algernon is my first name; my mother particularly fancied it, because, so she said, she found it so very English. She is French, as you most likely know," he added, in explanation.

"Yes, I was aware of the fact," replied Joanna, uncertain how to proceed. She recollected having been told by her grandmother how Lord Cholcombe had many years ago created quite a stir in London society by his marriage to a French actress.

"However, my mother never called me by it," proceeded Mr. Cholcombe. "She found it almost impossible to pronounce with a sufficiently English accent. On the few occasions when I have heard her make the attempt, the result was something like this —" and he produced a laughably Gallic version of the name.

His eyes lit up as he listened to Miss Feniton's rare laughter. Joanna was on the verge of asking him by what name his mother was used to call him, but she suppressed the question, fearing it might sound too pert and inquisitive at this early stage of their acquaintance.

"One can scarcely blame you for objecting to be called by a name other than the one to which you were accustomed," she said.

"You did not, at any rate! I was never more in need of a tender heart, either, for my appetite at that time was something prodigious!"

"In that you are changed, evidently," she remarked, watching him wave away the gooseberry tart.

"Not at all! It is merely that I have a rooted dislike of gooseberries," he answered. "Now, when I am asked to partake of that seductive looking dish of peaches over there, you will observe that it is quite another matter."

"Did I hear you say peaches, Algernon?" put in Lady Feniton, who had noticed his rejection of the one dish, and was anxious to ply him with another. "William —"

Miss Feniton raised her eyes at Lady Feniton's words, and in so doing, managed to intercept a glance which passed from Guy Dorlais, who sat at the opposite side of the table, to Mr. Cholcombe. It was full of mockery. She told herself, surprised, that there must surely exist a greater degree of intimacy between the two gentlemen than she had at first supposed, or than Guy had given Kitty and herself to understand.

"And how do you occupy yourself throughout the long winter months, Miss Feniton?" asked Mr. Cholcombe, having been helped to the fruit. "Do you have many private balls hereabouts, or must you rely solely upon the Assemblies at Totnes or Exeter?"

"It is but seldom that we venture as far as Exeter, sir, at this time of year. We dine with a number of families in the county, but, truth to tell, seldom enjoy any dancing. Our chief employments in company are music, cards and conversation."

"And which of these employments do you prefer?" he asked, smiling down at her.

"It is difficult to say," answered Joanna, wrinkling her brow. "I am neither a gifted singer nor instrumentalist, and I play but an indifferent game of cards. I suppose, therefore, that my choice must rest with conversation."

"'Pon my word, madam," he said, "I find you very modest! I fear you can scarcely be doing yourself justice. Since you will have it that you are not gifted in music, I take it that you must be most accomplished at drawing and painting?"

Joanna shook her head, smiling.

"What?" he raised his quizzing glass, and affected to study her through it. "Not even painting, my dear young lady?"

Again she shook her head, amused at his manner.

"I fear not," she answered, gravely.

He let the glass drop, and surveyed her sadly. "Miss Feniton," he said, in mournful accents, "I fear I must positively decline to know you. It will not do at all."

She started a little, for she was unused to raillery from anyone on so short an acquaintance. Then she began to laugh softly.

"You may laugh, ma'am, but I assure you that I am in deadly earnest. What, not even one single accomplishment? When I am informed on all sides that all young ladies nowadays are highly accomplished in every one of the arts? Indeed, it will not do, madam: you must see that my credit in the world would suffer, were I to prolong our acquaintance!"

"I am very sorry for it," she answered, still laughing. "But I cannot help the way I am made. However, if you should be interested in painting, my grandfather has an excellent seascape hanging in his library, which I'm sure he would be delighted to show you after dinner."

"Indeed? I must remember to ask him, later. But at present, I am far more interested in learning the reason for your having managed successfully to avoid becoming an accomplished young lady. Pray, how did you do it, ma'am?"

"Well, really, I don't know how it is," replied Joanna. "I was certainly offered every advantage, and had all the best masters. Perhaps I am more than common stupid."

"No, I cannot allow that." He sipped his wine thoughtfully. "I believe it is that you are unduly modest," he said, with the air of one making a discovery. "However, I shall very soon have an opportunity of judging your performance in some of these arts for myself. I will give you my considered opinion of your talents later on in my visit, I promise you."

"Such a promise throws me into a flutter of spirits," replied Joanna mockingly.

He regarded her seriously enough, but the twinkle in his eye betrayed him. "I believe you are laughing at me, Miss Feniton! It is a great deal too bad of you — and we are but just acquainted."

"It is too bad of me, is it not, sir?" she agreed. "But pray do not forget that you began it. Also, we have been acquainted before this, though that is many years ago."

"Did you at all remember me?" he asked, more seriously. "Am I as you imagined I would be?"

She shook her head. "It would be idle to pretend that I have any strong recollections of the boy who paid us a visit or two all those years since."

She looked up, and subjected him to a cool, appraising scrutiny for a few minutes. He smiled a little, letting his grey eyes meet hers.

"And yet, I fancy there is a certain familiarity," she said slowly, drawing her brows together in an effort of concentration. "However, it can only be imagination."

He assented gravely.

Lady Feniton, watching them covertly, had been pleased to notice the rapid progress of their conversation. It had not been possible to hear exactly what passed, but she had been particularly struck by the animation on her granddaughter's face. It was more usual in Joanna to appear either bored or rigidly correct, when conversing with newly-met acquaintances. It seemed there was nothing wanting in Algernon Cholcombe's address, she reflected, and he was not such an ill-looking young man, either: not perhaps so positively handsome as either of the other two young men who were at present sitting at her table, but for all that, a pleasant, attractive specimen of young English manhood. It was with complacent feelings that she gave the signal for the ladies to rise from the table.

Captain Masterman, too, had noticed the easy conversation between Miss Feniton and the new arrival to Shalbeare House. It had never been in his power, he thought bitterly, to bring that look of animation to the lady's face. But whenever he chanced to be in company with her, he invariably found himself stiff and awkward in his address, and only too conscious of the differences in their respective situations in life. He was not, at the best, an easy conversationalist, yet when Colonel Kellaway had remarked that Captain Masterman was asked everywhere in the county, he had stated nothing more than the truth. Hostesses valued the young man for his gentlemanlike qualities, while regretfully realizing that it was of no use to think of him as a match for their daughters, owing to his unfortunate lack of means. Still, he helped to make up their numbers, danced well, played a keen game of whist, and could be relied upon to toe the line in all matters of delicacy. Hosts found him a very good sort of a fellow, a bruising rider to hounds, a fair shot, and discreet in his cups. Discretion, indeed, was the keynote of his character. Even to Colonel Kellaway, who had known Masterman's father, the son remained something of an enigma.

After a brief interlude with the port, the gentlemen rejoined their ladies in the withdrawing room. When music was suggested, Mr. Cholcombe threw Miss Feniton a look of mocking challenge.

"Oh, that reminds me," she said, turning hastily to Sir Walter. "I was telling Mr. Cholcombe of your picture, grandfather, while we were at dinner, and he said then how much he would like to see it."

"Eh, my dear?" asked Sir Walter, vaguely.

"You know, sir — the one I was noticing the other day — the seascape of Turner's," explained Joanna.

"Oh, yes, to be sure. By all means, Cholcombe, I shall be happy to show it to you. Do you choose to go now?" he added, trying vainly to conceal his eagerness for a legitimate excuse to set foot again in his library.

Lady Feniton opened her mouth to say how little the scheme commended itself to her, but was forestalled by her guest's ready assent. She said nothing, therefore, not being minded to cross the young man in any way at present.

The rest of the company chimed in with assertions of interest, with the result that Sir Walter, somewhat to his disgust, found himself conducting a large party, instead of only his godson, to his holy of holies.

Once inside the room, the party spread out a little so that everyone might enjoy an equally good view of the painting. Every eye was turned studiously upon it, save only those of Lady Feniton and her granddaughter. Lady Feniton was regarding a candlestand which had been imperfectly dusted, and making a mental note to give a good set-down to the housemaid whose responsibility it was to do this room; while Joanna was studying the faces of the rest of the party. The picture had made a powerful impact upon herself when she had first seen it, and she wished to observe its effect upon others.

Her eyes went first to Mr. Cholcombe's face. He put up his quizzing glass, studied it for a moment with an inscrutable expression, then said, "Remarkable! Quite remarkable!"

Disappointed, she switched her gaze to the faces of those nearest to him, Captain Masterman and Guy Dorlais. The Captain was frowning, as though there were something about the picture that he could not understand: but she was just in time to catch Dorlais give a hastily repressed start, and thereafter maintain a fixed stare. She had seen, too, the flash of illumination which came all at once into his dark eyes.

At the time, she did not quite know what to make of this; but thinking it over afterwards, she decided that it was thus a man might look when he was familiar with the scene represented in the painting, yet did not wish anyone present to suspect the fact.

Chapter XI: The Building of a Ship

More than a week passed away, and the visitors to Shalbeare House had settled themselves in tolerably comfortably. Between Kitty and Guy the estrangement still persisted, in spite of a determined effort to dissipate it which was made on at least one occasion by the gentleman. A neighbouring family had been dining at the house on that particular evening, and dancing had been proposed. Neither party to the quarrel — if such it could truly be called — had any desire to parade it in the open: so Kitty did what was expected of her, and stood up with Mr. Dorlais for the first dance. He caught her hand, and squeezed it expressively as they came together after one of the brief separations which were part of the movements of the dance. She looked up at him and could not entirely fail to react to the eloquent message of his dark eyes.

"Kit, my love!" he whispered, as they went down the dance in close proximity. "Put an end to my suffering, and let us be friends."

She turned towards him, her heart in her look, at that moment entirely ready for reconciliation.

But as ill luck would have it, Georgina Masterman, who was in front of them in the formation, chose that very moment to turn back and make some jesting, trivial remark to Guy. It might not have been entirely luck, at that, for she had been quietly observing the pair during their recent brief interchange: however it was, it had the result of breaking the spell for Kitty, at least. Guy Dorlais was obliged by the rules of civility to make some answer, though noticeably curt. After that, they were again separated by the movements of the dance, and did not come together again until the music ended in a noisy scrape of fiddles and a round of hearty applause.

Try as he would, Dorlais could find no other opportunity, and was left to reflect uselessly that, if it had only been summer time, and the doors to the garden thrown open, he would have known how to contrive a *tête-à-tête* with his recalcitrant lady under a friendly moon.

The Honourable Algernon Cholcombe and Miss Feniton seemed to have established a footing of easy raillery which so far did not appear to be leading in the direction of the altar. Lady Feniton knew not what to think; nightly she poured her doubts into Sir Walter's unwilling — and frequently inattentive — ears.

"A jest is all very well," she remarked, coming into the library one evening after everyone else had retired except the three younger gentlemen, who were still engaged in playing a game of billiards elsewhere in the house, "but they will not come together by that road!"

"I am sure you are right, my love," he answered, looking up briefly from the book he was reading.

"Of course I'm right!" she said, somewhat snappishly. "When I warned her not to be too stiff with him, I never dreamed that it would ever come to my being sorry to see them on such easy terms together!"

"No, of course not," he agreed, absently.

"I'm sure I don't know what to do, Feniton," she went on, walking uneasily about the room.

"Don't you, my love? To be sure, that is an unusual quandary for you to be in."

"If only you could think of something!" she exclaimed, in near despair. "But there, you were never any help to me in a crisis!"

"A crisis, Augusta?" The one word seemed at last to penetrate his absence of mind.

"Yes, a crisis!" she repeated. "What else do you call this — this stalemate?"

He looked up at that, puzzled.

"I was not aware — surely, Augusta, you cannot be speaking of — chess? No —" This hastily, as he saw the look she turned on him — "No, of course not; how absurd of me!"

Her brow contracted in anger. "I do not believe that you've heard one word I've been saying, Feniton!" she accused.

"Oh, yes, I have, my dear," he replied, hastily. "Indeed, you misjudge me!"

"Do I, now?" Her accents were ominous. "Then perhaps you will have the goodness to inform me what I was speaking of."

"Certainly. You were saying that — you do not quite know what to do, that they are upon too easy terms for your liking. In short — there appears to be a crisis."

He repeated the words glibly, parrot-fashion: it was evident that he had no idea whatever of their significance.

She made a gesture of impatience. "It is just as I supposed, Feniton, you have not been attending to me! Oh, yes, I am aware that you are able to repeat my words, but you have no more notion of their meaning than a Chinaman might have, I imagine! It is a great deal too bad of you — but only what I would have expected!"

"In that case, my dear, you cannot be disappointed, can you? Will you please close the door quietly as you go out?" He added this as he saw her preparing to storm from the room. She made an exclamation of impatience. He looked at her wistfully. "I'm sorry, Augusta, but it seems I am doomed to be a source of irritation to your nerves. Never mind, my dear;

whatever it is that you're fretting over will most likely sort itself out in the end."

With this she had to be content. A day or so later, her alarms broke out with renewed vigour, however, when Mr. Cholcombe suddenly announced his intention of making a journey into Exeter for the sole purpose of getting his hair cut.

"Exeter! You surely will not travel all that way simply to have your hair dressed! I cannot believe, Algernon, that you could be such a frippery fellow!"

He smiled deprecatingly. "Ah, but I am ma'am; there is no gainsaying it."

"But you will be gone at least a whole day — and on such an errand," protested Lady Feniton.

He raised one eyebrow in languid surprise.

"I scarce think that one day will suffice," he answered, good humouredly. "However, I should not be absent longer than three days, I dare say. Let us hope not."

"Three days!" she was at once surprised and alarmed. "But — but surely there is no occasion to put yourself to so much trouble in the business? Cannot your man contrive to do it for you?"

"Fenchurch?" Mr. Cholcombe lifted his hands in horror. "I only wish you may suggest such a thing to him, ma'am, for I have not the temerity to do so!"

"But that is absurd!" replied his hostess, firmly. "Servants should be kept in their place; I have no notion of allowing mine to tell me what they will and will not do!"

"I congratulate you, milady. Evidently you are not so poor spirited as to be dependent upon your servants, but I must confess that to me life without Fenchurch would be a barren desert! He has a way with my boots that no valet of my

acquaintance can equal; while in the matter of tying a cravat —
!"

He made an expansive gesture of his hands to indicate the impossibility of finding words to do justice to his subject.

"Now that you mention boots," interposed Guy Dorlais, laughing, "I perfectly understand! It is evidently a matter of extreme delicacy, Lady Feniton, and not to be meddled with!"

"Thank you, Mr. Dorlais," she said, repressively. "I believe I am the best judge of that!" Then, turning to Algernon Cholcombe, she said: "Boots and cravats, indeed! But you are in jest — I know you are! There is a very good man who comes once a month to attend to Sir Walter's hair — otherwise, I assure you, nothing whatever would be done about it. If your host had to go all the way to Exeter for a haircut, he would rather adopt an old-fashioned pigtail! — however, this man Barlow is very good, and knows all the latest styles. I will send a groom over to ask him to call here this very day — or tomorrow, if you should prefer it."

Joanna, who was standing by listening with deepening amusement to this conversation, here mentally chalked up a point to her grandmother. So far, the honours lay fairly evenly between the two verbal combatants; but how was Mr. Cholcombe to answer this, she wondered?

"You are very good, ma'am," he replied, without a trace of irritation in his manner, "but I believe I must not put you to so much trouble."

"Trouble! Nonsense! I do not stand upon ceremony with you, Algernon!"

"I am very glad of that," he said, smoothly, "as it makes it easier for me to do something which I dislike — namely, to refuse a lady's request. However, in this instance, I regret infinitely that I have no choice in the matter. Vanity, my dear

Lady Feniton —" he sighed heavily — "is a hard taskmaster! And now, if you will excuse me, I'll step round to the stables myself, and see about my horses."

A graceful little bow, and he had quitted the room before Lady Feniton could think of anything further to say. Captain Masterman and Guy Dorlais exchanged glances. Joanna could not look at Kitty, for fear that they should both burst into laughter. It was rarely that anyone succeeded in getting the better of Lady Feniton: it must be confessed that, to most of those present, it was not a disagreeable sight.

A thin, grey mist was swirling in from the sea as Captain Jackson threaded his way through the narrow, cobbled lanes of the little fishing town. Here and there, the feeble rays of a lamp or rushlight burning within the cottages imparted a pale glow to the as yet unshuttered windows. The winding lanes themselves boasted no light, but Jackson stepped along smartly, as one who knew his way.

He halted at last before a mean and dingy alehouse, frowning a little. After a second's pause, he pushed open the door, which stood slightly ajar. A wave of warm air greeted him, made less acceptable by the stale odour of tobacco and unwashed human bodies.

The scene which met his gaze inside the tavern was ordinary enough. On either side of a generous log fire set in the hearth of a wide, open chimney, were placed high-backed wooden settles. Some half dozen or so fishermen lolled in these, very much at their ease. A few were indulging in the luxury of a whiff from a clay pipe, while some, with mugs of ale in their fists, were carrying on a desultory conversation. One, at least, was unashamedly asleep.

In the centre of the small room stood a narrow trestle table, evidently a stranger to the scrubbing brush, for it bore the old marks of countless wet tankards upon its grimy surface. A few rickety chairs were disposed around it, but these appeared to be out of favour, for only one man was seated there. He looked up at Jackson's entrance, and gave an almost imperceptible sign of welcome. After a quick, careful scrutiny, under lazy eyelids, of the others present, the Captain went and sat beside him, facing the door, and with his back to the rest of the company. The man nodded, and gave him good evening as one does to a casual acquaintance. After that, there was a moment's silence.

"You'll take something?" asked the first man, in a guarded tone.

The Captain grimaced, "I suppose so," he conceded, reluctantly, and rose to go into the tap.

He returned without delay, bearing a brimming mug of ale, and seated himself again at the other man's side.

"I have a room in a cottage not far from here," mouthed the other, draining his mug and setting it down noisily on the table. "To the left as you go out, four doors down the street. I'll wait for you there."

The Captain nodded, his face hidden by his raised tankard. To an onlooker, it must have appeared as though he bade the other a casual good night.

The first man rose, spat carefully on the sawdust which covered the floor, nodded to the men around the fire, and went out into the mist.

The Captain lingered a while longer. It would not do to follow the other too soon. Presently, he too, rose and repeated the performance.

The damp, clammy air caught at his throat as he pushed through the doorway into the street; but it was a welcome change from the foetid atmosphere of the tavern. He shivered

160

a little, rubbing his hands to warm them as he moved briskly in the direction indicated by his confederate. When he reached the fourth house along, a figure stepped out of the gathering shadows.

Jackson's right hand went swiftly to the leather belt which secured his breeches: it closed around the ebony haft of a knife.

"No need for that," a low voice warned him.

He let his hand drop to his side again, and followed his former companion into the house.

The door opened straight into a room that was poky and cheerless. A meagre fire dragged on a feeble existence in the grate, the floor was stone-flagged and uncovered, the furniture consisted solely of two battered chairs and a crooked deal table. On this stood an oil lamp, turned down low. The window of the room was fast shuttered.

Jackson's companion turned up the lamp, and secured both entrances to the room. Then he motioned to his friend to take one of the chairs.

"You're sure we can trust 'em?" asked the Captain, as he did so. "'Pon my word, we were almost better off in the alehouse!"

The other shrugged. "Needs must," he answered, succinctly. "At least we're in no danger of being overheard, here."

Captain Jackson nodded. "I've yet to find a suitable rendezvous in this place," he said. "The alehouse is splendid for meeting people, but impossible for conversation."

"Just so: we manage, though. Well, I think I've some news for you this time, Captain — but trust you can make more sense of it than I can. Maybe we're on the wrong track, though."

"Let's hear it, Number Three. Two heads are better than one, y'know."

"Three heads have had a go at this already, and it's all Dutch to us! However, here's the strength of it, Captain."

He leaned forward so that the rickety chair wobbled dangerously.

"It has come to our notice that there's a boat being built in a disused shipyard somewhere down by the quay. Nothing out of the way in that, perhaps you'll say; but these people are mighty private about the whole business. That was what first attracted Number Four's notice. He decided to investigate. It proved quite a long and ticklish business — they don't mean to be observed, I can tell you! Anyway, with the help of Number Two and myself, we evolved a plan. I won't weary you with the details; suffice it to say that we eventually managed to get a look at this vessel — and a reasonably good look, too." He stopped. Jackson, too, was now leaning forward eagerly in his chair.

"Yes?" he asked, impatiently.

"It was like nothing I've ever seen afloat," said Number Three, emphatically. "More like a damned birdcage than a fishing vessel! They'd almost completed it, by what I could tell, too."

"Describe it," commanded Jackson tersely.

"About twenty-one feet long, I should say — nothing extraordinary in size. Fore and aft, however, was a superstructure of ribs, over which was set tarred canvas, I tell you, the whole thing resembled nothing so much as a tunnel — the crew, presumably, must grope about in the dark on their hands and knees! In the centre of the contraption was set an odd sort of tower, with a hatchway at the top —"

Here Captain Jackson let out a startled exclamation.

"What is it?" asked the other, arrested in his train of thought. "Do you see a ray of light somewhere? Damned if I do!"

"I believe so — but go on."

"That's about all I have to tell. Except for the mast of this weird structure, which was collapsible, so that it could be used or shipped away at will. Though how far they can hope to go without even a mast, Heaven only knows! Either those who are building this ship must be stark raving mad, or else it isn't a ship at all! I suppose," he added, thoughtfully, "that there is just one other possibility, but that's too fantastic to utter —" He stopped.

"Suppose you let me hear it, just the same," encouraged the Captain.

"Well, I just wondered — can they possibly have discovered some new method of propulsion?" queried the other, in a puzzled tone.

"In a sense, yes, that is the answer," replied Jackson, slowly. "Not propulsion, though — that is the only thing lacking from their point of view. What they have discovered is a new means of transport. Have you ever heard of Robert Fulton, Number Three?"

His companion started. "Good God, yes! What a fool I've been not to see that for myself! That ship of his — what did he call it?"

"The *Nautilus*," supplied Jackson. "Yes, my dear chap, that — or its counterpart, rather — is what is taking shape in this disused shipyard you speak of. The question is —" he hesitated, and drummed a rhythm with his finger tips on the bare table top — "the question is, why?"

"That business in September," said the other man, suddenly. "I didn't hear the whole — what exactly happened?"

"Well, as you doubtless know already," replied Jackson, "this fellow Fulton's been at the game for years. No doubt about it in my opinion — for what that's worth — the chap's a genius.

As long ago as '94, he was granted a patent for this submarine of his by the Navy Board; but it never came to anything, owing to the fact that the vessel has to be cranked along by hand. Only let him find some other means of propulsion, now, and phew! There's no saying where the *Nautilus* underwater vessel will not go! However, that appears a distant target, at best." He broke off, and shivered slightly. "That damned fire's worse than useless for heating this room, Number Three! But to return to Fulton — his next effort was the torpedo, or infernal machine, as the Navy dubbed it. Having tried to market the invention first in France, then Holland, and obtaining no response in terms that were acceptable to him, he actually had the nerve to approach us afterwards!"

"As an American and therefore a neutral in the present war, naturally, all nations are one to him," agreed Number Three. "Still, it's a matter for wonder that someone or other hasn't yet tried to assassinate the fellow."

"Pity if they did," said Jackson. "Mark my words, he's a coming man! Anyway, the Navy Board consented to a trial of these torpedoes in September, and some of our ships took them in tow to Boulogne. The French had about one hundred and fifty boats lying in the harbour at that time; had the internals done their job, it should have been a massacre. But something went wrong, and the things refused to blow up — Fulton claimed that it was a fault in the construction, and wanted to try again. He found no enthusiasm for the scheme, however, and had to abandon all hope of doing anything with his invention over here. What he's been doing since, I couldn't say, but somehow I don't think he's had a personal finger in this pie. He was last heard of in France."

"Mm." Number Three considered this information thoughtfully. "Well, Captain, where does our secret boat fit into all this? If it is indeed a second *Nautilus* — and I must say that it seems very probable — where and how is it to be used? For us — or against us, would you say?"

"Not for us, that's certain. We should have had news of it before this — remember, I was lately with the Minister. But that's the only point on which I can be certain, I may tell you." He paused a moment, knitting his brows. "What news from the farm?" he asked.

"Little enough. A constant watch is kept, but so far no one has managed to effect an entry. The French agents who were there originally have been joined by others; reports keep coming in to suggest that their whole strength will eventually be concentrated there. Your mysterious kegs of brandy arrived in good order on one moonless night more than a fortnight since, but what's being done with them is more than we can discover at present."

The Captain pondered this for a moment in silence.

"I'll take a look there myself," he said, at last. "I'm due to visit the Cove, in any event. What meeting place is appointed for the others?"

"A disused fisherman's hut, about half a mile from the farm," replied Number Three, and proceeded to give detailed instructions for reaching it.

"I fear that I can do no more tonight in this mist," said the Captain. "I must wait for dawn. You've made arrangements for a boat?"

The other man nodded. "It's ready and waiting in the same place as before, under tarred canvas. Do you want a shake down for the night?"

"No, I think not; I must see Number One before I start for the Cove." He rose, then added as an afterthought, "Be at the tavern at the same time tomorrow, in case of need. Is it safe to send a message here?"

"Safe enough," replied the other man. "The old woman who lives here can neither read nor write, and is to be trusted."

"Well, that's only in case of dire emergency," replied Jackson. "Good luck, Number Three."

They clasped hands briefly, and Jackson stepped out into the night.

Chapter XII: A Declaration of Love

Faintly, Joanna heard the hall clock strike one. She turned over in bed impatiently. After close on two hours of sleeplessness, she found herself even more wide awake than at the start. She reflected wryly that, could her grandmother have known of her inability to sleep, it would have pleased that lady to imagine that it was on Mr. Cholcombe's account. But it was not thoughts of the Honourable Algernon Cholcombe which deprived Miss Feniton of her rest: the gentleman who had that honour was Guy Dorlais, although the thoughts were not of love.

Ever since her meeting with Captain Jackson at the cottage down by the river, Joanna's mind had been plagued by an uneasy suspicion. This French agent for whom the man Jackson was seeking — was it possible that he could be none other than Guy Dorlais? At first, she had shied away from the notion, too conscious of Guy as the boy who had grown to manhood amongst them all, liked and respected; and as the man whom her dearest friend loved. Her suspicion was not so easily silenced, though. Events moulded themselves to its growth.

The first of these had been her talk with Kitty. Although at that time she had laughed at her friend's doubts, some of them had succeeded in penetrating into her own mind. Kitty had said that she was uneasy because Guy made no attempt to join the Defence Volunteers. There might perhaps be good reasons for this, but for the life of her, Joanna could not think of any. At a time when almost every young man, even such an unlikely one as the poet, Walter Scott, was dashing into uniform and drilling on the beaches and meadows throughout the whole country, why should Guy Dorlais hang back? If ever there had existed a bold, fearless individual, surely Dorlais was that man.

Again, why was it that he did not ask Kitty to appoint a day for the wedding? There was no lack of love that Joanna could see, and she certainly did not believe that there could be any lack of means. But if he should in reality be a spy for the French, then all this was very easily explained. He could not hope to keep such a secret from a wife.

The second event which confirmed her in her suspicions was the disappearance of her letter. Sufficient time had now elapsed for her to be certain that it had not simply been mislaid, and she was satisfied that none of the servants had touched her reticule. Captain Jackson, too, had denied all knowledge of the theft in a way that carried conviction. The fact remained, however, that someone must have removed the letter from her bag; and Guy Dorlais had certainly seen her reading it, must have noticed the somewhat guilty manner in which she had quickly pushed it out of sight, and had observed the other unusual circumstances of that occasion. Why he should want possession of the letter, even supposing him to be a French spy, was not very clear to Joanna. He had certainly had the opportunity to take it, though, if he wished to do so. On the evening in question, she had left her reticule lying about in the drawing room until she had retired to bed, when it had reposed for almost an hour on her dressing table while she was out of her room.

Lastly, there was the incident concerning the painting which hung in the library. At the time, the full significance of this had not struck her. She had noted his expression, and instinctively analysed it as betraying knowledge. It was only afterwards that she had remembered Captain Jackson's description of the

Cove which was used as a post office by Boney's agents. Could this painting of Turner's depict that very same Cove? If so, then he had recognized it, and this in itself was an acknowledgement of guilt.

She reflected unhappily that there were so many things that would help to fit Guy Dorlais into the part of a French spy. He was of French origin, therefore his loyalties might be considered suspect, in spite of his avowals. The French agent whom Jackson was seeking would be a man who had the language at his command, and a thorough knowledge of South Devon, into the bargain. Dorlais had both; moreover, Dorlais was free to come and go as he pleased, a proviso very necessary to the wanted man. The more she considered it, the more likely it appeared.

It was considerations such as these which had lately prevented Joanna from trying to do anything to heal the breach between Kitty and her betrothed. If Dorlais were indeed a traitor, then the sooner that Kitty fell out of love with him, the better. Did people fall out of love as readily as they appeared to fall into it, Miss Feniton wondered? She had to confess her ignorance of the matter. She only knew what she had read, and that seemed to indicate a most distressing faithfulness on Kitty's part, entailing years of remorse and followed by either an early death or retreat into a convent. There was, of course, thought Joanna with a wry smile, yet a third possibility; that of a life henceforward devoted to good works.

None of these possibilities seemed to be suited to Miss Lodge. She might look vastly appealing, though, in a nun's habit, with her little, mischievous face peeping demurely out.

The lighter touch brought a less strained smile to Joanna's lips. This was absurd. If she must remain awake when everyone else slept, then at least she must find herself some rational occupation. This could not be done unless she was dressed, so she at once leapt from the bed, and began to don her clothes.

The room struck chill, for her fire had long since died away. For extra warmth, she fastened a green fur-trimmed pelisse over her gown, and pulled it close about her. When she was fully dressed, she stood still for a while in the middle of the room, debating what she might do next. There could not be a great deal of choice, at that hour of night.

It was while she was standing there, irresolute, that she fancied she heard a faint sound from outside the door of her bedchamber.

At once she stiffened, alert. There was no repetition of the sound, but she could not let matters rest there. Crossing the room quietly, she softly opened the door and peered outside.

All was in darkness. Her room was at the head of the staircase, and, if she leaned over the balustrade, she could look down into the hall. Knowing her ground so well, she ventured to do this.

The blackness dissolved a little, resolving itself into the dark shapes of things familiar by day. Across the void of the hall, a faint light was moving towards the passage which led to a side entrance of the house.

She caught her breath; but her mind was made up in an instant. She returned quietly to her room, and quickly changed her kid sandals for a pair of half boots. She snatched up the lamp from beside her bed, then quickly put it down again, as she realized that it would be of no use to her out of doors, and she would scarcely need it in the house, which she knew blindfold. In any event, a light might betray her presence; she must trust to luck that she would fare equally well outside without one. She trusted herself to find her way about that part of the grounds immediately surrounding the house without any difficulty. If the unknown person whom she intended to follow had a mind to venture beyond these limits, she could only hope for a moon on this particular night.

She ran quickly down the staircase with the ease born of long familiarity, and along the passage until she reached the side door. Sure enough, she found it unfastened. She slipped quietly through it, and into the garden.

For a moment, the intense darkness made her too uncertain to move. Then gradually, as her eyes became more accustomed to it, she could make out the shapes of trees and shrubs, and far ahead, a tiny pinpoint of light which was moving steadily away from her.

She began to run, trusting that, at this distance, she would not be heard. After a few minutes, she paused, breathless; but the light was much nearer now, a matter of only fifty yards or so away. She followed patiently. The distance between herself and her quarry lengthened as time went on, but she was always able to keep the light in sight. Her quarry seemed to know where he was going, and did not always make use of the paths. He had turned away from the formal gardens, and out into the parkland which sloped down towards the sea.

It was a long and tiring walk, full of unexplained rustlings which intruded now and then into the otherwise all-enveloping silence. At intervals, there was a hint of rain in the air, while the hoped for moon remained obstinately hidden by cloud. Miss Feniton would have been reluctant to admit the fact, but she did not feel altogether easy. The mystery of her errand, and of the tenebrous night, filled her with a sense almost of awe. She would not have been sorry to have found herself once more in her bed, and the whole episode no more than a bad dream.

Characteristically, she did not allow such thoughts to gain ground, but followed the winking light ahead of her with determined footsteps that could not help flagging a little as time went on.

Just when she was feeling that she could scarcely walk another yard, the light stopped, appeared to dart about a little, hesitated, and finally vanished.

She checked for a moment in dismay. What had occurred? Had the light been extinguished — or had its bearer entered one of the many ornamental buildings with which the grounds of Shalbeare House were embellished?

Even Miss Feniton, knowing the place as she did, could not say with certainty where she was standing at this moment. She moved forward cautiously in the direction where she supposed the light to have disappeared.

She had traversed a narrow path and crossed a patch of wet grass, when a building loomed up out of the darkness. She knew it must be one of the small temples which stood at intervals about the grounds, and according to her calculations, it was roughly at this spot that the light had vanished. She would most likely find her quarry, therefore, in the building.

By now, she was more than a little apprehensive, and for the first time wondered if she had acted wisely in coming out of doors in pursuit of whoever it was whom she had seen in the hall. Yet on whom could she have called for help, without raising the whole household, and revealing more of the matter than she cared to do just at present? She tried to put these thoughts away from her: she had come, she was here, and did not mean to go away again without knowing more of the affair.

Her heart beating fast, she began to make a stealthy circuit of the temple, seeking the entrance.

Suddenly, there was a whirr of wings close by her head, and an owl hooted loudly almost in her ear.

Even the intrepid Miss Feniton could not altogether repress a muted shriek as she ran forward a little way in the darkness.

She halted then, somewhat ashamed of her action as she realized what it was that had caused her alarm. She began to retrace the few steps she had taken away from the building.

Without any warning, she was suddenly seized upon from behind by two shadows which loomed up out of the darkness. A relentless hand was placed firmly over her mouth, so that she had the utmost difficulty in breathing, while her arms were pinioned in a strong hold behind her back.

"Good God, I believe it's a woman!" she heard someone gasp. A hand became entangled with her hair, and she protested faintly through the one which was clamped on to her mouth. "Yes, it is — well, I'm damned!"

The hold upon her relaxed a little, though not altogether. She heard the second man muttering something in his companion's ear.

"I'll handle this," she heard her captor answer. The accents seemed familiar, but at present she was too upset to be able to place them. "You'd best move off now. I have a suspicion —"

Here he dropped his voice, so that she could not hear what followed; but the other man moved away after they had conferred for a second or two longer.

She had at first been too stunned by the suddenness of the attack to attempt much of a defence. Now she began to struggle in earnest.

"Here, hold on!" adjured her captor, tightening his hold, though by no means brutally. "Let's have you into the light, and see who you are, first!"

He half led, half carried her into the small ornamental temple.

She was not altogether reluctant to go, for by this time she had recognized the voice. It was that of Captain Jackson, and she knew of no reason for fearing him.

It was dark inside the building, save for one patch where a shielded storm lantern stood upon the floor, close by a marble bench. He guided her towards the spot, then released her, turning her face to the light.

"Miss Feniton," he said, in tones of satisfaction rather than of surprise. "I guessed as much, but could not be sure."

She threw him an angry look, and tried to pin up her hair with fingers which trembled a little.

"May I inquire what you are doing on my grandfather's land? And how dared you treat me in that manner?"

"I can scarcely be blamed if I did manhandle you somewhat," he pointed out reasonably. "After all, how could I know that you were a female? I took you for an eavesdropper, most likely an enemy agent, and acted accordingly. I trust I have not hurt you, though?" he added, anxiously, scanning her expression.

"I dare say I shall survive," she conceded, somewhat mollified. "But I shall sit down, if you have no objection, I am a little tired."

She seated herself on the cold marble bench. Truth to tell, she felt almost exhausted. It was an hour of night when she was most often accustomed to sleeping, and she had just taken a long walk in nerve racking circumstances, quite apart from the shock of having been attacked.

He watched her with real concern. Her face was pale, her attitude one of the utmost fatigue. A disconcerting idea occurred to him.

"Miss Feniton!" he said, alarmed. "You — you are not going to swoon, I trust?"

A tired smile wavered on her lips. "I have told you before that I have not the trick of swooning. But I notice that you do not answer my question — what are you doing here?"

He hesitated for a moment. "History repeats itself, Miss Feniton. Do you remember that you also questioned me on the first occasion that we met?"

"With the same negligible result, it appears," she answered, dryly. "I recollect that the answers I obtained on that occasion were far from satisfactory."

"That bench can afford you little comfort," he said, suddenly, moving over to a corner where a dark travelling coat lay discarded in a heap. "Allow me to place this upon it for you."

She rose to her feet, and he folded the garment and laid it along the bench.

"There, that is better! Try if it is not."

She sat down again. He hesitated for a moment, then placed himself at her side.

"What on earth can you have been doing out of doors at this hour of night and in this season?" he asked, curiously.

She smiled wryly. "I see you are to answer my question by asking one of your own — a method common in Scotland, so I understand. It is no doubt very clever, sir, but it will not do. I was the first to ask, and am awaiting a reply."

"I must take you back to the house," he said, rising. "It is altogether undesirable that you should remain here."

"You fear to compromise me?" she asked, mockingly.

He studied her for a moment in silence. She could not see his face clearly, but she could tell that its expression was grave.

"If you truly thought of me as an equal, you would not ask that question, even in jest," he said at last. It was her turn to be silent.

"I am sorry," she answered, after a pause. "I know you to be — sufficient of a gentleman — not to harm me in any way."

"Sufficient of a gentleman!" he repeated, ironically. "You do not grant me the full title, then, madam?"

"How can I?" she asked, in surprise.

"How indeed? I suppose you will argue that gentlemen do not demean themselves by participating in smuggling, spying, or other such low activities; I imagine that they would scorn to appear in such attire as this —" here he indicated with a gesture the fisherman's garb which he was wearing — "or speak, as I do, in the homely tones of Devon! Is that what you mean, Miss Feniton?"

"Perhaps it is." She faced him squarely, a candid light in her hazel eyes. "Since you prefer plain speaking, Captain Jackson, let me say that you have given me no choice but to believe that you and I belong to two totally different spheres of life. You have consistently refused even to tell me your real name."

"I know. There is something in what you say." He knitted his brows in thought. "The devil's in it, but I must not," he added, quickly. "I'm afraid the little I've been able to tell you of myself must suffice: you will have to take me on trust."

"But I observe that you are not to repose a like confidence in me," she retorted. "You do not mean to trust me at all with your secrets!"

"You little know," he said, earnestly, leaning a little towards her, "how greatly I have already shown my trust in you. Only consider for a moment, Miss Feniton! Do you seriously suppose that in the ordinary way I would be likely to confide in anyone to the extent that I have done in yourself? On such a short acquaintance, too! Can you imagine that I would have lasted a day in this dangerous game, had I been in the habit of making such revelations? Why, even my nearest relations have no notion —" He broke off abruptly.

"Your nearest relations," repeated Joanna, thoughtfully. "Can you not at least tell me who they are?"

He shook his head. "It is difficult to make you understand. Already I am suspected by the French of playing a double game; it becomes increasingly important that I should preserve my anonymity. That is my one sure defence. In these times, it is impossible for a man to know himself just who are his friends and who his enemies: how should you with less experience in such matters than I, be able to tell who is or is not to be trusted? If you were to know more of me, a chance word of yours — a look, even — might give the clue to one of these hidden watchers."

"Surely you do not mean to suggest —" she began, then broke off, frowning. "At least there is one thing you can tell me," she continued, eagerly. "Someone came from the house to meet you tonight, I know — I saw a light being carried across the hall in the direction of the side door, and when I examined the door, it had been left unfastened. I could not see who it was, but you did have another man with you when — when I arrived on the scene, though you sent him away almost at once. Who was it — who is your confederate in Shalbeare House?"

He shook his head, frowning.

"Was it one of the servants?" insisted Joanna. "Is it possible that any of the domestic staff who came here with Sir George Lodge are connected with your smuggling gang?"

"Believe me when I say that it is wiser if you remain in complete ignorance of the whole business," he said, firmly.

"But tell me, was it this which brought you out here tonight — did you follow this person? How comes it then that you were not abed?"

"You are much better at asking questions than at answering them," she pointed out, with a flash of her green eyes. "However, I will give you a lesson in openness. I was unable to sleep, and had got up again, with some idea of finding a way of employing the time until I should feel more like settling down, when I heard a noise outside my room. I looked out after a moment, and saw the light. I followed it to this spot — and you know the rest, I fancy!"

"But why on earth should you do such a —" he fumbled for words — "such a foolhardy thing? Why did you not rouse the house — though I must say that I am thankful you did not," he added, in heartfelt tones.

"Perhaps for the same reason that I did not rouse the house when I discovered you that night," she said mischievously. "I am a woman, and have my full share of feminine curiosity, after all."

"You have an uncommon share of courage," he said, warmly. "But you mustn't do such things, indeed you must not! There is no saying what dangers you may be led into!"

"Into such hazards as this, no doubt?" she asked, with a little crooked smile.

He looked into her face. The hazy light of the lantern threw an enchantment about her, a suggestion of mystery that was heightened by the silence and darkness of the world outside their small shelter. Her eyes were soft and mellow in the white oval of her face. He felt a quickness in his blood, a disturbing sense of her femininity. He drew a little away from her, until the heady feeling should have passed.

"I must take you home," he said, without any real conviction.

"You are very anxious to be rid of me; am I such poor company?" she asked, mockingly.

"Quite the reverse," he said abruptly. He was still feeling the challenge of her presence.

Almost as though she sensed this, some impulse moved Joanna to be provocative. She turned towards him, so that what little light there was fell upon her face.

She was smiling, with a whimsical twist of her red lips; twin devils of light danced in the green flecked eyes. He caught his breath.

"You do not sound very convincing," she accused, softly.

Something flamed within him. He leapt to his feet, drawing her to him, crushing her body relentlessly in his strong embrace. Before she could prevent it, his lips had found and held hers in passionate demand.

For a moment only, she lay inert in his arms. Then she tore herself away, and dealt him a stinging slap across his cheek.

"How — how *dare* you!" she stormed, the hazel eyes flashing with fury. "How dare you!"

"'I dare do all that may become a man'," he quoted, quietly.

"No *gentleman*," said Joanna, in biting accents, "would dream of behaving so to a lady situated as I am at present!"

"Evidently you know little of the sex, madam," he replied, dryly. "But I accept your reproof: perhaps I did in some sort take advantage of your situation. If it eases your mind at all, I am willing to beg your pardon."

"Willing!" repeated Joanna, in fury. "Let me tell you, sir, you beg like a very tyrant! If I had anyone to avenge me, you should not go unscathed for this!"

His lips twisted ironically. "Do not concern yourself, Miss Feniton. A sharper sword has entered my heart than any a champion of yours might produce!"

"Do not be flowery," she said, scathingly, subsiding a little. "I have warned you before that it is not in my style."

He shrugged. "That can scarcely matter."

She stared, uncertain whether to be affronted or not at the bitterness of his tone.

"Not matter? Upon my word, you are a very strange man, allow me to tell you! I suppose you think it no great matter, then, that you have just offered me an insult?"

His expression hardened. "Do you take an honest man's love for an insult, Miss Feniton?" he asked, in a brittle voice.

"Love!" she effected a scornful laugh. "I can think of another word for it!"

"Then you would be wrong," he said, quietly. "This is no moment to be making you a declaration, I realize, but I am scarcely in a position to stand upon form. I do in truth love you, Miss Feniton. The conviction has been growing upon me ever since our first meeting."

"Pray continue!" she goaded him, mockingly. "You should now offer me your heart and hand!"

"That I cannot do at present, as you very well know."

"Upon my word!" she exclaimed, tartly. "This is a vastly fine declaration, to be sure! What answer do you expect me to make to such a piece of effrontery, I wonder?"

"Effrontery?" He considered her for a moment in silence. Her manner was quieter now; the first fury had vanished, leaving only a trace in her slightly flushed cheeks. She had become the Miss Feniton of their first meeting, the cold, disdainful young lady whom nothing could touch.

"It may perhaps appear so to you," he said, in a voice charged with feeling. "You do not think me your equal in rank and fortune, and what right has an ordinary man to the affection of one such as Miss Feniton of Shalbeare House?"

"It is not altogether that," she said, defensively, discarding her mocking tone. "Leaving aside such matters, you surely cannot expect that I would form an attachment to you after the very few meetings we have had together — more particularly when you consider the nature of those meetings!"

"Few or many, what does it signify?" he asked, with a touch of scorn. "Do you feel that love comes only after a proper interval, and solely to those who have been properly presented to each other in some ballroom or other public place? I had thought that Joanna Feniton had a soul above the conventions!"

"Conventions are very necessary, and a woman flouts them at her peril," replied Joanna, in a practical tone. "We cannot all fling our bonnets over the windmill."

He stepped forward impetuously, and took her hands in his.

"But you can, Joanna! Think of the bonnet which you flung into the river Teign! I still have it, you know, though I was obliged to burn the scarf with which you bandaged my arm."

"You kept my bonnet?" she exclaimed, for the moment so diverted by the idea that she forgot to withdraw her hands from his.

He nodded, looking into her eyes.

"That poor bedraggled wreck of velvet and satin ribbons was all I had as a reminder of you," he said, softly.

She returned his gaze for a moment, the hazel eyes widening. A faint blush came to her cheek; then she pulled her hands impatiently from his grasp.

"Then you had much better burn it!" she said, with a snap. "And I advise you to put these foolish thoughts of me out of your head! I must tell you that I am already as good as affianced to another."

These words did not produce quite the effect that she had hoped for: it crossed her mind that perhaps he had learnt as much already from one of those mysterious sources of information which he appeared to have at his command.

"May I inquire who the man is?" he asked, in even tones.

"It is no business of yours, of course," she pointed out, coldly. "Still, I see no harm in telling you. His name is Cholcombe — he is the son of a nobleman."

"Algernon Cholcombe!" he repeated, scornfully. "You know him?" she asked, quickly.

"Let us say rather that I know of him."

"You seem to have a knowledge of everyone in these parts," she said, musingly. "Though I recollect that you did not know Kitty Lodge by sight, for you took me for her."

"It is my business to know such things," he replied, shortly. "What did you mean when you said that you were 'as good as affianced' to this man?"

She looked away, unable for some reason to meet his eyes.

"He has not spoken as yet," she said, in an uncertain tone. "It is — a family arrangement."

"A marriage of convenience!" he exclaimed, scathingly.

"If you like to call it so."

"And you would be content to enter into such a contract?" he asked, incredulously. "You, who have the spirit for high adventure, the courage to flout those conventions which you affect to prize! I tell you it is — it is —" he struggled for a word, and brought it out at last, vehemently — "prostitution!"

"If you are to use such unsuitable language," she said, coldly, advancing towards the exit, "I think it high time for me to go. I wish you good night, Captain Jackson."

"No, wait!" In two strides he was before her, blocking the way. "I am sorry if you should mislike my choice of words, but someone must tell you the truth! Cozened by that old battle axe of a grandmother of yours, you may slip into a marriage which can only be a source of disgust to one of your disposition! My lovely Joanna —"

She made a gesture of distaste at these words.

"Very well," he said, in a quieter tone. "I promise I will not be flowery! But ask yourself if you can honestly give any better word to a marriage such as you contemplate at this moment! Do you truly consider it worthy of your highest ideals?"

"I have had little to do with such matters," said Miss Feniton, sensibly. "It seems to me that a suitable match is capable of yielding as much happiness as one between two people in the throes of a violent passion, who may be as incompatible as — as night and day!"

"May I ask what you consider a suitable match?" he asked, gravely.

"One where rank and fortune are nearly equal, and there is not too much difference in age," she answered, unconsciously quoting her grandmother. "Both parties, of course, should be of good character," she added, on her own account. "And if the families are known to each other, so much the better."

"A very sensible arrangement," he approved, mockingly. "I think it provides for everything. Choosing a husband, then, partakes of something of the same nature as choosing a new bonnet? The colours and materials must tone with the rest of one's wardrobe, and it must have just the right number of ribbons and fal-lals!"

"Captain Jackson," said Miss Feniton, wearily. "This conversation is not leading us anywhere. I am very tired, and would like above all to return to the house. Will you kindly allow me to pass?"

He stood aside at once.

"I am sorry," he said, contritely. "Of course, you must be dead tired. I will escort you back to the house — and promise to plague you with no more questions or homilies."

She protested a little, insisting that she could go alone. He was not to be moved this time, however, and she was not altogether sorry. The prospect of the long walk back alone in the dark was not a pleasant one in her present state of mind.

He picked up his coat and placed it about her shoulders, paying no heed to her protests. He took the lantern in one hand, and offered her his other arm. She was about to refuse, but thought better of it, and placed her hand upon his sleeve.

They made the long walk back in silence, both wrapped in thoughts which apparently could not be shared. As they stood in the shadows close to the side door of the house, he released her arm, and, taking her hand, carried it gently to his lips. She permitted the gesture, but unresponsively. She felt unutterably weary.

She slipped the coat from about her shoulders, and handed it to him.

"I must go in. Thank you for accompanying me. Good night," she whispered.

He watched her while she softly opened the door, and stepped into the passage. She turned for a second, smiled, then closed the door upon him.

He heard the bolts being gently eased into place, but it was some time before he turned to go.

Chapter XIII: The Trap

The grey day was not far advanced when Captain Jackson beached his boat on the thin strip of sand which had been exposed by the outgoing tide. There was no beauty here in Kerswell Cove on this cold morning of December; even the tawny Devon sand seemed drained of colour. He made towards the low, dark cave in the cliffs, and, flinging himself down on hands and knees, crawled laboriously into its depths. After a short distance, he was able to stand upright.

The interior of the cave was pitch black, but he could find his way comfortably along its narrow, winding ways with the aid of a small lantern which he carried attached to his belt. He had not far to go. The first bend in the path brought him to a wider section of the cave. Here he paused, turning towards the wall on his left hand. With the ease born of long practice, he reached up to a natural shelving of the rock, his hands closing around a small wooden box which rested there.

He lifted down the box, and fitted into the miniature lock a key which he drew from the pocket of his sea-stained breeches. He raised the lid, and inspected the contents of the box by the light of his lamp.

He saw at once that there were no dispatches inside. This did not surprise him, for it was understood that he would not be making the voyage to France for another few months, unless in case of urgent need. It was customary for him to remain in England until the contraband which he had lately brought over the water should have been disposed of, and the money for it collected. Only then would he set out for the shores of France once more.

There was, however, a thin strip of folded paper lying in the box. This could only be one of the orders for which he had of late looked in vain. His pulse quickened a little; did this mean that he was not suspect, after all? But perhaps it was not for him. He picked it up, and saw the letter "J" marked plainly on the cover.

Hastily, he unfolded the paper, reading its brief message by the light of his lamp. As usual, the text had been made up of words cut from a printed page, and stuck on to a sheet of plain paper.

"Go as soon as possible to Babbacombe," he read. "Show your pass to the blacksmith there. You will be told what to do."

His mouth twisted grimly. There was an ominous ring about the last sentence. He read the words again, then pocketed the paper, and replaced the box on the shelf, after relocking it.

He did not linger, then, but returned to the boat. He climbed in, and bent his back to the oars, taking a southerly course. It was some time later that he fetched up in a cove farther down the coast. This was larger than Kerswell Cove, and could be approached from the land by those who did not mind a steep descent down the cliff face, and a stiff scramble over rough, jagged rocks to reach the beach. Possibly in the summer months there may have been those who would have made the attempt, but at this season, the place was deserted.

Captain Jackson beached his boat behind one of the jutting rocks, and covered it carefully with a length of tarred canvas. Then he began the tricky ascent to the top of the cliffs.

A while later, panting a little, he crouched on the sparse grass above the cove. He surveyed the surrounding country carefully through a pair of perspective glasses. Satisfied at last that not a soul was in sight, he rose, and, keeping to the cliff edge, walked along it some distance until he espied a rough track. This he took, following it for almost a mile, until it dipped down to lead into another tiny cove, which lay in the hollow between one cliff and another. Here there were signs of habitation; two or three rude huts could be observed on the rough ground beyond the shingly beach. He raised his glasses, and scrutinized these buildings carefully as he approached them.

They were constructed chiefly of timber, and appeared to be derelict, one of them at least being roofless. He drew closer; putting away the perspective glasses, and keeping one hand ready on his knife. The first hut to which he came was a mere shell. Nevertheless, he was not prepared to take any chances. Having approached cautiously to the opening where, no doubt, a door had once stood, he peered tentatively inside. There was nothing at all to be seen other than a heap of rubble and miscellaneous rubbish on the floor.

Satisfied that he was leaving no lurking enemy here at his back, he made the same cautious approach to the second hut. This stood a little further back, at some distance removed from the first, and was obviously in much better condition. Before he could reach it, however, the figure of a man emerged, and stood motionless outside the building, as though awaiting his arrival.

Captain Jackson's muscles tautened warningly, but he continued to approach with his habitual light step, poised for instant action, if need be. His hand rested upon the hilt of his knife.

At a distance of five yards from the hut, he relaxed. He had recognized the figure waiting at the door, and it was that of the man whom he had expected and hoped to meet here.

They nodded wordlessly to each other in greeting, and wasted no time in entering the hut. Inside were three other men, who evidently had lately been playing cards. A fourth was sleeping heavily on a pile of sacking at one corner, and never stirred. The rest looked up eagerly at Jackson's entrance.

"He's been on reconnaissance most of the night," explained Jackson's companion, with a nod at the recumbent form in the corner. "What news, Captain?"

"I was about to ask you the same question," parried Jackson.

"Precious little," replied the first man, with a rueful shrug.

"They keep very close at Randall's Farm, and even at night always have a man on sentry go — so it's impossible to get near the house. We've tried various ruses for keeping the sentry out of the way for a bit, but so far without success. To overpower him is, of course, out of the question — we must not show our hand, or the alarm would be raised.

Jackson nodded. "There must be a way," he said, thoughtfully. "We'll put our heads together over that presently. Has anyone so far been observed to visit this farm?"

"No one of note," was the regretful reply. "Certainly no one who could be supposed to be their leader. The 'brandy' arrived some weeks since, as no doubt you were informed by Number Three — and they've had a quantity of timber delivered there by night on several occasions."

"Timber!" Jackson started. "Did you say timber?"

"Why, yes," replied the other, looking at him in surprise. "Can you see any particular significance in that? Damned if I can!"

"Perhaps," said Jackson, frowning. He paused a moment, and when he spoke again, it was with an undertone of excitement. "What do you think of this, gentlemen?" he asked. "I believe I have the answer to our problem!"

The other men came to their feet, and gathered eagerly about him.

"The deuce you have!" exclaimed one of them.

"What is it?" asked the ringleader. "It will be worth something not to be working all the time in the dark!"

"I make no doubt that Number Three passed on to you the information that he had acquired from the other source?" asked Jackson. "You already know about the boat which they have constructed on similar lines to Fulton's *Nautilus*?"

"What of that?" asked one, but the ringleader eyed Jackson thoughtfully, saying nothing for the moment.

"Do you think they're doing something of the kind out at the farm, then?" asked another, doubtfully.

"Not that, but the other half of it," said Jackson, somewhat cryptically. "It's my belief, gentlemen, that they are constructing a number of torpedoes at Randall's Farm!"

There was a stunned silence for a moment or two. Then the leader nodded slowly.

"You may be right," he said. "Indeed, I begin to see your trend, and think it very likely. With a boat capable of submarine travel, and those damned infernals of Robert Fulton's, they are all set for an attack by water! But what is their target? Can you answer that, Captain?"

Jackson shook his head.

"I can think of nothing hereabouts," he answered, in a puzzled tone. "Perhaps one of you others has some notion?"

"Unless they want to blow up the quay at one of the fishing ports," suggested one man, diffidently.

Jackson considered this for a moment in silence.

"Possible," he decided slowly. "Though how it can benefit them is not easy to see, unless that is only part of a larger scheme Naturally, it would throw a scare into the neighbourhood concerned, but do you really suppose that such a motive would be weighty enough to justify the great expense and risk of discovery which their exploit must have entailed?"

The rest thought this over, and could not but have the same doubts.

"If perchance they were to destroy some of the fishing vessels," went on Jackson, "it might have a more adverse effect upon the morale of the people hereabouts; but even that could —" He broke off. It was evident from his expression that a momentous idea had occurred to him.

"Well?" asked the leader, seeing how it was.

"Suppose their target is not yet available?" asked Jackson, gravely.

"You mean —"

Jackson nodded. "They know — and we know — that sooner or later, the Fleet must put into Torbay. At this time of year, with frequent bad weather in the Channel, they may be expected any day. I'm willing to lay you any odds, gentlemen, that the Navy's the target for which all these elaborate preparations are being made!"

"Damned if I don't think you're right!" exclaimed the leader.

The rest echoed him, their faces grave and concerned.

"What shall we do, then?" asked one. "Have these people placed under arrest, and blow their infernals sky high?"

"And let their chief go free?" asked Jackson. "We have no lead to him as yet, remember. All our watching of the rest has not given us a single clue to his identity. No, if we have conjectured aright, they can do no harm at present. The Fleet is still out there, guarding the Channel, and as you know, they cannot take their submarine vessel so far! It is capable of covering only very short distances, owing to the fact that it has to be propelled by hand. There can be no danger until the Fleet puts in: and that may give us just the interval we require to find this man."

A short and heated debate followed this speech; but in the end the verdict was unanimous.

"And now I have something to tell you which may perhaps help us to that end," continued Jackson. "I have today picked up this message. You may like to see it."

He handed over the paper which he had taken from the box in the Cove. His companions scrutinized it carefully.

"Sounds deuced like a trap to me," said one.

"Almost sure to be," agreed another. "You won't go, Captain?"

"I am of your opinion," conceded Jackson. "Nevertheless, I believe I must go."

There was a general outcry at this.

"What, put your head voluntarily into a noose?" asked the leader, incredulously. "Good God, you must be mad, man!"

"I see no other way of coming to grips with my man," returned Jackson.

"But even this may bring you no nearer to him," expostulated one of the others. "It's my belief that the smith will have a bullet waiting for you, and that will be the end of the matter."

"You may be right. But there is just a possibility that I am still trusted by them, and that they wish to allot me some part in this affair. If it should be so, I obviously cannot afford to miss such a chance."

One of the men let out an oath. "You are willing to hazard your life on odds like that?" he asked. "Number Six is right, you know; you are indeed mad, and should be shut up in Bedlam with the best of 'em! You can never hope to return alive from that smithy!"

"If it is their purpose to kill me, they can find easier ways than this," replied the Captain, nothing daunted.

"I'm not so certain of that," demurred the leader. "Unless they make an appointment of this sort, they have no means of coming at you, have they?"

"It is known that I visit Kerswell Cove in the first se'nnight of every month, however," pointed out Jackson.

"Tell me, my dear chap, would you choose to lurk in that cave for seven days, with the sea washing into it at every high tide? I think not."

Jackson grinned. "There is the cliff," he said, without conviction. "But I think you have proved your point, Number Five. There is not a shred of cover in the vicinity, and they have no means of knowing on which of the seven days I may arrive. Very well, then, they may have made this appointment with the object of putting a period to my existence."

"And so?" asked Number Five, challengingly.

"And so we must make a plan," replied Jackson. "I never had the slightest intention of walking blindly into any trap of theirs, I can tell you! I have it in mind that there may be a way to discover just what kind of a reception they have in store for me at Babbacombe. That will mean delaying my visit there for a day or two. Listen, and give me the benefit of your invaluable opinions."

They put their heads together.

Chapter XIV: Miss Feniton's Suspicions are Verified

Mr. Cholcombe had been two days absent from Shalbeare House when Lady Feniton came into the morning room where Joanna and Kitty were sitting alone after breakfast. She looked flustered, a thing unusual with her.

"Such a to-do!" she began. "Here's your grandfather almost beside himself with rage, Joanna, over what he terms a most outrageous act of vandalism!"

Joanna looked up in amazement, while Kitty Lodge could not help staring at her hostess.

"Grandpapa vexed?" asked Joanna, incredulously. "Pray, ma'am, whatever can have happened to put him into a taking? He is in general the most placid person of my acquaintance!"

"You should see him at the moment," recommended her grandmother, "and you would not say so! And all over a book, too! Mind you, I think it a great deal too bad of whoever is responsible; but it is only one of those stupid travel books, after all — nothing of the least value!"

"But what exactly has happened?" persisted Miss Feniton. "Can it be — can someone possibly have torn up one of my grandfather's books, then? I cannot imagine who would do such a thing!"

"It has not exactly been torn," said Lady Feniton. "Only a piece cut out of it, neatly, as if with scissors. Indeed, I defy anyone to notice it, unless they should happen to be paying particular attention to the text — and who would be likely to, with a book of that kind? No one but your grandfather, I'll be bound!"

Joanna's heart missed a beat. "Do I understand you to say that it is simply one page of the book which has been mutilated?" she asked.

"Not even one whole page!" exclaimed Lady Feniton. "A single word is what has put Feniton in such a bother! Why, whatever is amiss, Joanna? Do not tell me that you are to fall into a taking over the stupid affair, too!"

These words caused Kitty to eye her friend sharply. She was just in time to catch Joanna's quickly controlled look of concern.

"Is there anything wrong, Jo?" she asked, curiously.

"Only that I cannot at all understand the whole silly affair," replied Miss Feniton, lightly. "Has Grandpapa made any effort to discover who is responsible for the outrage, ma'am?"

"You may be sure that he has! Never have I seen him bestir himself so over any matter in my recollection! He is even now questioning all the servants in turn. I came away, for I cannot waste half the morning in such a foolish commotion! For all we can know, it may have been done many years since — perhaps, even, Geoffrey may — but, there, I do not really credit such a notion!"

"Possibly Mr. Cholcombe may have done it when he was on a visit here as a boy," suggested Kitty, with a mischievous look in Joanna's direction.

"Mm!" Lady Feniton considered this for a moment in silence.

"I doubt if there would be enough devilment in such an action to appeal to the boy that he was in those days," she said, at last. "In any event, it's of no consequence that I can see. The thing is done, and no one a mite the worse for it, except for your grandfather's choler."

She swept out of the room, leaving Kitty and Joanna sharing an amused glance.

"What a silly trick!" said Kitty. "Do you suppose someone can have meant to spite Sir Walter, Jo?"

Joanna shook her head, hesitating to reply. She was saved the necessity of thinking of something to say by the sudden entrance of three other members of their party. It was evident from the expressions on their faces that they had something of special interest to impart.

"Here is the most splendid news!" exclaimed Georgina Masterman, radiant in a morning gown of white muslin trimmed with blue ribbons and lace. "They tell me that there are five or six men-of-war at anchor in the Bay!"

"If it is true," said Guy Dorlais, "I must go down and take a look. If it should chance to be some of Cornwallis's lot, many of them are known to me, and I should not like to miss the opportunity of renewing our acquaintance. What do you say, Masterman? Shall we step down to the quay, presently?"

"I should like it extremely," replied Captain Masterman, in an apologetic tone, "but for the fact that I am engaged to accompany my sister to Totnes today. We must leave soon after luncheon, Georgina," he added, turning to her with a smile.

She did not return it. "But, William, surely there can be no occasion to leave today! I am promised to the Radletts for any time during the rest of the week — there is nothing definite — tomorrow, or the day after, will suit me just as well. There is no need of haste."

He looked a trifle put out, but soon overcame the emotion.

"I believe that it must be today," he said, with quiet insistence. "I am sorry, Georgie, but I really must look in on

Colonel Kellaway to see if there is anything he wishes me to be doing. I have had a long spell of leave, you know."

"Oh, you and your stupid playing at soldiers!" she said, with a petulant shrug. "As though they may not manage very well without you!"

This waspish speech caused Joanna to look at Masterman with a hint of sympathy.

"I am afraid I must insist," he said, in a different tone. "Perhaps you had best start your packing now, my dear sister."

Somewhat to the surprise of everyone present, Miss Masterman raised no further objection, and very soon left the room to do as her brother suggested. Guy Dorlais repeated his intention of going down to the quay. He did not request Kitty to accompany him, and she tried not to look as if she had expected such an invitation.

When Captain Masterman left the room in order to see about transport for himself and his sister, Guy accompanied him. After sitting still for a moment, moodily gazing into the fire, Kitty sprang suddenly to her feet.

"I am going to walk for a little in the shrubbery, Jo," she announced with a flurried air.

"Should you like me to come, too?" asked her friend, starting from her chair.

"No — no, thank you," said Kitty, hurriedly. "The fact is, Joanna, I wish to be alone for a space. I — I want to think."

Miss Feniton gave her a compassionate look. "I understand, my dear. But be sure and wrap up warmly, for the wind is very keen today, and we must not have you taking cold."

The tears came suddenly to Kitty's eyes.

"You — you are so good, Jo!" she stammered, incoherently, and made a dash from the room.

Joanna made as if to follow her, but subsided into her chair again. It was of no use for her to try and advise Kitty. Her friend must come to terms with herself. Besides, she had another idea in mind, though for a time she struggled to resist it. It offended all her notions of propriety, but she was almost certain that this was one time when what was proper must yield to what was necessary. She reflected that if the man Jackson had been available, she could have left such an unpleasant undertaking in his hands. There was no saying where he might be, and meanwhile she was the only person on the spot. She must act, little as she liked it.

She had been seriously disturbed by Lady Feniton's account of the mishap to one of Grandfather's books. Idle act of vandalism though it must seem to her grandparents, to her it wore a very different and more sinister appearance. She had not forgotten Captain Jackson's description of the orders left for him in the Cove by the enemy; judging by the evidence, it would appear that the man responsible for composing those orders must have been at some time under her very own roof.

She fancied, too, that she knew who he was. All her former suspicions of Guy Dorlais came rushing back in full force. She felt that she must make some push to confirm or deny them, and now was her opportunity to do this. With Guy Dorlais and Kitty out of the house, and Captain Masterman and his sister busily engaged in their own concerns, it should be possible for her to gain access unseen to Guy Dorlais's bedchamber. Sir George Lodge would no doubt be assisting her grandfather in the inquiry which was being conducted in the library, while Lady Lodge had not yet risen. As for her grandmother, at this hour of day she was usually closeted with the housekeeper.

The glimpse which she caught through the window of Kitty toiling along against the wind on the path which led through the shrubbery, hardened her resolve. For Kitty's sake, she must try to discover the truth.

She rose quickly from her chair and took her way upstairs, before she could change her mind. Even now, she was not fully convinced that she ought to pry. Had there been the least difficulty over gaining access to Guy's room, she might have faltered in her purpose; but when she reached his door, there was not a soul in sight in the passage.

She opened the door, heart beating fast, and slipped quickly into the room. Then she paused, heartily disliking her self-appointed task.

The room allotted to Guy Dorlais was large, and had evidently recently received the attentions of a housemaid. A bright red silk coverlet was disposed neatly over the bed, the fire had been tended, the hearth swept, and the contents of the room set in order. The flap of the dressing table was shut down, and nothing stood on its brightly polished surface.

It was to this article of furniture that Joanna went first, timorously lifting the hinged leaf which held the looking glass. She set it upright, revealing the space beneath. It contained the usual articles for a gentleman's toilet — razors, brushes, a comb, a bottle of Macassar oil and a pair of nail scissors. The only thing which Joanna had any difficulty in identifying was a small bottle of dark brown liquid with which she did not concern herself for more than a second, as it seemed little to the purpose of her quest. A few moment's search was sufficient to convince her that there was nothing more sinister here than she might find in her own grandfather's dressing table. She closed the leaf again, and opened the drawers of the table one by one.

Here again, she found nothing unexpected. Cravats, handkerchiefs, hose, all were lifted and carefully replaced without anything of the least interest being uncovered.

She was again assailed by a violent dislike of her task, and was half minded to give it up then and there. Supposing anyone should enter the room, and find her there? What possible excuse could she make? Supposing she had been mistaken about Mr. Dorlais, and he was in reality innocent of any traitorous activities?

She squared her shoulders, in that moment looking, had she but known it, very like her grandmother. She might as well finish what she had come to do. If Mr. Dorlais were innocent, then he had nothing to hide. If not, then it was plainly her duty to try and unmask him.

There was a closet set in one wall of the bedchamber. She walked towards it, and resolutely pulled open the door.

It was here that Mr. Dorlais kept his suits and outdoor garments. She passed them all in review, wondering where to start. It seemed improbable that she would have time to look through every pocket of all those coats, waistcoats and small clothes. Neither did the notion of tackling such a task appeal very greatly to her. There was something so particularly repulsive about searching in the pockets of a guest.

Perhaps that was why she picked up one of a pair of boots which was standing in a rack to one side of the closet. She could have had no notion of finding anything of interest in a boot. Yet that is what happened. She caught hold of the boot by its heel, and it swung in her hand. Amazed, she turned the boot upside down, and subjected the heel to a long scrutiny.

She made the unexpected discovery that it was screwed on to the boot. A second's thought, and she was unscrewing it feverishly. It came off in her hand, revealing a small opening underneath. She caught the glint of something metallic inside, and probed with an exploratory finger. She produced what she took to be a large coin.

She dropped the boot, and, stepping outside the closet, walked over to an adjacent window. Holding the object to the light, she studied it carefully.

Suddenly, all her senses became alert. She had heard the tiniest of sounds from the direction of the door to the room. She glanced across, and saw to her horror that the doorknob was slowly turning.

Quick as thought, she slipped behind the thick folds of the full length red damask curtains. Her heart was beating so loudly that she was certain it must be heard by whoever was now about to enter the room.

She did not dare to look, but she heard the soft closing of the door, and the quiet footfall of the newcomer on the thick pile of the carpet. She waited, hardly daring to breathe, hoping against hope that it was not Guy Dorlais returned. This seemed scarcely likely if he had carried out his original intention of going down to the quay. She could not imagine, though, who else it could be. The housemaids had evidently done their rounds, and it was unlikely that they would return again until the evening.

It seemed that she waited there for an eternity. She could hear the newcomer padding about the room, and finally stepping through the open door of the closet. A smothered exclamation reached her ears, then a quick footstep.

Before she could open her mouth to let out the startled ejaculation which rose to her lips, the curtain which concealed her had been dragged ruthlessly aside. She found herself looking into the surprised eyes of Captain Masterman.

There was a moment's silence. He was the first to break it.

"Miss Feniton! What are you doing here?"

She did not ask what business it was of his: instead, she echoed his question.

"I just dropped in for a moment, hoping to find Dorlais before he went off," was the unhesitating reply. "But why on earth —"

"If that is true, a single glance into the room must have told you that Mr. Dorlais was not here," she said, accusingly.

She had read somewhere that attack is the best method of defence. She meant to give him something to think about other than the matter of her presence in the room: after all, why had he been poking about in there for so long? Let him explain himself.

"It did," he acknowledged, readily. "But I took a second glance. That disclosed to me your slipper peeping from under the curtain. Evidently you hid there when you heard my approach. But why, Miss Feniton? What errand could you possibly have in here?"

She knew that she was caught; she could make no satisfactory answer to this. It was unthinkable that a virtuous young lady should under any circumstances enter a gentleman's bedchamber, even in his absence.

"One which I cannot explain to you," she said, with a touch of hauteur. "You must believe what you choose. Moreover, it appeared to me that you were taking a long time over your second glance, as you put it — neither did you immediately come over to the window!"

He studied her appraisingly for a moment in silence. Then he appeared to make up his mind.

"You are quite right, Miss Feniton," he said, quietly. "And I believe that you, too, entertain a suspicion that Guy Dorlais is not all he seems to be."

She started, staring at him in silence.

"I wonder, ma'am," he continued, "whether you and I might not contrive to trust each other?"

She found her voice at last. "What do you mean?"

"Simply this — I am nearly certain that you know of a man who calls himself — Captain Jackson."

He watched her face intently as he spoke the name. The colour ebbed from her cheek, and she raised her chin a trifle, as though in defiance.

"I do not see, sir, what concern it is of yours to interrogate me about my acquaintance," she replied, in her most distant manner.

He bowed. "I accept the reproof, ma'am. I merely thought it a pity that you and I should be at cross purposes, when we have the same interests at heart. I, too, am acquainted with Captain Jackson."

She gasped. "You are? Pray, sir, do you know where he can be found?"

He studied her once more, without making any immediate answer.

"I collect that you do not?" he asked, at last.

She shook her head.

"Yet I had the impression," he continued, still watching her closely, "that you entered this room because you believed that Mr. Dorlais and Captain Jackson were one and the same man."

Again she started.

"No!" she exclaimed, involuntarily. "Such a notion never entered my head! It was because I thought that Mr. Dorlais — " She stopped, realizing that she had said more than she intended.

"You do not know the true identity of the man Jackson, then?" he asked.

"No," she answered, uncertainly. "Why do you ask? Are you a friend of his? Do you know who he is?"

"Possibly," he said, smiling, "but his true identity must for the present remain a secret. Tell me, Miss Feniton — if you did not take Guy Dorlais for Jackson, what suspicion did you entertain of him?"

Her thoughts had been moving at lightning speed. It was evident that Captain Masterman knew a great deal about Captain Jackson. Was it possible that it had been he who had stolen from the house that night to meet Jackson in the temple? If so, then he must also know of the French agent whom Jackson was pursuing and he might possibly have entered this room for the very same purpose which had brought her here.

"Are you a helper of the Captain's?" she asked, bluntly.

He nodded briefly. "But this information is for your ear alone, Miss Feniton," he warned.

"Naturally," she answered, impatiently. "If that is so, however, then you must share my suspicions of Mr. Dorlais?"

"Tell me what you have noticed," he invited.

She frowned. "It is difficult to put a finger upon anything definite. First of all, of course, he seems an obvious suspect by reason of his birth."

"You mean because he is a Frenchman? Then what you suspect is that he is an agent for the French?"

"Do not you? The Captain has told me that he is on the lookout for a man who is the ringleader of a number of agents who are collected here in Devon. This man must have a sound knowledge of the French language, besides being intimately acquainted with the area. Only Guy Dorlais would fit — besides, there are one or two other little circumstances which lend colour to the notion. For instance, my friend, Miss Lodge —"

Haltingly at first, but with gathering fluency, she retailed the occurrences on which her suspicions of Dorlais had been founded. He heard her out in silence, frowning a little, and studying her face attentively as she spoke.

"Yes, well, as you've guessed," he said, when she had finished, "I've had the same notion myself. But I see that you have been conducting a search of this room — did you find anything, ma'am?"

She smoothed back a lock of thick, black hair which had fallen over her forehead.

"Yes — this," she said, holding out her hand, and disclosing the small object therein. "I have not had time to study it properly — your entrance interrupted me."

"May I?" he asked, taking it from her.

His eyes looked intimately into hers as their hands touched. She hastily fixed her glance upon the medallion which he held. For a while; they stood shoulder to shoulder, looking down at it.

"Do you know what this is?" he asked at last, raising his eyes from the medallion and looking into her face.

She met his gaze, a puzzled expression in her eyes. "It — it seems to be some sort of Victory medal," she said, doubtfully. "But surely —

"It was certainly intended originally for that purpose," he answered, gravely. "But it is now used as a token between Napoleon's agents."

"So that Mr. Dorlais —?"

They were so intent upon each other that they failed to notice the door of the room slowly opening.

Chapter XV: Miss Lodge is Adamant

"A vastly pretty picture!" approved a cool, mocking voice, and Algernon Cholcombe stepped lightly into the room, and softly closed the door behind him.

The couple started apart with guilty looks. Masterman's hand closed tightly over the medallion.

"You must not suppose — all is not as it may appear!" he began, jerkily, then finished, in a calmer tone: "If you have any question to ask me, I am sure you will excuse Miss Feniton. I believe you and I will do better alone."

"Questions, my dear fellow?" drawled Cholcombe. "The only question I was about to ask was as to the whereabouts of Dorlais. Knowing him for a bit of a sluggard in the mornings, I came to his room expecting to find him still here."

"He is out," replied Masterman, tersely, obviously still ill at ease.

"I had guessed as much," said Mr. Cholcombe, raising his brows ironically. "You could not say when he is likely to return? I fancy you might be possessed of such knowledge."

He was conversing as though he had found them in the most ordinary of circumstances. Joanna, whose cheeks were flushed scarlet, could not meet his gaze.

"He has but just gone down to the quay," replied Masterman. "There are some men-of-war at anchor in the Bay, and he was hoping for news of some old acquaintances, so I believe."

Cholcombe nodded easily. "Well, you see I am returned," he said, airily. "I suppose I had better go and present myself in form to my lady. Can you tell me where I can find her?

Possibly in my own bedchamber? Give you my word, I shall not be surprised at anything!"

Masterman took a step towards him. His handsome face was stern.

"Do you mean to insult Miss Feniton, Cholcombe?"

Mr. Cholcombe's eyebrows arched delicately in surprise.

"Certainly not, my dear fellow!" Then, with a change of expression — "Do you?"

For a moment, their eyes met in a challenging glance.

"This is absurd!" said Joanna, in her most matter-of-fact manner. "I don't propose to stay here any longer, listening to such nonsense!"

"You are quite right," approved Cholcombe, gently. "Allow me to open the door for you, madam."

He did so; she left the room with her head held high, but with cheeks that still burned.

"*Au revoir*, Masterman," murmured Mr. Cholcombe, lightly, as he prepared to follow.

"No, wait!"

Masterman signalled with one hand. Mr. Cholcombe halted on the threshold. After a brief glance around the passage, he again entered the room, closing the door.

"I don't know what you may be thinking —" began Masterman.

"That is one of life's fascinations," agreed Cholcombe solemnly.

"Don't jest, man! I trust you don't seriously suppose that Miss Feniton and I — that is to say —"

"I am never serious if I can possibly avoid it," suggested Cholcombe, helpfully.

"I wish you will not avoid it now!" was the tart retort. "Miss Feniton's honour is at stake. I desire you to believe me when I say that our meeting here was the purest accident; and I would like your word that you will not blab it about to the other members of the party — or, indeed, to anyone."

"Dear me!" interrupted Cholcombe, blandly. "Do you really suppose that I would blab, as you so forcefully express it? You must hold a regrettably low opinion of me, my dear chap!"

Masterman made a gesture of impatience.

"I am insufficiently acquainted with you, sir, to hold any reasoned opinion. I make my appeal in the full expectation that you will respond favourably to it. I am obliged to go away from here this very day — my sister is promised to some friends in another part of the county, and I must escort her. It may not be in my power to return for some days — if at all. That I cannot say at present. The thing is, I do not wish to have any unpleasantness for Miss Feniton in my absence."

"Very creditable, Masterman, I'm sure," drawled Mr. Cholcombe. "Might it not perhaps have been better to have thought of that first?"

"I tell you, it was an accident that brought us here together! I had slipped into the room as you did, thinking to find Dorlais still here —"

"And you found Miss Feniton instead?"

Masterman nodded, and cleared his throat. "I imagine she had come here on some errand from Miss Lodge," he said, huskily, "or perhaps from her grandmother. I did not have time to inquire — it was only a few minutes before you arrived —"

Mr. Cholcombe had been looking over towards the open door of the closet. His lazy glance rested upon a boot flung carelessly down upon the floor.

"Quite," he said, in a bored tone. "No doubt the housemaids were too busy at that moment to run errands. Well, my dear chap, I really must tear myself away from this — er — popular spot, and go in search of my hostess. I wish you and Miss Masterman a pleasant journey."

He opened the door, and stepped out into the passage.

"But I can rely upon you?" asked the Captain anxiously.

Cholcombe nodded gently. "Oh, yes," he said, with a faint smile, "you may rely upon me completely."

He closed the door, Captain Masterman stood looking at it, frowning deeply. Then he turned, and hastily crossed to the closet. He picked up the boot, replaced the medallion, and screwed on the heel. This done, he laid the boot tidily alongside its fellow and closed the door.

One swift glance around the room assured him that none of its other contents had been disturbed. With a feeling of strong relief, he left the apartment.

When Joanna had gone out of the room, she had proceeded at once to her own bedchamber. Her feelings were in such confusion that for the moment she could not think coherently on any subject at all. She poured some cool water into a basin, and bathed her hot cheeks. Then she tidied her hair, pausing to study herself objectively in the glass.

She was not truly pretty, she decided: her mouth was too wide, her nose too long, and her hair not really black. Her teeth — well, she admitted reluctantly, perhaps her teeth were not so much to be deplored as the rest of her face.

At this point in her reflections, she dropped the comb she was holding poised uselessly in mid-air. She was only concentrating on her appearance to hold back other, more important, considerations, she told herself sternly.

It would not do: she must face the facts.

The most outstanding fact which required facing was that her worst suspicions were now confirmed. There could be no doubt that Dorlais was the French agent for whom Captain Jackson was seeking. If she had only known earlier that Masterman was working with Jackson, she might have spared herself all the trouble she had taken to find out this. But Masterman had been so very circumspect: he had not betrayed himself in any way. Thinking back over the past events, she realized all at once that when he had seen the open window and the bloodstains on the carpet on that occasion in Teignton Manor, he must have had a very good notion who it was who had been there. Had he guessed at once, when the Colonel and he had met the drunken Militia man on their way to the Manor that night, and heard his incoherent story? It was very likely, but if so, he had given no sign of it at any time. And was it possible that Jackson had been lurking in the grounds of the Manor on that occasion in the hope of seeing Masterman, knowing in some way that he and Colonel Kellaway were to spend the night there? Jackson had told her at that time that he had entered the grounds to escape from someone; that could have been only part of the truth.

Perhaps it was as well, after all, that she had been ignorant of Masterman's complicity. Captain Jackson had been quite in the right when he had refused to divulge the secret of the identity of his helper in Shalbeare House. It was suddenly borne in upon her that, if she had been in the secret, she would almost certainly have betrayed it to the experienced eye of such a man as Guy Dorlais must be.

Her heart contracted as she thought of Kitty. Dear, pretty little elfin Kit, how would she bear it? But at least the breach had already begun; even now, Kitty was beset by doubts. Joanna knew that she must go to her friend and tell her the truth. It was an unpleasant task, but it must be faced. A long friendship brought responsibilities as well as pleasure.

A definite purpose helped to clear her mind of its confusion. She rose purposefully, donned a dark red pelisse trimmed with ermine, tied a bonnet of the same shade under her chin, and, snatching up a muff from her wardrobe, ran from the room.

On her way downstairs, she encountered her grandmother.

"Are you going out, Joanna? Then you surely cannot know that Algernon is here again. I have already spoken with him, and he is at present in the library with your grandfather, hearing all about that stupid affair; I expect he will be asking after you in a few minutes."

Joanna did not expect any such thing, but she contented herself with saying that she had caught just a glimpse of Mr. Cholcombe on his way to see Lady Feniton.

"If anyone should want me, I shall be walking in the shrubbery with Kitty," she concluded.

"Oh, very well! I suppose you are right in taking exercise, though the air is very bleak this morning. However, I observe that you are warmly clad. Do not stay out too long, child."

Joanna promised, impatient to be gone. It was not long before she came across Kitty wandering aimlessly through the shrubbery. There were tears in her eyes, Joanna noticed at once. She took her friend's arm.

"I judged you had been long enough alone, Kit. Besides, I wish to talk to you."

"And I to you," replied Kitty, despondently. "Oh, Jo, I have thought and thought until my head goes round like a whirlpool! I do not know what is to be done!"

"You will know, dearest, when I have told you what must be told," said Joanna. Her voice was gentle, but firm, and she pressed the arm which rested on her own. "I mislike what I have to do, Kitty, but I have decided that it is only fair to acquaint you with something that at present is known only to myself — and one other, whom I shall come to presently," she added, remembering Captain Masterman.

This hint of mystery momentarily diverted Kitty's thoughts.

"What can you be talking of?" she wondered.

Quietly, Joanna told her story. She started with her first meeting with Captain Jackson, and worked down to their last encounter in the grounds of Shalbeare House. So far, she had been heard in a stunned silence; but when she spoke of Captain Jackson's declaration of love, Kitty could contain herself no longer.

"Joanna! This is not at all like you! It is all so — so romantic!"

"I am not telling you this, Kitty, to stir your feelings for romance, but for quite another reason. The man Jackson can be nothing to me, as you will speedily realize: his declaration was the wildest piece of folly! But did you mark what he told me of this French agent who controls the activities of the others of his kind — and did you notice what I said concerning the way in which this man delivers his orders to Jackson?"

"Yes, to be sure," said Kitty, with a shiver. "It sounds vastly unpleasant! This Captain Jackson must be a very brave man, Jo!"

"He is indeed," replied Joanna, with a reminiscent smile. "But pray do pay particular attention now, Kitty. As I mentioned before, these orders were made up of words cut from a printed page, and stuck on to a sheet of letter paper."

Kitty frowned. "It must be a tedious task —" She broke off, staring at Joanna as a sudden thought struck her. "Good Heavens, Jo! Your grandfather's book!"

"Exactly," said Miss Feniton, quietly. "That was how I came to realize that this French agent must be staying in my home as a guest."

An odd expression came over Kitty's face.

"Do you see what I am trying to tell you?" asked Joanna. "Piece together the evidence, Kitty, and you will be bound to come to the same conclusion as I have reached. And as if that were not enough, there is one final circumstance —"

She retailed the incident which had just taken place in Guy's room. Kitty listened in complete silence, watching her friend's face with considering eyes.

"So you see," concluded Joanna, in a gentle tone, "there can be no mistake. Mr. Dorlais is undoubtedly the man, and it is perhaps for the best —"

"No!"

Joanna drew back a little, startled by the other's unexpected vehemence.

"You are wrong, Joanna, wrong, wrong, wrong!" reiterated Kitty, passionately. "Don't ask me for reasons, for I have none — and anyway, they are the stupidest things, and can prove nothing! I only know that Guy is good and honourable, and not a traitor! I know it with that special part of me that tells me when such a one is to be trusted, while another is not! I do not deny that he has acted strangely, for you are well aware that his behaviour has almost persuaded me that he no longer cares for me: but whatever the motive for his actions, I dare swear that it's not the one you impute to him! No, there is something else which holds him back from me — I don't know yet what it is, but I am confident that I shall do so in time. Meanwhile, I must simply trust in him!"

"Trust!" echoed Miss Feniton, dismayed. "You poor child, what is the use of hoodwinking yourself? You cannot continue to believe in him in face of all the evidence!"

"But that's just what I can do, Jo, for that is what love means," replied Kitty. She was quiet and confident now. "I should thank you, my dear, for you have at last made me realize that I love Guy in spite of anything he may do! I have had my doubts, but they are over, thank God. I have only to wait patiently, and I know that he will make it all clear to me in time."

It was in vain that Joanna tried to reason her friend out of this dangerous attitude of mind: Kitty was firm. Where before she had doubted, she now trusted implicitly. Joanna's story had produced quite the opposite effect from what she had intended.

"You may as well give up, Jo, for you won't change me," Kitty advised her. "I know my own mind, now — but are you certain that you do?"

"In what way? If you are speaking of Mr. Dor—"

"I am not; I am speaking of Captain Jackson."

"Oh," replied Joanna, and was silent.

"Are you quite sure, my dear, that you do not return his regard — just a little?"

"How could I do so?" asked Joanna, in surprise. "He is not of my world; he — he is not, as far as I am aware, a — a gentleman."

"I understood you to say that you did not know his real identity?"

"No more do I. But it is obvious, from all manner of little things —"

"Does it really matter?"

"Matter? My dear Kitty, whatever can you mean?"

"Only that you must take love where you find it. That may not always be where you expect — or wish — to find it."

"Oh, if you are to speak in riddles, I have done!" exclaimed Joanna, with a touch of anger. "As you are so ready to persist in nourishing an affection for a traitor, I suppose you think it nothing that I should entertain one for a nameless smuggler!"

"No more do I," said Kitty, sticking out her chin. "And if we are to remain friends, Miss Feniton, you will say no more of traitors, if you please!"

"Oh, Kit!" exclaimed Joanna, contritely. "We must not quarrel — we are each other's only confidante. And besides, we are the proper complement each of the other. I need your romanticism — and you, my dear, need my common sense!"

They looked into each other's faces, and laughed.

"Well, that's very true," said Kitty, taking her friend's arm once more. "But do you know, Jo, I think we each possess more of the other's chief characteristic than we have ever realized until now!"

They walked in silence for a little while.

"Can I say nothing to make you change your mind?" asked Joanna, timidly.

"Nothing," was the firm reply. "But we are not to quarrel on that account. Let's decide never to mention this subject again."

"Very well," replied Joanna, with a sigh. "It must be as you wish."

"Good! Then let us return to the house. I had not thought of it before, but I am pretty near frozen to death! There should be a good fire in the morning room, too, by now."

They turned towards the house, arms closely linked together.

Chapter XVI: Mr. Cholcombe Makes a Declaration

Guy Dorlais did not return for luncheon, but his absence was felt by no one except Kitty. Joanna was thankful for the opportunity of postponing a meeting with the man whom she now knew to be a traitor: as for the rest of the party, they were too much occupied in discussing the subject which claimed so much of Sir Walter's thoughts.

"Well, there you are!" pronounced Sir George Lodge. "I'm tolerably certain that the servants know nothing of the matter, Walter. One cannot escape the conviction that the offence must have been committed some time since — perhaps years ago."

"Certainly it is some years since last I opened that book —"

"I should think it is!" interrupted his wife. "I'm sure it would not signify if no one ever opened it! Such a to-do about a book which could not have cost more than a few shillings at most! Your guests must find it more than a little tedious, Feniton!"

"Not at all," said Mr. Cholcombe, in his pleasant drawl. "Mysteries are always entertaining, do you not agree, Masterman?"

Captain Masterman nodded briefly, but did not speak. Miss Masterman was more voluble, saying that for her part she dearly loved a mystery.

"So you see, ma'am," remarked Cholcombe to his hostess, with a smile, "you need have no fears on that score." He turned to Sir Walter. "I myself have not seen the book, sir. Tell me, are you sufficiently acquainted with the text to know what the missing word would be? Was it perhaps — could it be —"

he smiled deprecatingly — "something which was removed so that it could not offend the eyes of, let us say, a female reader?"

Sir Walter looked a trifle impatiently at the speaker.

"My dear young man, *I* imagine there is nothing particularly offensive about the name of a village."

"So that is what it was!" exclaimed Georgina Masterman. "How very odd, to be sure!"

"I believe I told you that the book was a traveller's account of various districts of England and Wales," explained Sir Walter. "The particular page which was damaged —" his voice shook a little with anger — "dealt with our own county of Devon. The missing word was 'Babbacombe'."

There was a lengthy silence. Lady Feniton was the first to break it, determined to change the subject. She turned to Mr. Cholcombe.

"I collect that you, also, have the intention of renewing acquaintance with some of the officers whose ships are just arrived in the Bay?" she asked him.

He bowed. "I thought of walking down there this afternoon, and seeing if I could run across anyone I know."

"Then perhaps you will like to bring some of them back with you to dinner? Sir Walter and I generally offer hospitality to any officers who may put in here; we are always glad to see company at Shalbeare House. With Captain and Miss Masterman leaving us, we shall be but a small party; and I have a strong conviction that we would all benefit from a change of conversation."

He bowed again, and undertook to carry her invitation to his friends.

At the conclusion of the meal, Captain Masterman and his sister rose to take their leave.

"Do you expect to be able to return to us later on?" Lady Feniton asked the Captain. "It will be dull for you at home without your sister, you know, and you are very welcome here."

He thanked her politely, and said that it must all depend upon Colonel Kellaway. If he should find himself free nothing would make him happier than to return to Shalbeare House.

"Of course, we realize that you have important work to do," replied Lady Feniton. "But do not stand upon ceremony with us. If you should be at liberty for as little as one day — either you or the Colonel, or both — do pay us a call. I shall keep your room ready, in the hope of seeing you back with us before long."

He thanked her again, the final farewells were said, and the Mastermans departed.

Miss Feniton had been unable to take any particular leave of the Captain, though there was much she would have liked to say to him privately, many questions she could have asked. She consoled herself with the thought that he would know just what to do concerning Dorlais, however: there was no longer any need for her to take action in that matter. She felt it highly probable that he would return to them in a few days; his eyes had seemed to promise this when he was taking leave of her. It did not escape her notice that Mr. Cholcombe had appeared to be observing them both very narrowly at that particular moment: she wondered if he was thinking of the encounter in Guy Dorlais's room. Did he mean to make any reference to that, she asked herself? So far, he had been given no opportunity of private speech with her since that occasion. They had been always in company with the rest.

She and Kitty passed a quiet afternoon with the two dowagers. By common consent, nothing more was said between the friends on the subject of Guy Dorlais. Some copies of *La Belle Assemblée* were scanned, and the latest fashions debated. Lady Feniton waxed indignant over the wearing of pink silk stockings, which she categorically declared to be scandalous.

"It is all of a piece," she proclaimed, "with these disgracefully filmy gowns which are all the go at present! Why, when I was at an Assembly in Exeter last year, there was an abandoned female there who could not have been wearing a stitch under her gown, so close did it cling to her form! You must remember, Joanna, for I pointed her out to you at the time," she added, turning to Miss Feniton.

Joanna nodded. "Yes, I do recollect it; I believe she had most likely damped the gown slightly, grandmama, to make it cling like that."

"*Damped?*" asked Lady Lodge, in horror, "My dear child, you surely cannot mean that young women do such foolish things? I can't imagine what the young are coming to — only think of the risk of taking a chill!"

Both young ladies permitted themselves a laugh. "That is a small price to pay for being in the first stare of fashion!" said Kitty. "All the same, I do not quite like to follow so extreme a vogue."

"I should think not, indeed," declared Lady Feniton. "As for pink silk stockings, I hope I shall never see either of you wearing them!"

Joanna and Kitty exchanged guilty glances. Then Miss Feniton, bolder than her friend, lifted the hem of her dress just enough to allow her grandmother's eye to rest upon her ankles.

"Well, of all things!" exclaimed the outraged dowager. "You must go at once, and put on something more modest, Miss!"

"Oh, please, ma'am!" Kitty produced her most charming smile, and at the same time unveiled her own pink ankles. "Dear Lady Feniton, it's all the go, and one simply must be in the fashion, you know! Mama actually sent all the way to London for these, and I gave Joanna those she is wearing."

Lady Feniton eyed her friend severely. "I should not have thought it of you, Letitia —" she began, in a moralizing tone.

"Oh, well, girls will be girls!" replied Lady Lodge, hurriedly, avoiding her friend's eye. "And I must say that when we were young, we did not like to be dowdy, now did we, Augusta?"

This brave speech produced the desired effect. Lady Feniton, after an expressive snort, said no more about Joanna's going to change the offending articles of clothing, and instead launched herself into a bitter attack on the latest novel which had been conveyed to them from the Circulating Library in Exeter.

It was late in the afternoon when Mr. Cholcombe returned to the house in company with Mr. Dorlais. They promised company for dinner. Between them, they could muster several acquaintances among the ships' officers, and of these, no less than four were at liberty to take advantage of Lady Feniton's invitation on that very evening. This was good news to Lady Feniton; she liked nothing better than to fill her house with visitors.

Miss Catherine Lodge was not so well pleased. She was anxious for a quiet talk with her betrothed. She had no intention of breaking her word to Joanna, and making any mention of the extraordinary revelation which had been unfolded to her that afternoon; but her heart swelled with affection and loyalty towards Guy which must be expressed in some way. Her manner towards him was, therefore, very different from what it had been of late. Although they had few occasions of conversing in private, he could not help noticing the change. He, too, wished the party could have been smaller.

"Do you still keep your old interest in theatricals, Cholcombe?" one of the officers asked him at dinner. "We had famous fun at Pompey with 'The Triumph of Friendship', if you recollect!"

"Yes," said another. "And what was the name of that other piece — the one where you came on dressed as an old washerwoman? 'Pon oath, you brought the house down on that occasion!"

"I had no idea, Algernon," said Lady Feniton, in a disapproving tone, "that you indulged in theatricals!"

"But yes, ma'am, you must have done!" said Kitty. "Do you not recall that Guy — Mr. Dorlais — mentioned the fact, when we were questioning him about his acquaintance with Mr. Cholcombe — I mean, of course, before Mr. Cholcombe arrived," she added, feeling that perhaps she had not made herself very clear.

"We played together in 'The School for Scandal' at Trelawney's house," volunteered Dorlais. "He was the leading man on that occasion: I tell you, he's a deuced versatile chap, this Cholcombe!"

"I never before suspected you of toad-eating, Dorlais," replied Cholcombe, with a drawl.

"Only fancy! But I suppose it is scarcely surprising," said Lady Lodge, thoughtlessly, "that you should be an accomplished actor, Mr. Cholcombe. After all, it's in the family — I mean your Mama, you know!"

Lady Feniton coughed loudly, and glared at her friend. Lady Lodge caught the look, choked a little over her fish, and subsided. Augusta was foolish, she thought resentfully: after all, it was a very old scandal, and my Lady Cholcombe was now an acknowledged leader of fashion in London, and everywhere received.

"I see that the Pope has at last crowned Napoleon as Emperor of France," remarked Sir George, thinking to create a diversion. "According to report, it was a most magnificent ceremony."

"The newspapers seem to have more to say on the subject of Master Betty's prodigious success at Covent Garden," remarked Cholcombe, nobly seconding Sir George in his attempt.

"Master Betty?" asked Joanna, who was seated beside him.

He looked down at her gravely for a moment.

"He is a boy actor who's created quite a furore in Town," he said. "He appeared a few days since in a tragedy of Dr. Brown's entitled Barbarossa. I'm told that there was a regular stampede to get into the theatre. Apparently His Royal Highness was there, and showed his approval by applauding frequently — and loudly."

She smiled. "I can well imagine that he might."

"Prinney has few inhibitions," he agreed. "But it really does seem that, this youth is something out of the common way. I must see him for myself."

"You like the theatre?"

"So much," he answered, "that I could almost have chosen to enter the profession."

"But that, of course," she said, questioningly, "was not to be thought of?"

"No," he replied; abruptly, and fell into a reverie which was presently broken by Lady Feniton signifying that it was time for the ladies to rise from the table.

When the gentlemen rejoined them later in the drawing room, Guy Dorlais went immediately to Kitty's side. She looked up at him, her brown eyes warm with affection. He managed to catch her hand and give it a quick squeeze before anyone could notice.

"Am I forgiven, Kit?" he asked in a low voice.

"Stupid," she whispered back. "There is nothing to forgive!"

"You're not going to pretend that you have not been vexed with me this long while?" he asked incredulously.

"Oh, Guy, if I was, indeed I am sorry!" she answered, contritely.

"My love! There are many things in my conduct which must puzzle you sorely — but I hope the time is not far distant when I can explain them all satisfactorily to you."

"I —" she began, then broke off, as she noticed Lady Feniton's eye upon them.

She fancied that she heard Guy let drop a mild oath as he moved away from her side, but she was well content.

It was not until after their guests had departed that Mr. Cholcombe found a much sought for opportunity of being private with Miss Feniton. She had gone upstairs to fetch a shawl for her grandmother's shoulders; on her way down again, she encountered him loitering in the passage outside the drawing room.

"I have been desiring a word alone with you all evening," he said, his expression more serious than was usual. "If you can spare me a moment, we might perhaps go in here." He indicated the door of a small anteroom nearby. She hesitated a second. No doubt he wished to speak to her of this morning's incident. She did not see what business it was of his, but she might as well hear what he had to say, and have done with it.

"Certainly," she answered, coldly, and passed before him into the room.

There was, a small fire burning in the grate; he indicated a sofa which was set before it.

"Shall we sit down?"

She obeyed, holding her grandmother's shawl in her lap, and waiting for him to speak. He seated himself beside her, but gazed into the fire in silence for so long, that at last she turned her eyes upon him in surprise.

"I have something to say to you, Miss Feniton," he began, presently, with rather less than his customary assurance. "Though how to begin, puzzles me somewhat, I must confess!"

Her heart missed a beat. Perhaps, after all, he was not about to speak of their encounter in Dorlais's room that morning. This sounded to her ominously like the beginning of a declaration.

"This man Masterman," he went on, abruptly. "What is he to you?"

She was considerably startled. "You have no right to ask such a question," she pointed out, after a pause.

"But I wish to have the right!" he said, emphatically. "Miss Feniton — Joanna —" Her eyes widened a little, but she gave him no help. "You must allow me to tell you," he said, more quietly, "how very much I admire and respect you. Will you do me the honour to become my wife?"

She looked full into his face. There was no trace now of the laughing gallant who had continually jested with her during his stay at Shalbeare House. His grey eyes were deep and serious. She took a quick breath.

"I — I scarce know what to say —"

"At least you cannot say that it is so sudden," he remarked with a trace of his former manner. "You must be aware that I came to Shalbeare House with the intention of making you an offer."

"I will not pretend to you," she said, slowly. "I did know, of course."

"We have no disapproval to contend with," he remarked, a certain irony in his tone. "Both my parents and your grandparents desire the match. Everything is as it should be in that respect."

"Ye-es," she answered, hesitantly.

"So you see," he said, watching her closely, "you owe it to me to say if Captain Masterman means anything to you."

"You are thinking of what happened this morning," she said, quickly, not sorry to change the subject. "I know that you found me — us — in a situation of — of — seeming intimacy — but, believe me, things were not what they may have appeared."

"Might I venture to ask for an explanation? You are not obliged to give one, of course, if you do not wish."

She hesitated for a few moments, thinking what answer to make.

"I — it is difficult to explain. He and I went quite separately to Mr. Dorlais's room, for a purpose that — for something which —" She stopped, completely at a loss. He continued to watch her face and its changing expressions, but made no remark.

"It is a secret," she said, at last, desperately. "I cannot tell you more. But this much you may know — there was no connivance in our meeting there, neither is there any attachment between Captain Masterman and myself. I think I owe it to you to inform you of that much, at least."

He nodded. "I wondered, seeing you so close together," he said, apologetically. "Watching your parting earlier today, too, the same doubts assailed me. Whatever may be your feeling towards the gentleman, I think that he is certainly in love with you."

"Perhaps," replied Joanna, uncomfortably. "It cannot signify — he means nothing to me. Are you satisfied now, sir? For Grandmama will be wanting her shawl."

"Not quite," he said, smiling a little. "You have not yet given me your answer."

"Oh!" Dismay spread over Joanna's countenance. She was silent for a while. "Must I answer you now, sir?" she asked, in a timid tone.

He looked a trifle chagrined.

"Not if you do not wish to do so. Perhaps I have been too hasty in speaking — but I could not wait —" He broke off, and appeared to be labouring under some emotion.

"I cannot quite understand you!" said Joanna, impulsively. "So far, you have never given the smallest sign of being — of being —"

"Attached to you, you would say? No, perhaps not. I suppose I care as little as any man for making a parade of my emotions, and we have been seldom left alone together of late. You cannot bring yourself to believe, then, that I care for you? Is it such a new idea to you?"

"I have no wish to give you pain, Mr. Cholcombe, but I must insist that it is. We have had a vast deal of amusement together, and have been from the first on the easiest of terms: but as to anything of a deeper nature; I can only say that I have seen no sign of it."

"No," he said, rising abruptly and pacing uneasily about the room. "No, of course not: I forget —" He broke off, and swung towards her. "Do I understand that you do not positively wish to reject me, Miss Feniton?"

The tone was controlled and formal. She shook her head.

"No; I — in a way, I was prepared for this, and perhaps not sufficiently ready to hear your proposals. I need a little time, sir —"

"You shall have it." He spoke shortly. "I will say nothing for the moment to your grandparents. When can I come for my answer, Miss Feniton?"

"You mean to go away again?" she asked, alarmed. Her grandmother would not like this, she knew.

He nodded brusquely. "You must see that I could not remain, under the circumstances. I shall leave tomorrow. Will a se'ennight suffice, do you think, to show you your mind? It shall be longer, if you wish."

She gave him one of her compassionate looks. The soft hazel eyes twisted his heart.

"I will tell you by then," she promised, softly.

He bowed low, and opened the door for her to walk out.

Chapter XVII: The Enemy Revealed

A thin mist lay over the Bay, obscuring the lights on shore. The ship rocked gently at anchor, her timbers creaking slightly. Down in the cabin, two men faced each other across the table. One was wearing the uniform of His Majesty's Navy: it bore an imposing amount of gold braid. The other was a fisherman. He was bareheaded, his black hair curling crisply back from a face that looked curiously pale in the light of the lantern which hung from the rafters.

"You really mean it?" asked the officer, incredulously. "I can believe this fantastic story?"

"No doubt about it at all, sir," replied the younger man, standing stiffly at attention.

"Well, I'm damned!"

The officer fingered his chin thoughtfully.

"And when can we expect this visitation?" he asked, at last. "Any notion of that, eh?"

"Not as yet, sir. We're working on it."

"Humph! There isn't all the time in the world! Mind, I realize it's difficult —"

"The difficult we do at once, sir: the impossible may take a little longer."

The mahogany-coloured face before him relaxed into a smile.

"Yes, well — that's the spirit! Of course, we shan't be here for long, I trust. They may not arrive in time to catch us. Still, best to be prepared. We'll plan a reception committee."

"May I ask what your scheme is, sir?"

"Eh?" The older man had relapsed into thought, and now came to with a jerk. "Oh, yes — certainly. Nets, I think, don't you? Go fishin' for 'em, y'know! Have to do the thing with caution, or we may frighten 'em off. I'll consult the others, of course, but I'll lay any odds that's the best way — nets. Tell you what, Jackson — or whatever that dam' silly pseudonym of yours is — I fancy they'll get hoist with their own petard this time, eh? What d'ye say?"

Jackson replied that he thought it inevitable. He refrained from remarking that the idea of nets as a protection against the submarine had also occurred to him. He mentioned that he must be on his way before long.

"Got to go, then, have you?" asked the officer. "Get on with the impossible, I suppose?" He laughed briefly. "Not bad, that," he conceded. "But is there anything we can do to help, my boy? There are enough of us, and my fellows are pretty sick of inaction, give you my word! If only these Frogs would come out and fight!"

Captain Jackson commiserated with him. "There is one thing sir," he said. "There's a man called Kellaway — a Colonel in the Volunteers —"

The Naval man snorted. "Toy soldier, eh?"

"No sir, this is a Regular Army man, retired. Good sort of fellow. I need his help, but he does not know me — at any rate, not in this capacity. A word from you, however —"

"You shall have it. Give me his direction. What exactly is it you require?"

Jackson briefly explained his needs. The officer nodded, and made a quick note.

"When?" he asked, shortly.

"There is some urgency," replied Jackson. "I propose to step into a hornet's nest before nightfall tomorrow. By that time, I must know if the Colonel will be ready and waiting. My plans depend upon it."

"He will," promised the other, "even if we have to keelhaul him. I'll send at first light, then, Captain, and let you know the outcome. Where can I reach you?"

Jackson gave directions for reaching the nearby cove where his friends were encamped.

"But you will most likely see me back here again, sir, before dawn — with your visitor."

"Visitor?" The bushy eyebrows shot up. "Ah, yes, the fellow you want me to clap in irons. Got any useful information out of him?"

"He confirms all that we have guessed, but has little to add. He denies all knowledge of the identity of their leader — and in this I believe him to be telling the truth. One thing he has revealed, and that is that this leader himself will be in the submarine when the attack is made."

"By God, we have him, then!" exclaimed the officer. "We shall net a fine catch there, Captain!"

"To be sure, sir. That is why we have allowed matters to proceed so far. To let their plan come to fruition seemed to us the only way to smoke out this man, and destroy once for all time this nest of spies in the West of England."

The other man nodded. "Damned if you don't have the best of it, Jackson," he said, enviously. "If only we could see some action at sea!"

"Your time will come, sir, never fear! Sooner or later, they must come out and make a stand. When that day comes, I trust I'll be with you."

"There is no man I'd sooner have in my command," was the reply. "Well, bring up your spy, and we'll see him safely stowed away."

"It is all quite settled, then?" asked Number Six. "You are to go alone, Jackson?"

"Ask yourself, my dear chap! There is no cover in a place like the village of Babbacombe. Besides, there can be no danger; we are aware of their plan."

"But suppose they change their minds?" asked Number Six, dubiously. "It may somehow leak out that we are holding one of their men, and they may change over to another scheme."

Jackson shook his head. "I should suppose it to be too late for that. It is some days since I first picked up the orders, do not forget, and their arrangements must have been already made then. Our captive told us that it is no part of the plan to shoot me out of hand. Their way is a deal more clever than that; it is all perfectly legal, on the face of it."

"But they must hold you there until their chief comes," protested Number Six. "Lord knows I've no wish to cast you into the doldrums, Captain, but there's no saying what state you may be in by then."

"Wonder how it is that they're now so certain you're no longer on their side of the fence?" asked another man, slowly. "By all the evidence, they were uncertain in the matter until very recently. What's happened to confirm their suspicions?"

"I fancy I can tell you that," said Jackson. "I can hazard a guess, too, as to who this chief of theirs will turn out to be."

They gathered round him eagerly at this.

"Some of you may chance to know the name," he said, and told it.

"Good God, impossible!" exclaimed one of them.

"Yes, I am a little acquainted with him, and — but are you sure?"

Jackson shook his head. "I cannot say that. But I have the strongest grounds for my suspicion."

The other man whistled. "But why in the world should a man like that take such a course?"

"I can only conjecture. But now we must get some sleep. The night is already far advanced, and there's brisk work ahead of us tomorrow."

They did not sleep, though, but played cards until the first streaks of dawn appeared low over the grey, turbulent sea. Only then did they lie down, fully clothed, for a few hours, leaving one man to keep watch.

They were awakened by him just short of nine o'clock.

"There's someone approaching from the cliff," he said, quickly.

"It may only be the messenger I'm expecting," said Jackson, leaping to his feet. "Give me the perspective glasses, someone."

They were quickly put into his hand. He stood at the door of the hut, carefully scanning the track which led from the cliff.

"Would a man reach Totnes and back so soon?" asked one man, doubtfully, coming to his side.

"Four hours?" asked Jackson, his eyes still upon the advancing figure. "Egad, man, we're speaking of the Navy!"

The other grunted: he was an Army man, himself.

"I can't be sure," went on Jackson, frowning. "He's not in uniform, of course —" He drew the other man back within the shelter of the door, and closed it. "Let him knock," he said, "He's outnumbered, be he friend or foe."

The minutes passed, tension mounting. Number Six produced a pistol, and trained it on the door. Jackson nodded, his hand poised on the latch.

Footsteps sounded clearly on the stony track outside. They halted, and there followed a quiet tapping on the door. Three knocks, then silence; this was followed by a single, sustained knock.

Jackson suddenly flung back the door. Number Six stepped forward smartly, covering the newcomer with his pistol.

"The password," said a voice familiar to all, "is Horatio!"

Number Six lowered the pistol, and laughed. The rest, after one startled glance at the newcomer, followed suit.

"My dear chap," protested Jackson, clapping the visitor on the shoulder, "not that fungus again!"

"I know what it is with you," retorted the newcomer. "You're envious — you couldn't wear a beard, not with those features. Come to that, I can't think how you contrive to go on with them at all — but, there, everyone has his trials."

"Come to the point, Number One. I must say, I never looked to see you as our messenger! Is everything arranged?"

"As right as a trivet. Mark you, Kellaway almost went off into an apoplexy — was for making an arrest there and then, once we'd managed to convince him of the truth."

"I should imagine he's a difficult man to restrain. How did you manage it?"

"Acquit me. The Admiral made no trouble of it at all. Kellaway is now standing by, ready for marching orders."

"Then there is nothing else to hinder me," remarked Jackson, with a sigh of relief. "Except a little matter of breakfast."

This remark found general approval, and the matter was attended to with dispatch. While they were busy eating, Jackson gave a few last minute orders.

"Let me come with you," said Number One. "Something may go awry, and at least there'll be two of us to meet it."

232

Captain Jackson shook his head. "If anything's to go wrong, then it had better be for one alone," he said, firmly. "More cannot be spared."

After the rough meal was over, Jackson made his simple preparations for departure. They were soon concluded: then he drew Number One aside.

"There's just a remote possibility," he said, in a low tone, "that this affair may finish otherwise than we have planned. If that should be so, and you should know for certain that I am not to return, will you deliver this for me?"

He pressed into the other's hand a letter. Glancing down at it, Number One saw that it was directed to Miss Feniton.

"I will," he said abruptly, frowning. "Good fortune go with you — Peter."

He lowered his head, and they clasped hands for a moment in silence.

Then Jackson broke away, bidding an easy farewell to the others. That done, he left the hut, and turned his steps inland.

It was not quite an hour later that he came to the village of Babbacombe. He glanced sharply about him as he made for the smithy, but the sleepy little hamlet seemed deserted.

The door of the forge stood open, so that he could see the glow of the fire, and hear the blows of the smith's hammer on the anvil. He hesitated for a second on the threshold, then, squaring his shoulders, walked inside.

The smith at once left his work, and came forward, a hammer in his hand. Jackson eyed this warily, keeping his own hand on the knife in his belt. The smith was a burly man, after the way of his kind, but it seemed that his immediate intentions were not aggressive. He threw down the hammer, and looked inquiringly at his visitor.

"I came to show you this," said Jackson, and produced the French victory medallion.

The man inspected it carefully, then motioned with his hand to a door leading through to the back of the house. He handed back the token, picked up his hammer, and went on with his task which Jackson had interrupted, without uttering a single word.

The Captain hesitated again. A man needs his full share of courage to walk knowingly into a trap. Then he went forward resolutely, and opened the door. It closed quietly behind him.

He found himself in a small, dim room, sparsely furnished. He looked about him sharply; there appeared to be no one there. He noticed another door at the far end of the room. This he tried, but found it locked.

He waited for perhaps ten minutes, not knowing quite what action to take. A strong instinct warned him to make his escape, while he yet had the chance. He repressed the feeling sternly. He had come as far as this in order to confirm his suspicions as to the identity of the man who was at the head of this spy ring. He must not falter now — and, anyway, no doubt the tension was all part of their game.

At last, he heard the smith's hammer cease its metallic din. He waited, expectantly.

Behind him, his quick ears caught the slight creak of the door which led into the forge. He swung round quickly, his knife half drawn from its sheath.

A man stood there in the opening. Jackson knew him for one of the agents whom he had brought over from France to do the enemy's work on the Devon coast. He shut the door carefully behind him, and stood facing Jackson, a mocking smile on his mouth.

"Ah, *mon capitaine*. But it is enchanting to meet you again! We began to fear that you could not come," he said, in French.

"My apologies for the delay," replied Jackson, speaking in the same language with a faultless accent, "but I have been extremely occupied of late. As you doubtless know, I have other duties to perform."

"Ah, yes." The tones were silky. "We are very interested in these other duties of yours. They seem to take you into some strange places — and among some strange company, *mon capitaine* — if that is what you are."

"Smuggling, of course, does take a man into strange places, *c'est entendu*," answered Jackson, with a Gallic shrug, ignoring the final thrust.

"No doubt. But does it in general lead him into assignations with young ladies of quality?"

"My private life is my own concern," snapped Jackson.

"Assuredly," replied the other, smoothly. "But it is all too often a mistake, *mon capitaine*, to mix business with pleasure. In this instance, it has cost you dear."

"What do you mean?" asked Jackson, sharply.

"Why, simply this," said the other, speaking very deliberately, and watching his face, "that the young lady to whom you entrusted so much of your story has betrayed you."

"Betrayed me! Impossible! You lying dog —" His words broke off, as some instinct warned him of someone standing behind him. He turned sharply; but it was too late.

Even as he moved, the butt end of a pistol was brought down upon his head. For a moment he tottered, not completely succumbing to the blow.

"You did that extremely well, Poindé," approved a voice. "He was so engrossed in what you were saying, that he did not hear my approach."

The voice was familiar, though was not using the language which Captain Jackson was accustomed to hearing from that source. As he sank into unconsciousness, he carried with him the sound of that voice, and the image of that face towering over him, its expression one of savage triumph.

Both voice and face he recognized, in that brief moment before the darkness engulfed him.

They were those of Captain Masterman.

Chapter XVIII: Joanna's Trust is Misplaced

The next morning Miss Feniton was sitting quietly with Lady Lodge in the morning room. Kitty and Mr. Dorlais had been invited to spend the day with one of the Naval officers whose wife had obtained lodging in a cottage down by the quay. As the cottage was small, the officer concerned was unable to invite a larger party from Shalbeare House in return for Lady Feniton's hospitality to him: Guy Dorlais was an old friend of his, and as such, the natural person to be asked.

It was always a relief now to Joanna not to be required to be in company with Mr. Dorlais, so she could not feel sorry at their absence. Lady Lodge, however, had some lingering doubts as to the propriety of Kitty's being allowed to visit a family with whom her parents were not thoroughly acquainted, solely in the company of her affianced. She mentioned the matter hesitantly to Joanna.

"I do not think, ma'am," replied Joanna, "that you need be in any alarms. Lieutenant Ridge was here to dine the other evening, and you found him everything that was amiable."

"Yes, so I did — did I not?" asked Kitty's mother, pleased at this reflection. "Indeed, he was quite the gentleman — there was nothing that one could take the least exception to, don't you agree, Joanna? I dare say his wife will be just such another person — a ladylike, pleasing young woman, who will make a very proper chaperone for my girl."

"Just so," replied Joanna, soothingly. "You need have no further worry on that head."

She felt a pang of conscience as she said the words. She was far from being completely easy herself about her friend, but for very different reasons from those of Lady Lodge. Knowing what Guy Dorlais was, how could she be certain that Kitty would come to no harm in his company? True, he loved her: Joanna was confident of that much, at least. She could only hope that his affection was sufficiently strong for him not to involve Kitty in any of his misdeeds. But it was surely absurd to imagine that any harm could come to Kitty in a visit to a cottage in Tor Quay, only a short walk away from Shalbeare House? Her mind wavered this way and that, trying to rationalize a growing unease of spirit; but there was no point in allowing Lady Lodge to share her fears.

"Such a pity our party is quite broken up!" declared the dowager, turning her mind to a fresh topic of conversation. "First Captain and Miss Masterman being obliged to leave, and now Mr. Cholcombe, too, is gone! I declare, we shall be quite dull."

"You are scarcely flattering to those of us who are left," said Joanna, with a little smile.

"Oh, how you do take one up, my dear. You are such a quiz, you know! It all comes of being clever, I suppose, for I never had any talent for it — but you know well enough what I meant. It is pleasant to have a good company about one during these dreary winter months — and Mr. Cholcombe was so very lively always, was he not?"

"I suppose he was," replied Joanna. To her annoyance, a faint blush came to her cheek.

Lady Lodge gave her a penetrating look. "I rather fancy your Grandmama did not quite like it that he should leave so soon," she said, tentatively. "Even though he did ask if he might return in a few days' time, when his business should have been concluded."

"No, perhaps she didn't," answered Joanna, shortly.

She bent her head studiously over the magazine she was holding, and hoped that her companion might take the hint. Lady Lodge was evidently not to be put off, however, for she laid her own book aside, and leaned forward confidentially.

"My dear Joanna, I've no wish to be impertinent, but after all, I am a very old friend. I have wondered — did Mr. Cholcombe make you an offer? Augusta has said nothing but I know you would not object to tell me."

Joanna winced. She had been obliged to answer the same question from Lady Feniton, and been involved in quite a scene as a result. There could be no possible harm, though, in telling Lady Lodge how matters stood. She was not one to gossip about other people's concerns, however dearly she loved to pry into them. Besides, Joanna knew that she had a very real affection for this one-time schoolfellow of her daughter's.

"I dare say Grandmama may have wished to wait until my own intentions are clear. Yes, Mr. Cholcombe did speak — though only to me, not to my grandparents."

"He did? My dear, how very —" She stopped dead, seeing from Miss Feniton's face that congratulations were not in order. The significance of Joanna's first words gradually penetrated her mind. "Am I — am I right in thinking that you did not give him his answer on that occasion?"

Joanna nodded, unable to meet her questioner's eye.

"Well, to be sure," said Lady Lodge, doubtfully, "in my day, we were always taught never to assent the first time we were asked — it was considered immodest, you know, to do so! But I should have supposed that you, in particular, might have set such conventions aside. You are so very sensible, my dear — and it is always possible that a young man may not ask twice!"

"You are quite right, ma'am," said Joanna, vigorously. "And I have no use at all for such elegant nonsense! But in this instance, you see —" her voice tailed away — "I did not perfectly know my own mind."

"Not know your own mind? But surely it was all decided before ever Mr. Cholcombe arrived? I certainly understood —"

"I — oh, yes, it was agreed upon beforehand," said Joanna, in some confusion. "But it is one thing, you must know, ma'am, to contemplate such a serious step as matrimony, and quite another to take it. Especially when one's knowledge of the other party is so small as in this case."

"You find, perhaps, that Mr. Cholcombe is not to your — not quite what you had expected?"

Joanna hesitated.

"If there is any doubt in your mind at all, my dear," said Lady Lodge, in a burst of confidence, "do not allow yourself to be persuaded! Augusta and I have known each other for a good many years, so that it is impossible for me not to know that hers is a — somewhat forceful character. As you may realize, I myself am not a particularly courageous person: but I will undertake to lend you what support I can, should you decide that you cannot possibly accede to your grandparents' wishes in this matter."

At this kind speech, Miss Feniton's eyes filled with tears. She could not wholly account for such an unusual occurrence, and was trying to compose herself sufficiently to return an answer to her visitor's kindness, when Lady Feniton herself suddenly entered the room. It was evident that she had news to impart.

"What do you think?" she began. "Sir George has just met one of the officers on his morning stroll, and he has given him some astonishing news! A French spy has lately been arrested in Babbacombe village!"

Joanna started violently. Her first thought was of Guy Dorlais, and her second of Kitty. Lady Lodge gave a little shriek, and dropped the book she was holding.

"Augusta! So close to us! How dreadful!"

"There is no cause for alarm, Letitia," went on Lady Feniton, "for he has been removed to Totnes, and lodged in a cell at the Guildhall. He won't find it easy to break out of there, I fancy."

Lady Lodge continued to make incoherent murmurs of alarm, however, and at last Lady Feniton turned somewhat impatiently to her granddaughter, with the rest of the story.

"It happened yesterday," she said, evidently relishing her role of informant. "It seems that an information had been laid against this man, and it became known that he could be found in Babbacombe. Accordingly, some of the local Volunteers went to the village, and surprised him at the smithy. He was searched, and some highly incriminating documents were discovered concealed upon his person — treasonable matter, by what I can hear. I trust he will speedily meet the fate he deserves!"

"Babbacombe!" exclaimed Joanna, struck by a sudden thought. "Why, if you remember, ma'am, that was the word which was cut out of Grandpapa's book!"

Lady Feniton frowned. "Why, yes, so it was! But I don't see how it can signify: there can be no connection with this affair."

Lady Lodge emitted a frightened squeak of protest. "For Heaven's sake, Joanna, do not say that there are spies in this house! Oh, dear, we live in such troubling times, that one cannot feel safe anywhere!"

"Nonsense, Letitia!" reproved Lady Feniton, sharply. "You must know very well that Joanna could mean no such thing! Spies in Shalbeare House, indeed!"

"Besides, Lady Lodge, this man would be a Frenchman," pointed out Joanna, in a soothing tone. "All our servants are English, you know."

She was feeling easier herself now that she had been told that the man was arrested yesterday. At any rate, he could not be Mr. Dorlais.

"Nothing of the kind," interposed her grandmother. "That's what is so very shocking about the business. The man was English, so I am informed."

"English!" repeated Joanna, sharply. "Pray, ma'am, do you recollect what his name was? Or were you not told?"

Lady Feniton pondered for a moment, then looked a trifle annoyed. "La, the name has gone right out of my head, child! I fear my memory is not what it used to be. However, Sir George will no doubt be able to tell you, though I fail to see what it can possibly benefit you to know."

She continued to speak further on the subject, though there was little to add to what had already been told. Joanna was only half listening, and presently made some excuse to leave the room.

She quickly ran Sir George Lodge to earth in the library, where he and her grandfather were deep in the morning's newspapers. Sir Walter was never anxious to have the privacy of the library invaded by the female portion of his establishment, and this particular hour of day had always been considered sacrosanct. He looked up in faint annoyance as his granddaughter entered.

"I do not mean to keep you from your newspaper," she said, in apology. "I have just this minute heard from Grandmama of the spy who was taken yesterday in Babbacombe, and I thought that you might possibly be able to add something to her account."

"Oh, yes," said Sir George, who had risen reluctantly at her entrance. "A smart piece of work on someone's part, though no one quite seems to know who was responsible for laying the information."

"Was the man concerned — the spy, I mean — a local man?" asked Joanna.

"According to what I heard from Smythe, no one appears to know much about the fellow at all. It seems that he will have to answer charges on two accounts — there is evidence that he has been engaged in smuggling, as well as spying for the enemy. But his confederates are not known, nor his previous history — apart from his traitorous activities, that is to say."

Joanna's heart gave a painful leap during this speech: a dreadful conviction was growing in her.

"I suppose you did not think to ask — that is to say, you were not told his name?" she asked, trying hard to keep all expression out of her voice.

Her grandfather had long since returned to his newspaper, and Sir George still held his copy, glancing surreptitiously at it from time to time while he was answering Miss Feniton. He looked briefly down at it now as he spoke.

"His name, you say? Oh, if my recollection serves me it was — let me see — Jackson. Yes, Jackson, that's it."

She nodded, not trusting herself to speak, and turned towards the door as though all her interest in the subject had been satisfied. But the indefinable sympathy which exists between two people who hold each other in affection told Sir Walter, preoccupied as he was, that something was amiss with his granddaughter. He looked up, and exclaimed at sight of her bloodless face.

"Joanna! What's wrong, child? Do you not feel well?"

"I — it is nothing —"

She stumbled a little. Sir Walter went to her and put an arm about her waist, while Sir George thoughtfully pulled the bell rope to summon a servant.

Hardly knowing what happened, Joanna was guided to a chair. A short while later, Lady Feniton herself had, her granddaughter in charge, and was settling her into her bed.

"Upon my word," she chided, as she tucked the covers around Joanna, and dispatched a maid for a warm beverage, "you are as poor a creature as Letitia, it seems! All this talk of spies appears to have quite overset you! I had thought better of your stamina, my dear, I must confess. But there, young ladies are often in the megrims on the slightest excuse — you will grow out of it in time. Lie there quietly, my love, and I promise that no one shall come near you until it is time for dinner, when you may get up again, if you are recovered."

Joanna made no reply to this, nor did she attempt to resist or aid anything that was done for her. She meekly drank the hot milk when it arrived, and lay down upon her pillows as though composed for sleep. She watched her grandmother and the maid tiptoe from the room without any change in her set expression of vacant misery.

She must try to think. Captain Jackson had been taken at last, and she must find a way to free him. The idea of his not being saved sent a pain through her heart that seemed almost to stop her breathing. For a while, she could go no further than this — in her thoughts — that it might not be possible to save him, that he might have to pay the penalty.

She *must* think. There was a way, there must be a way, to bring him safely off, if only she could use her wits to find it. But her wits seemed no longer at her command: they ran hither and thither, following now one, now another, useless train of thought. There were — there must be — people in authority who knew of his real activities, who were aware that he was innocent of the charges made against him. Who were these people? He had never mentioned them to her, and she could not conjecture who they would be. Mr. Pitt, perhaps, she thought vaguely, and let her mind wander over the other members of the Government who might be supposed to make foreign intelligence their business. How was she to reach them? Through her grandfather, or Sir George? She could not convince herself that either gentleman would hear her tale with any credulity. At best, they would suppose her to have been imposed upon by this French agent. It would take time — perhaps a long time — to persuade them to act: and by then, it might be too late for Captain Jackson. Even if she could speedily win them over, there would be the inevitable delays attendant on any Governmental proceedings. Captain Jackson's life could not be allowed to rest on so doubtful a scheme as that: she must think of something more speedy, more certain of success.

She sat up in bed suddenly, her panic receding as it came to her what must be done. There was one man who could help her, one man to whom tedious and delaying explanations would not be necessary. That man was Captain Masterman: why had she not thought of him before?

She became quite calm again, the mists of confusion lifting from her mind as it fastened upon a definite course of action. She did not know for certain where Captain Masterman was to be found. Presumably he had returned to his home after accompanying his sister to the house where she was to make a visit: Masterman's home was in Totnes.

It might as well have been somewhere a thousand miles away, thought Joanna despairingly, for all her hope of reaching it. How was she to do so? To order the carriage was out of the question, even if her family had not supposed her to be ill. Lady Feniton would desire to be told exactly where she was going. It might be easier to sneak away unnoticed if she rode.

She turned this notion over in her mind. It was a long ride to Totnes, more than eight miles. Moreover, it was not usual for females to ride the high road alone. This was not the time to be thinking of the proprieties, but, from a practical viewpoint, would it be wise to go alone? There might be obstacles to be met with on the way which would be better overcome by two people. She would be obliged to bring herself to the notice of one or more of the stable hands before she could obtain her horse; might it not be wiser to allow one of them to accompany her, thus disarming suspicion? It was no unusual thing for Miss Feniton to ride in the morning, but to ride without a groom in attendance would cause comment.

In the end, she decided to take one of the lads with her. The next, more pressing problem to be solved, was how to reach the stables without being seen by anyone in the house.

While she was puzzling this out, she rose, and quietly began to dress again. She chose a dark red riding habit with frogged buttons, and pulled a hat tightly over her dark curls. The curtains had been drawn before the windows of her room. She left them as they were, and hurriedly arranged the bedclothes so that it might appear to a casual glance that the bed was still occupied. Then she opened the door of her bedchamber, and peeped cautiously out.

It was by this time after eleven, and the servants had long since finished the routine tasks which took them into the family part of the house. Sir George and her grandfather were still shut up together in the library: Lady Lodge and her hostess were in the morning room, comparing notes about the vagaries of their respective charges. There was no one about in the passage outside Joanna's room, or on the staircase.

She ran lightly down the stairs, turning to the right along the passage which led to the side door which she had used on the night when she had followed the unknown person to the temple. There would almost certainly be a servant within reach of the front door, but here she might be fortunate enough to escape unnoticed. She slipped like a shadow along the passage, heaving a sigh of relief as she saw that the door was unguarded.

She stepped quickly outside, feeling almost jubilant. Even the hint of rain which was in the air could not damp her spirits. She managed to reach the stables without meeting anyone, and calmly gave good morning to the two or three hands who were gathered there.

As she had expected, it caused no comment that she should wish to ride. Her horse was saddled and led out for her, and she was assisted to mount.

"Shall I go with you, ma'am?" asked the groom who had conducted the business.

She assented, and presently he followed her from the yard and down the drive which led to the rear entrance of the house.

She noticed that he showed some surprise when they eventually turned into the high road; but it was not until they had covered some miles that he ventured to ask if Miss Feniton meant to turn back now.

"No," she answered, shortly.

"Very good, ma'am," he said, woodenly. "I only wondered seeing it was close on luncheon, an' the rain beginnin' to set in "

"I must reach Totnes," replied Joanna, firmly.

"Totnes, ma'am?"

The man gaped at her for a moment, then rode on a little way behind her without saying anything more, but frowning a little.

By this time, the rain was falling steadily, and both of them were very wet. She appeared not to regard it, however, merely urging her horse to a better pace. The groom, thinking that his mistress must have taken leave of her senses, kept up with her.

They had been riding for some little time longer when they heard a carriage approaching. Rounding one of the frequent bends in the narrow road which they were travelling, they almost met it head on: it was a curricle, and being driven at breakneck speed.

Just in time, the driver reined in expertly. Miss Feniton swerved, and a collision was narrowly avoided. In a moment, the groom was at her side, and had put a hand upon her horse's rein, lending his strength to hers to control the animal. She was not looking at her mount, though, but at the driver of the curricle, who had also recognized Miss Feniton in that brief moment when they had almost collided.

"Miss Feniton! I trust you are not hurt, ma'am?"

She disclaimed hurriedly.

"What brings you abroad in such inclement weather?" he continued, almost without pause.

"That is soon told, sir," she said, briefly, "for I came to seek you."

"To seek me, madam? How can I serve you?" he asked, swinging himself down from his high perch. He looped his horses' reins, and came to stand at her side, gentling her mare to quieten the animal.

"Captain Masterman, it is a matter of the utmost urgency! When I tell you that it is connected with one whom we both know, and who is called —" She paused, and threw a glance at her groom, who was standing nearby, uncertain what to do. "Who is called Jackson," she finished, in a low tone. "You will not need me to say more, I am sure."

"No, indeed."

He stood still for a moment, while the rain fell softly about them, making a melancholy sound on the miry road. Then he roused himself, speaking with energy.

"But what am I thinking of? My vehicle affords some shelter from the rain — you must allow me to escort you to some place where we may discuss this matter in private. Do you think it best to retain your groom? Or shall we send him home with your horse?"

"I think it wisest to be rid of him," whispered Joanna. "I could not avoid bringing him with me, but what I have to say to you must not be overheard. I shall have to ask you to put me safely on my way home after our talk."

He nodded, and gave the order to the groom. The man glanced uncertainly at his mistress, but could not do other than obey. The thought entered Joanna's mind that she was flouting all propriety, and storing up trouble for herself later on with her grandmother; but she dismissed it instantly. She could think of nothing but the danger which threatened Jackson, and how best to help him.

She was soon seated under the partial shelter of the curricle's hood, pouring out her tale. Captain Masterman had drawn a travelling rug about her shoulders, and listened intently while she spoke. At the end of her recital, his face was grave.

"Yes," he said, slowly. "I feared this might happen at some time, and I fancy we both know who was responsible for it. The thing is, what's to be done now?"

"In God's name, think of something quickly!" cried Joanna. "I rely utterly upon you — if you fail me, he is lost indeed!"

"He means so much to you?" he asked, glancing at her with an expression she could not define.

"I — oh, what does it matter?" she stammered, desperately. "What can we *do*? There must be some way to save him — for he is innocent, after all!"

"That's true," he said, frowning, "but it may be difficult to convince anyone in authority of it, in time to accomplish anything to the purpose. The people who can prove his innocence are far enough way — in London. It will take too long to reach them."

"Then think of something else!" she pleaded, in her intensity laying a hand upon his arm, and looking into his face with trouble in her green-flecked eyes. "For the love of Heaven, think quickly!"

"If I should succeed in saving him," he asked, studying her lovely, disturbed face, "do you mean to marry him?"

"Marry?" She drew a deep breath, then shook her head violently. "Such a thing is impossible! We are poles apart! But I must save him, if I can."

"I think I see a way," he said, laying his hand briefly upon hers. "Listen — if I were to ride to Totnes at the head of a body of Volunteers, I believe I could persuade the gaoler there to hand his prisoner over to me."

"But that is capital!" she said, breathlessly. "What would you do then? Where could you take him that would be safe?"

"To a farm not far from here, where he would be amongst friends. There he could lie low, until we can get word to London of his plight, and orders can be sent to quash the charges."

"But in that case you must go at once to Totnes!" cried Joanna pulling at his arm. "We are heading in the wrong direction — did you realize?"

"I am taking you to the farm I mentioned, Miss Fenton we can reach it in half an hour. There I shall leave you; making all speed to Totnes and returning later with Jackson — if all goes well."

"So that I shall see him once more," said Joanna, in a low voice.

He assented, and whipped up the horses.

She fell silent, thinking of the man called Jackson. She was at peace for the first time that day since hearing of his arrest. Captain Masterman now had matters in hand, and he was a man to inspire confidence. She believed that he could save Jackson, if anyone could, and was content.

She was so deep in thought that she scarcely noticed which way they were going. Early on in their journey, they passed the groom trotting the two horses back to Shalbeare House; but she paid scant attention, although the groom looked curiously after the curricle which bore his mistress and one of the recent visitors to Shalbeare House.

It seemed scarcely any time before they pulled up before a farmhouse. Captain Masterman helped her down from her perch, and led her to the door. It opened before they could knock, and he ushered her quickly inside.

"*Diable*!" exclaimed the man who had admitted them. "A woman!"

"Keep a civil tongue in your head!" rasped the Captain: "The others — they have gone?"

"Yes, *mon capitaine*," replied the other, in a more subdued voice. "Some hours since — I am the only one left."

"Wait here," ordered Masterman, and tried to take Joanna's arm in order to lead her into a room on the left of the passage where they were standing.

But she shook him off: with blinding clarity, too late she saw what she had done. The conversation in French could mean only one thing.

Captain Masterman saw from her face that she knew. He motioned with one hand to the other man to depart. The fellow obeyed, vanishing silently.

"I am sorry, my dear lady," he said, with real regret in his voice. "I had to deceive you, for several reasons."

"*You* are that man for whom Jackson was searching!" she cried. "And I — fool that I was — thought you were helping him!"

He nodded. "I had to make you think so, that day when we both attempted to search Dorlais's room. Otherwise, you might possibly have guessed the truth. Besides, I had to find out if you knew the true identity of Jackson. I have known of your connection with him for some time now — in fact, ever since I read the letter which he left for you that night."

"So it was you who took the letter!"

"I apologize, but again you must see that it was necessary for me to know more of the man whom we had good reason to suspect was false to our cause."

"Thank Heaven I did not — still do not — know who he really is! I might have unwittingly betrayed him to you!"

"You tell me that there can be no question of a marriage between you," he said, ignoring this. "That encouraged me to hope."

"You?" She laughed, putting all the scorn at her command into her voice.

He coloured faintly. "Apart from my lack of fortune, I am your equal in birth, Miss Feniton."

Her grandfather's words flashed across his mind.

"The man is more important than the birth," she said. "What kind of man are you, Captain Masterman? A traitor, a spy, a hypocrite!"

"There are reasons for that," he said, hotly. "Reasons of which you can know nothing! You do not know what it is to try to keep up an appearance to the world on insufficient means, Miss Feniton — nor to watch another man pay court to the woman you love, knowing that you may never approach her, because of your lack of fortune! Money, Miss Feniton, money — that is the reason for all I do!"

Even at this moment, she could not entirely withhold a pang of that compassion which was so strong a part of her disposition.

"You are not to blame for the conventions of our present day society," she said, quietly. "That much I allow: but there are other ways in which your fortunes might have been mended, without injury to your honour: You have chosen the most ignoble way of all!"

"As much as anything else, it was for your sake," he said, between set teeth. He was now as pale as he had before been flushed.

"If that is true," she answered, seizing her opportunity, "and you have any genuine regard for me, then allow me to return home without delay. You can do nothing that will raise you more in my estimation."

He shook his head regretfully. "Impossible," he said, shortly. "You know too much now to be allowed to go free. I fear you must reconcile yourself to a long separation from your relatives, ma'am."

She felt the colour ebbing from her cheeks. "What do you mean to do?" she cried, sharply.

He laid his hand upon her arm. "Do not be alarmed, Miss Feniton. I could never harm you — but I must constrain you to remain here, until I have finished what I set out to do."

"What is that?" she gasped.

"There can be no harm now in your knowing. We have constructed a special kind of offensive weapon which will enable us to destroy the ships at present anchored in Torbay — and that without any risk of our being apprehended!"

She stared at him in horror.

"You do not believe me?" he asked, watching her pale face. "Yet you, too, were present when Colonel Kellaway — a pompous ass, that man! — spoke of Robert Fulton's inventions."

Light broke in upon her, as she recalled the conversation which had kept her in the drawing room of Teignton Manor that evening when she had wished to go downstairs to the man whom she had left in hiding.

"But — you cannot do it!" she gasped. "You cannot send so many of your own countrymen to their deaths!"

"In a new country, I may perhaps stand a better chance," he said, grimly. "I disclaim all allegiance to this one."

"You are mad!"

"Never more sane, I assure you, Miss Feniton. And now, I must go, for my plans will not wait to be put into execution. I shall be obliged to leave you here for some hours alone, but you will come to no harm, that I can promise. When I rejoin you, it will all be over, and we can begin a new life together, over the water."

By now, she had herself in control. There could be no benefit in behaving hysterically: she must be calm, and use her head.

"A new life?" she forced herself to ask.

He nodded, pleased to see her accepting matters so quietly.

"In France, I will have some status," he replied. "And I shall be paid well for my services. We may be married as soon as we reach Boulogne. Have no fears, Miss Feniton: I mean honourably by you. And now, if you will be so good as to go with me —"

She did not move.

"It is better that you should do as I ask," he reminded her. "I have no wish to lay violent hands upon you, but I am in haste, and cannot stay to parley. Now, will you go, ma'am?"

He offered her his arm. She declined it with a gesture of distaste, but moved forward in the direction which he indicated. There seemed nothing to be gained at present by opposing him. Once he had left the farm, she might possibly discover some way of escape. Perhaps the other man, the Frenchman, might be susceptible to a bribe? She had not brought a great deal of money with her, but she could promise more, and hold out strong hopes of a pardon if he turned King's evidence.

Masterman led the way along the passage and to the top of a winding, rickety stair. This terminated in another passage, out of which opened several doors. He chose one, opened it, and ushered her into the room beyond.

She looked around her, trying to master her panic by a scrupulous attention to detail. It was a tiny room, lit only by a small skylight in a sloping roof. There was a truckle bed along one wall, and a plain wooden chair set against another. The floor was bare of covering, and dusty.

"I must apologize for your accommodation," said Masterman. "It's the best I can devise at such short notice. You need not fear to be intruded upon by the man downstairs: I myself will lock the door, and keep the key. I will leave you a lantern, for it will shortly be dark, and I know you will not care to be without a light."

"I beg of you, change your mind, and let me go!" she said, making one last desperate appeal. "You cannot do this thing — you have been bred a gentleman, after all — release me!"

"No," he answered, harshly. "Haven't I told you already that I cannot afford to be a gentleman?"

"'The man's the gold, for a' that'," she quoted, sadly.

He made no answer, not fully understanding her words. He went outside for a moment, returning with a lantern ready lit.

"Farewell, for the present, Miss Feniton. I will be with you again before long," he said, in parting.

She made no answer. He shut the door upon her, and she heard the key turning inexorably in the lock.

Chapter XIX: The Passing of a Traitor

It was mid-afternoon when a small fishing vessel sailed into the bay, and anchored off Tor Quay. Word was passed down to the cabin on the Admiral's ship. The man who had been waiting there in expectation of this event went on deck to take a look for himself. He studied the new arrival carefully through a telescope.

"It could be what we're looking for," he murmured, thoughtfully. "Yes, I believe it is."

He handed the telescope to the man who stood at his side.

"Watch her carefully," he ordered. "In particular, keep your eye on that mast. If they should lower it, call me at once."

"Aye, aye, sir."

He went below again. A number of the officers were gathered round the table in the cabin, the Admiral at their head. They turned round as Jackson entered, their faces expectant.

"Well, Captain?" said the Admiral.

Captain Jackson nodded. "I think this is it, sir. We had a signal when she started on her voyage, and the time would be right."

The Admiral turned to the others: "Well, gentlemen, I imagine we're to play a waiting game once more — God knows we've lately had plenty of practice! What happens now, Captain?"

"We're watching for her to lower the mast, sir. Once that's done, she can submerge totally in a very few minutes. It's my belief that they'll wait until the light's beginning to fail —

which should be in less than an hour from now — when she would be invisible from a distance of more than a few yards."

The Admiral grunted. "Give it half an hour, then, and we'll go on deck, gentlemen," he said. "Not going to miss the only bit of action that's offered in God knows how long, are we?"

There was general agreement at this: the watchdogs of the Channel were straining at the leash.

Desultory conversations sprang up, in the way that occurs at such moments. The man Jackson was soon the centre of a group of officers, answering their animated queries. There was laughter, and an underlying sense of excitement well controlled.

Time passed. The Admiral glanced at his watch. He nodded, and there was a general movement towards the door of the cabin.

As they came up on deck, the light of the short day was wavering: already the houses on the quayside were dark shadows relieved here and there by pin points of illumination. The waters of the bay slapped monotonously against the sides of the ship as the men on her deck peered through the gathering twilight towards the shore.

The fishing boat was a smudge of grey against the darker background of the buildings surrounding the quay.

"I believe she's moving," said someone, in a low voice.

For a moment, the rest could not be sure. The point was debated, as though it were only of academic interest.

"Yes, she is!" exclaimed another man. He clamped his telescope firmly to his eye. "And they're lowering the mast," he added, after a moment.

There was a faint stir at this, and all conversation abruptly ceased. Everyone's eyes were fixed upon the small vessel.

The grey smudge changed shape, and appeared to shrink; gradually, it merged into a shadowy sea. In a few moments, there was nothing to be seen where once it had stood.

"They've submerged! How long d'you reckon it'll take them to come close enough to be caught in the nets?"

"It's a slow business," demurred Jackson. "They have to crank the thing along by hand. Say twenty minutes — half an hour, possibly."

"It'll be dark by then," said another, in a disappointed tone. "We shan't be able to see anything."

"I fancy you will," replied Jackson, grimly.

They waited silently after that, while the shadows gathered thickly about them. The sky darkened, the lights sprang up more abundantly on shore. The silence was tense with uncertainty. Would the submarine, after all, manage to evade the nets? They had no other means of defence against this insidious enemy: this was not a warfare they understood. To remain inactive while the foe crept steadily upon them, unseen, unheard — this was a new experience for them, something uncanny.

And then their straining eyes caught a glimpse of a vague object bobbing up and down in the sea, not far from where the ships were anchored: it might almost have been the head of a strange whale-like creature. For a moment only they caught a glimpse of it; then suddenly a flash of searing flame leapt across the dark waters, and the quiet of the bay was shattered by the reverberating thunder of an explosion. The man of war rocked violently in the resultant swell. The whale's head disappeared in trails of blue-streaked, ruddy fire.

"The nets!" exclaimed the Admiral, triumphantly. "B'God, we've caught them! So much for the new weapon of war!"

Jackson lowered his telescope. "The day may come when it will present a very real menace," he said, soberly. "But for the moment, they have failed."

When the explosion was heard in Shalbeare House, a great commotion ensued. Servants screamed and ran hither and thither, declaring that the French had come at last. Lady Lodge, who had been comfortably dozing before the fire in the withdrawing room, awoke and went immediately into strong hysterics. Her hostess, after a useless attempt to rouse her from this state, finally left her in the more experienced hands of Sir George Lodge, and hurried to the library. There she found her husband placidly reading, as though nothing out of the way had occurred.

"Feniton, how can you be so calm?" she asked, in the exasperation of a strong spirit who will not admit to fear. "Did you not hear that dreadful noise just now? The servants are saying that the invasion has begun, and it may very well be true! How can you sit there, as though nothing was toward?"

He rose, and put an arm about her. "My dear, I am too old for heroics. If the invasion has indeed started, we must simply await the event. But I do not credit it."

"Then what can it be?" asked his wife, impressed in spite of herself by his calmness and rational mode of speech. "Here is Letitia going into hysterics in the withdrawing room, and all the servants nearly off their heads with fright!"

"I do not need to tell you, my dear, that your friend is a silly woman, even though she may be a sweet person," he said. "I believe that the noise may have been occasioned by nothing more serious than the military manoeuvres of our Naval friends in the Bay. Why look for a dramatic explanation, until one has exhausted the rational possibilities?"

"I wish you will go and tell the household so! The housekeeper can do nothing with the females of the staff; and the men are rushing about, erecting barricades, and seizing upon anything which could conceivably be pressed into use as a weapon!"

"I'll have a word with them," he promised, pulling the bellrope. "One of them can go down to the quay, and take a message to young Dorlais. He will be able to tell us what is really afoot."

Lady Feniton let fall a startled exclamation.

"Joanna!" She made quickly for the door. "If she should have been roused from sleep by this uproar, she must be very nearly frightened out of her wits, poor child! I must go to her at once!"

She went hurriedly upstairs, and threw open Joanna's door.

All was quiet within. The curtains were still drawn across the windows from which the light had long since faded, and the room was dim. A casual glance at the bed gave the impression that its occupant was still there. She paused uncertainly for a moment, then trod softly across the room, reluctant to disturb the sleeper.

"Joanna, child —"

She broke off, as she saw that the bed was empty. An exclamation escaped her, and she rushed from the room to seize a candle from a stand in the passage. She returned, and held the light so that it fell across the room. She at once noticed her granddaughter's discarded nightgown lying over a chair; but there was no sign of the former occupant of the room having been there recently. Evidently Joanna must be up and dressed, and in some other part of the house.

She went in search of Miss Feniton's maid, knowing that at the present time it was useless to ring the bell with any hope of its summons being answered. She found the girl at last in tearful colloquy with some of the other abigails.

"Where is your mistress, Betty?"

Betty stammered incoherently that she had not set eyes on madam since helping her into bed after she was taken poorly earlier in the day.

"There need be no more alarms!" said Lady Feniton, peremptorily. "The master is of the opinion that the noise was nothing but that of Naval exercises in the Bay. You must go about your concerns as usual. Search the house for Miss Feniton, and inform me at once where she is to be found."

This speech had the desired effect upon the abigails. They hastened to do her ladyship's bidding. Lady Feniton returned to the drawing room, where her friend Letitia still lay stretched upon the sofa, looking like a ghost. Sir George was holding a vinaigrette to her nose, while a trembling maid pressed a wet cloth upon her brow.

"You may be easy, Letitia!" she said with something of a snap. "Feniton considers that we need have no alarms, and attributes the explosion to Naval exercises. He has sent for more certain information to Mr. Dorlais, and hopes to have your daughter back here with him presently."

"He is very likely right," said Sir George, his brow clearing. "Good old Walter, he never misses a trick, for all that he deceives one into thinking that he takes no heed!"

This was evidently a new view of her husband to Lady Feniton, for she was quiet during the next few minutes, while she weighed it.

"Perhaps so," she said, at last. "However, I am uneasy about Joanna at present. She has left her room, and I cannot discover where she has gone."

"Oh, she will most likely be rushing around the house, trying if she can to restore order," replied Sir George, carelessly. "Come, Letty, come, my love! That's a good girl, now!"

Lady Lodge gave a faint moan, and sat up weakly.

"Where am I? What has happened?" She clutched her husband's arm convulsively. "For the love of Heaven, George, don't leave me!"

"I tell you it's all right, Letitia," repeated Lady Feniton, while Sir George hastily disclaimed all intention of deserting his wife in her present state. "Feniton is confident that it is *not* an invasion! We shall —"

At that moment, voices were heard outside the room, and in walked Sir Walter, with Kitty and Guy Dorlais at his heels. Kitty rushed across to her mother, and enfolded Lady Lodge in a warm embrace.

"Oh, Mama! Were you very frightened? Poor darling! I was too, only you see, I had Guy with me."

She looked up at Mr. Dorlais, and it was evident that any trouble which had existed between the lovers was now resolved.

Sir Walter closed the door, and drew Sir George to one side.

"I have the explanation," he said. "Dorlais brought it. Prepare yourself for a shock, though."

In a few low words, he told his visitor the tale. "But I think," he concluded, "that for the time being, we will keep to my original explanation as far as the rest of the household is concerned. The truth will probably have to come out later — that can't be helped: but your wife, for one, is in no state to learn of this at present."

Sir George could not but be in wholehearted agreement with this point of view.

"Masterman, though!" he said, in bewilderment. "It's — it's incredible!"

"A bitter man," said Sir Walter, shaking his head. "Such people are seldom to be relied upon for sound judgment."

At this point there came a knock on the door, and one of the maids who had been deputed to search for Miss Feniton entered.

"If you please, y'r la'ship," she said to her mistress, "we've looked all over for Miss Joanna, an' she bain't in the house."

"Nonsense! Where else could she be?" asked Lady Feniton, sharply. "Are you sure that you've looked everywhere?"

The maid replied timidly in the affirmative, and after a few moments' more questioning, she was dismissed.

"Where on earth can she be?" asked Lady Feniton, turning to Kitty, who had now taken over her father's duties with the vinaigrette, and in consequence had not had much leisure for attending to the conversation with the abigail. "She was taken unwell earlier in the day, not long after you had left, and I took her up to her room to lie down. I thought she must be sleeping, and did not trouble to disturb her until this explosion occurred, when I found her gone from her room — and now they say she is nowhere in the house!"

"Unwell? Jo?" asked Kitty, much struck by this. "That is unlike her."

"Oh, well, anyone may have the headache," said Lady Feniton, defensively. "Although I did think myself at the time that she seemed unduly put about over a stupid scare. I expect you heard that a spy was apprehended yesterday in Babbacombe village?"

"Why, yes," said Kitty, quickly. "In fact, Guy —" She broke off, and flashed a guilty look at Dorlais.

"Well, I guessed you might have done," continued Lady Feniton. "Only Joanna seemed to be vastly disturbed by the news — which is not in her character, you must agree. I have not brought her up to have a fit of the vapours just when there is a crisis! I have no patience with such ways of going on!"

She glanced meaningly at Lady Lodge as she spoke. Feeling the weight of her hostess's disapproval, the invalid sat upright with a groan, and declared in martyred tones that she begged no one should concern themselves with her sufferings.

"I shall do very well presently," she continued, in failing accents. "To be sure, I am not strong, but then one must not think only of oneself —"

Before anyone could reply to this brave speech, or, indeed, before it could be completed, the door burst open, and Mr. Cholcombe strode into the room.

His entrance created a minor sensation. Lady Feniton and the gentlemen stared, Kitty exclaimed, and Lady Lodge gave another faint moan, and motioned for her smelling-bottle.

"I am aware," said Cholcombe, quickly, after the first brief bow of greeting, "of all that is going on — I had the news as I passed through the village. I must make my apologies for arriving at such an ill-chosen time."

"Algernon Cholcombe!" muttered Lady Feniton, under her breath. "It wanted only this to make the day complete!"

He had turned to inquire after Lady Lodge's health, although it must have been obvious from the evidence that he could not hope for a favourable reply.

"Poor Mama is quite overset!" explained Kitty. "When she heard that dreadful explosion, she was convinced that the French had landed in Devon, and really, one cannot blame her, you know."

"I think it very foolish and wrong of the Admiral," complained Lady Lodge, feebly, "to permit his men to shatter the peace of a small fishing village with — with things of that nature. And merely for the sake of putting in a little practice, too! Sir George, I wish you will have a question asked in the House concerning it — such things should not be!"

"But where is Miss Feniton?" asked Cholcombe, having paid his respects to everyone else in the room. "I trust the affair has not alarmed her unduly?"

"That is just what I have been trying to ascertain," said Lady Feniton, with a frown. "Joanna was not feeling well earlier in the day, and I sent her back to bed. When the explosion occurred I went at once to see if it had alarmed her, and found her gone."

"Gone?" asked Cholcombe, knitting his brows.

"Gone from her room," explained Lady Feniton. "Naturally, I supposed that she would be found in some part of the house, and sent her maid to look for her. Now I am told that she is nowhere to be found at all."

"Perhaps Betty is mistaken, ma'am," said Kitty, handing the vinaigrette to her mother, who was now looking much more herself. "I will go and look for her myself."

"I don't believe there can be any mistake," replied Lady Feniton, with a worried air. "Betty was aided in her search by several of the other girls. Besides, Joanna would surely not remain in a room alone at such a time as this? Unless she had suddenly become much worse, and swooned, or some such thing."

Lady Lodge shuddered. "Who could blame her, if she has?"

"I have never known Joanna to swoon in her life!" exclaimed her hostess, with a snap. "She has not been reared in such fainthearted style, I assure you!"

"Has anyone searched out of doors?" asked Mr. Cholcombe, still frowning. "Miss Feniton may have decided to take a stroll."

"It seems unlikely, in view of all the circumstances —" began Lady Feniton, who by now was beginning to feel more than concerned. "However, no one has actually been outside to look."

"Then I will do so now. Do you care to assist me, Dorlais? Between us, we should soon cover the likely ground — for I imagine that Miss Feniton would not venture far from the house in this weather?"

Both Lady Feniton and Kitty were in agreement with this.

"But there is no saying for certain," finished Lady Feniton. "She was acting so very strangely today. What exactly occurred in the library, Feniton? She seemed perfectly as usual when she left the room where we were sitting, did she not, Letitia?"

Lady Lodge nodded, without any real conviction. She found nothing extraordinary in the fact that the mere mention of spies being in the neighbourhood had been enough to prostrate Joanna. She wondered now how she herself had managed to keep up her spirits so well in face of the dreadful tidings.

"She asked a question or two concerning the affair," answered Sir Walter, with troubled eyes. "In particular, she wished to know if we were acquainted with the man's name."

"Were you able to answer her, sir?" asked Dorlais, sharply.

"As a matter of fact, I was," replied Sir George. "Smythe gave me a very full account of the business — told me the fellow's name was Jackson. No one seemed to know anything of him, though."

"So you passed that information on to her?"

"Naturally."

267

"And after that," asked Cholcombe, breaking in upon this conversation, "Miss Feniton became unwell?"

Sir Walter directed a sharp glance at the speaker. For a moment, their eyes met in silent understanding. Then Cholcombe strode to the door.

"Are you coming, Dorlais?" he asked.

Guy Dorlais nodded, and started to follow him.

"I think we will go, too, eh, George?" said Sir Walter. "Four of us will cover the ground more quickly than two, even if you and I are not quite so active as these youngsters."

They all quitted the room without more ado.

"Upon my word," said Lady Feniton, roundly, "there is something going on here which I do not at all comprehend!"

Lady Lodge acquiesced weakly, and reached once more for the vinaigrette.

Chapter XX: The True Identity of Captain Jackson

For some time after Captain Masterman had left, Joanna could hear no sound in the farmhouse. She had examined her prison carefully for any chance of escape, but had reluctantly been obliged to admit defeat. The small skylight was wedged so that it would not open; and even if she should succeed in breaking the glass without injury to herself, the resultant aperture would not be sufficiently large for her to pass through. She next had the notion of trying to pick the lock with a hairpin, only to give up in disgust when she had ruined all the available tools for this purpose. She searched in vain for a piece of wire which might be stronger, but at last had to give up the idea altogether, and sat down upon the hard chair which had been provided for her use with feelings very near to despair.

It was imperative that she should escape from here without delay. There was no one other than herself who could save the man Jackson from whatever punishment would fall to the lot of a supposed traitor. What a fool she had been, she thought bitterly, to allow herself to be deluded by Captain Masterman! But her suspicions of Dorlais had been so strong that she had not kept a sufficiently open mind. When Captain Masterman had questioned her about Jackson, she had jumped to the conclusion that he was Jackson's helper: considering his words now, in the light of what she knew, she saw that he had, in reality, been as uncertain as she was of Jackson's identity. He had quickly taken advantage of her false assumption, like the accomplished deceiver he must be. Well, there was no help now for that. Her folly had brought her into her present predicament, and she must trust that her wits could help her out of it again.

As far as she could see, there remained only one possibility; she must somehow persuade the man downstairs to help her. She searched feverishly among her belongings, and brought to light the total sum of money of which she was at present possessed. She shook her head sadly. No one would be likely to think much of a bribe of twenty-three shillings. Still, she could promise more; and there was always the inducement of a possible mitigation of punishment if he should help her. At any rate, it was her only hope, and she must try it.

She listened intently. She could hear no one moving about downstairs, but she was certain that the man was still somewhere about the place. If he had left the house, she would certainly have heard the shutting of the outer door, as she had done when Masterman had departed.

"Hullo, there!"

Her voice rang clearly through the door, as she stood with her lips to the keyhole, and shouted. The sound shattered the silence of the house, making it seem even more profound as the echoes of her call died away.

She waited a moment, hoping for a reply. None came: she called again, several times in rapid succession. At length, she heard heavy footsteps ascending the stairs.

"Why is it that you make so much din?" growled a voice, in French. "It can avail you nothing! Close your trap!"

"Will you not help me?" pleaded Joanna, in the same tongue. "I have not much money about me at present, but I can promise you —"

"*Blague*! Is it likely that I shall trust your promises, woman? Anyway, I am getting to the devil out of this place, and at once, *je vous assure*! In a little while, you'll have only the rats to keep you company, which is fitting!"

Joanna attempted to expostulate with him, but it was soon evident that she was wasting her breath. Even veiled threats as to what might befall him when it was realized that she was missing, and a search should be made, failed to produce any effect.

"It is partly for that reason that I go now. If I am not here, I cannot be blamed! Me, I am nothing; it's our chief whom they require, and those about him when they find him will come in for their fair share of trouble. I do not mean to be one of them, that is all!"

So saying, he stamped downstairs again, and she heard his footsteps receding into the lower half of the house. Barely five minutes later, she heard the slam of a door. Miss Feniton was now quite alone in Randall's Farm.

For the first time, a blind panic seized her. She caught hold of the doorknob and rattled it frantically, at the same time calling for help in wild accents. She paused at last, breathless and ashamed, her black hair tumbling in disorder over her shoulders. Her throat ached and her hands were sore. This was the worst kind of folly, she told herself sternly. She could accomplish nothing but her own discomfort by such exhibitions of emotion. All the same, she felt better for her outburst, and more able to think rationally.

Now that the Frenchman had left, gone, too, was her last hope of escape. Her eye measured once more the width of the skylight, now a dark square in the cobweb hung rafters. She shook her head; it would not serve. She stooped to turn up the lamp, and looked thoughtfully at the rickety chair on which she had been sitting.

Obviously, she could not hope to break down the door with such a feeble battering ram, but might it not have other uses? She felt a quickening of excitement in her blood, as she weighed the possibility of an attack upon Masterman with the chair as a weapon. It seemed most probable that he would return here as he had gone, alone; and there was now no one in the farmhouse to come to his aid. If she were to stand to one side of the door, with the chair at the ready, with good fortune she might have a fair chance of stunning him as he entered the room. She would be waiting for him, hearing his footstep upon the stair: but he would be all unprepared, and surprise might carry the day for her. Once she had won free of the farm, she could —

Her thoughts halted abruptly, and the flood of elation ebbed away from her, leaving her drained and empty. Even if she succeeded in escaping from the farm, how could she save Jackson, now that there was no one to aid her?

She sank back on to the chair, her tears not far away. Once more she was back at the point where she had started when she had left Shalbeare House. Meeting Captain Masterman had then seemed to be the end of her problems, for she had thought he was Jackson's friend. Now that she was acting alone, it was impossible that she could achieve anything — and there was no time to reach those who could. It appeared, therefore, that Captain Jackson was doomed.

The realization was like an acute physical pain. Now that she would see him no more, she knew at last how much he had come to mean to her. She tried to recall his face, but could not. She had never seen him for more than a few moments in a really good light, and the features escaped her memory. Only a general impression of his expression remained, too vague for her aching heart to be satisfied. She could recall his voice, though, perfectly: the tones that were not quite those of a gentleman, with their rich, warm Devon strain. In her imagination, she could hear them now, repeating the words in which he had told her of his love.

"Can you be content with a marriage of convenience?" he had asked her. "You, who have the spirit for high adventure?"

She had answered him coldly then, she remembered with a pang, telling him that she was well content to wed Mr. Cholcombe, for whom she felt nothing but a warm friendship. If he could have asked the same question now, at this very minute, she thought, with the warm tears stinging her eyes, she would have made a very different reply.

But it was too late. She would never see him again — he could never know —

She bowed her head in her hands, and for once the indomitable Miss Feniton gave way to tears.

Presently, she roused herself, and found her handkerchief. She dried her eyes, and, rising from the chair, paced slowly about the room. She determined to keep to her original plan of campaign. Even if she could do nothing else, she might at least escape from Captain Masterman to the safety of her own home. Then she would tell the whole story to her grandfather, beg him to do something for Jackson, even if it should prove to be useless. At least he might be able to obtain permission for her to visit the prisoner in Totnes gaol. Then she could say to Jackson all the things which now burned within her: he should not go to his death without knowing that she loved him.

This brave resolution made her almost resigned to her present lot. She sat down again, and allowed her fancy to conjure up the scenes in which Jackson had played a part. Who was he, this man who had literally stumbled into her life, and obstinately refused to back out of it again? Was he indeed no more than he seemed, an adventurer, a soldier of fortune? Or was he —

She jumped violently. In the distance, the echoes of an explosion rent the silence. She leaped from her chair, her heart beating furiously. A dreadful fear assailed her — the fear that she had just heard the death signal of those men on board the ships at present anchored in Torbay. For a long time she stood rigid, waiting for any other sound which might come.

The silence was oppressive, bearing down upon her: only her thoughts were noisy, brawling inside her head. She felt for a moment that she must go mad if she could not know for certain what had happened.

She must calm herself. She lifted her trembling hands from her sides, and regarded them scornfully. She had work for them to do presently, when Masterman should return, fresh from his triumph.

And then a childish memory came to her aid. Whenever she had been in low spirits as a child, she had been wont to sing. At that period of her life, there had been occasions when she had been shut in her bedchamber as a punishment for some minor misdemeanour: she used to sing softly to herself to keep at bay her fears of loneliness and silence. She had told Mr. Cholcombe that she had no accomplishments, but it was only partly true. She was possessed of a clear singing voice that could give pleasure to others, as well as herself. Now she warmed the chill silence of the lonely house with the notes of an English folk tune, a simple air which might have been heard in many a Devon lane on a summer day.

How long she sat there singing, she could never afterwards be sure. She thought presently that she had heard a shout from downstairs, and stopped for a moment to listen. It was not repeated, and she concluded that she had imagined it. She continued with her song.

But all at once, there was the unmistakable sound of footsteps mounting the stairs.

She broke off, and, seizing the chair, trod quietly across the room. Her heart was beating as though it would choke her, but she did not falter in her purpose. She took up her station by the door, raised the chair above her head, and waited, eyes fixed upon the doorknob, for the exact moment when she must act.

The knob was seized, and rattled violently. She trembled, but stood firm.

Then she heard her name being called by two voices in unison. For a moment, she was too agitated to recognize them, although it flashed across her mind that neither spoke in the tones of Masterman.

"Are you in there, Miss Feniton? Can you unfasten the door?"

It was the voice of Guy Dorlais which she recognized first. She knew now that she had nothing to fear from him, and quickly answered.

"No, I can't: Captain Masterman locked it, and has taken the key."

"Stand back then: we'll have it open in a jiffy. Keep right away, though."

She obeyed, retreating to the far side of the room, and taking her chair with her. There followed the sound of some heavy object being dashed against the door. It held for a moment, shivered, then splintered down the middle. The gap was quickly widened, and two men thrust their way through, panting a little with their efforts. One of them was Guy

Dorlais; she saw with surprise that the other was Mr. Cholcombe.

"Are you all right, Miss Feniton?" he asked, his voice sharp with anxiety as he came towards her. "They have done you no harm?"

She shook her head. "No, I am quite safe. What has happened? How did you find me? And where is — Captain Masterman? I thought — I thought that you were he —"

"You poor child!" he said, quickly. "You must have had a wretched time of it." He turned to Dorlais. "Will you see if there is any kind of conveyance in the stable suitable for Miss Feniton?" he asked. "We must get her home without any delay."

Dorlais glanced at Joanna, smiled reassuringly, and left the room in obedience to Cholcombe's request.

"Sit down, Miss Feniton," urged Cholcombe, gently. "You will not have long to wait now."

But she shook her head. "No, I am tired of sitting. Tell me, sir, how did you find me? And is there any likelihood that — that Captain Masterman will come upon us?"

"You have no longer anything to fear from that source," he answered, gravely. "Masterman is dead."

"Dead?" She caught her breath. "What — what happened?"

"You knew, of course," he said, looking at her keenly, "that he was a traitor to his country?"

"Yes." She breathed the word.

"He tried to destroy the British ships which are lying in Torbay — and perished in the attempt," he said, briefly.

"I — I see. Then the explosion I heard — I feared at first that he had succeeded — it was dreadful —"

He shook his head. "No, thank God! But he and his confederates paid the penalty."

She shivered. "He was a wicked man, I know, and yet — oh, his poor sister!"

"Yes, it is hard on her, I agree. But I fancy there was little sympathy between them — indeed, Miss Masterman seemed to me to go in fear of her brother. I imagine the affair will not be noised abroad for security reasons, so she may at least escape unpleasant repercussions of that nature."

"How do you know all this?" asked Joanna, curiously.

"I returned to Shalbeare House at the height of the alarm," he said. "The attempt had just been made, and the resultant explosion had thrown everyone into a state of confusion. Dorlais had been with one of the Naval officers all day — but, of course, you know that — and he had the whole story at first hand. He brought it to the house, where you had been missed, and together we set out to find you."

"Mr. Cholcombe," she said, only half attending to his speech, "there is something I must implore you to do for me!"

"Anything in the world, ma'am I assure you," he promised, soberly.

"I had thought that my grandfather would be the only one who could help, but now I see that you may be much better able to serve me," she said, rapidly. "You may think my story strange, but I must ask you to believe what I say without asking for too many explanations. I have not time for them, you see! There is a man, at present lodged in Totnes gaol — his name is Jackson —"

"I know of him," he interrupted, quickly.

"You do?" She was too surprised for a moment to continue.

He nodded. "What have you to say concerning Jackson, Miss Feniton?"

"I must find someone with the authority to set him free! He is innocent of the charges made against him — Masterman was responsible —"

"Why should you concern yourself with this man?" he asked, eyeing her keenly.

She coloured faintly. "Surely no one would willingly connive at an injustice —"

"Is that your only reason for wishing to help him?"

"Oh, do not waste time in asking questions, I implore you!" she begged, placing a hand upon his arm, and looking up into his face with pleading eyes. "While we are talking, he may be —" She could not finish, but bowed her head, fighting against the tears.

He put his fingers under her chin, tilting her face upwards, so that she was obliged to meet his eyes.

"Tell me, Miss Feniton," he said, quietly, "the real reason why you wish me to do what I can to save Jackson."

She met his glance firmly, in spite of her trembling lips.

"You may as well know," she answered, as coherently as she was able. "Indeed, you will have to know at some time. I — I love him."

He was silent for several minutes.

"Then it is only right that I should set your mind at rest," he said, at last. "Jackson is no longer in gaol, ma'am: he is as safe as you — or I. He was released yesterday by Colonel Kellaway, who is in command of the security arrangements in this area, as no doubt you already know."

"And he is really free?" she asked, overwhelmed by this information. "There are no charges to be brought against him?"

"Thanks to the splendid work of Dorlais and a handful of other British agents, it was possible to make arrangements to bring him safely off."

"Dorlais?" she repeated, at a loss.

He nodded. "I am aware that you once suspected him of being a spy for the French. Quite the reverse is true — he has all the time been acting as Jackson's right hand man. It seems that they were at school together."

"He — he has?" She paused, as all kinds of recollections came back to her. "Then that is why he did not join the Volunteers — nor seem to wish to hasten his marriage to Kitty! Of course, he would have been obliged to let her into the secret, and I suppose that would never have answered! And Kitty thought —"

"I know. However, they have reached an understanding at last. There will be no more need now for Dorlais to postpone his wedding day, for Masterman is finished, and the rest of the spies in this area apprehended. The work of the local British agents is at an end."

"Then Captain Jackson, too —"

"He will return to the Navy, where he belongs. Before long, we shall see some action at sea, you may depend."

"He really is a Naval man, then?"

He nodded, watching her face. So far, the welcome news of Jackson's release had suspended her critical faculties. Now they were once more coming into play, as he could read from her expression.

"Tell me," she asked, with a puzzled frown, "how do you come to know all this?"

He shrugged, smiling. "Jackson is a very old friend of mine — I might almost say, my oldest friend."

"He is?" she said, eagerly. "Then perhaps you can tell me where I may find him?"

It was at this moment that Guy Dorlais returned.

"I've come across a gig in the stable," he said, abruptly. "It's a poor thing, but I fancy it will get us there. The Volunteers have turned up, by the way: they've taken that fellow who was here with Miss Feniton, so there goes the last of that little lot!" He turned to Joanna. "Are you ready to go, ma'am?"

"I — if you could wait but a moment —" she stammered, turning appealing eyes upon Cholcombe.

"Dorlais, my good chap," said Cholcombe, airily, "run away and amuse yourself for ten minutes or so. Feed the hens — commune with nature — show the Militiaman your beard — there must be something you can find to do!"

"Oh, very well," replied Guy, with a grin. "But don't be too long about it, for it's deuced cold in this place, and the Fenitons will be getting into a state, remember!"

He vanished promptly, leaving them alone. Joanna repeated her question impatiently.

"Certainly I can," he answered, gravely. "Whether or not I will, is quite another matter."

"What — what do you mean?" she asked, uncertainly.

"What will you do, if I tell you?" he countered.

"Go to him, of course." There was no hesitation in her reply.

"A man you do not know — a one-time smuggler?"

"I do not care," replied Joanna, defiantly, "what he may be! I only know that life without him is impossible for me!"

It seemed to her that his eyes lit up: but this might have been a trick of the flickering light afforded by the lantern.

"You would do much better to marry me, after all," he said. "I can offer you the things you most require in marriage."

"I thought so, once," she said, wistfully, "but now I know better. I do not wish to give you pain, Mr. Cholcombe, but I could never wed you."

"Could you not, m'dear?"

She started violently at the sound of the rich, Devon burr.

He took her hands, and drew her towards him, so that her face was looking up into his. His grey eyes danced.

"Do you still ask me where Captain Jackson is?"

She stared at him incredulously, catching her breath. "You? But —"

"Do you mind very much if you are to wed a prosperous nobleman instead of an indigent smuggler?" he asked. "It is not near so romantic, I realize, but then you have always been known for a sensible young lady!"

"You are absurd!" she said, with a tremulous smile. "But — I don't altogether understand — how is it that I never recognized you before? Although," she added, thoughtfully, "I must say that I did notice a certain familiarity, which I put down to my recollections of you as a child."

"I like to think," he said, with a quizzical look, "that it was my art which succeeded in carrying off the deception. However, I will admit — grudgingly, mark you! — that I was aided by two facts. One is that you were not looking in me for a resemblance to Jackson: the other, that whenever you met that man, it was at night, or in a poor light, so that you never saw him properly. For the rest, you know that acting is in my blood."

"Your hair, though!" she exclaimed, looking at his well-groomed brown head. "It was black — that much I am certain of!"

"Yes." There was a tinge of regret in his voice. "Did you prefer it so? I am sorry, if such should be the case: it was my only concession to the art of disguise. I wore a wig. But I suppose I could always dye my hair, if you have taken it in dislike —"

"No." She put up her hand, and gently stroked his head. "I like it as it is."

Quickly he caught the hand, and carried it to his lips.

"Dare I hope that you will like me, also, as I am?"

She laughed softly, blushing a little. "But I do not know which is the real you, sir — Captain Jackson or Mr. Cholcombe."

"It is something between the two — but both, Miss Feniton, love you very dearly. You must recollect that we have both told you so on other occasions."

His arms were about her, now, and he was bending his face towards hers. For a moment, she held back a little.

"Why 'Jackson'?" she asked, irrepressibly curious.

"My father's name is John," he answered, tightening his hold.

"And what is yours? I mean to say — what did your mother call you?"

"Peter," he murmured, a trifle impatiently. "But, dearest, can't we come into port?"

"If that is one of your Naval expressions for this," she said, smiling: and she gave him her lips.

It was some time later that Guy Dorlais once more entered the room, this time treading heavily upstairs, and first knocking on the door.

"Are you ready yet?" he asked, smiling broadly. "Have you unveiled the mystery of your two identities? But I scarcely need ask?"

"My dear chap," drawled Cholcombe, squeezing Joanna's hand, "I've now assumed a third. You see before you Miss Feniton's intended husband."

A NOTE TO THE READER

It's wonderful to see my mother's books available again and being enjoyed by what must surely be a new audience from that which read them when they were first published. My brother and I can well remember our mum, Alice, writing away on her novels in the room we called the library at home when we were teenagers. She generally laid aside her pen — there were no computers in those days, of course — when we returned from school but we knew she had used our absence during the day to polish off a few chapters.

One of the things I well remember from those days is the care that she took in ensuring the historical accuracy of the background of her books. I am sure many of you have read novels where you are drawn out of the story by inaccuracies in historical facts, details of costume or other anachronisms. I suppose it would be impossible to claim that there are no such errors in our mother's books; what is undoubted is that she took great care to check matters.

The result was, and is, that the books still have an appeal to a modern audience, for authenticity is appreciated by most readers, even if subconsciously. The periods in which they set vary: the earliest is *The Georgian Rake*, which must be around the middle of the 18th century; and some are true Regency romances. But Mum was not content with just a love story; there is always an element of mystery in her books. Indeed, this came to the fore in her later writings, which are historical detective novels.

There's a great deal more I could say about her writings but it would be merely repeating what you can read on her website at **www.alicechetwyndley.co.uk**. To outward appearances, our mother was an average housewife of the time — for it was usual enough for women to remain at home in those days — but she possessed a powerful imagination that enabled her to dream up stories that appealed to many readers at the time — and still do, thanks to their recent republication.

If you have enjoyed her novels, we would be very grateful if you could leave a review on **Amazon** or **Goodreads** so that others may also be tempted to lose themselves in their pages.

Richard Ley, 2018.

Sapere Books is an exciting new publisher of brilliant fiction and popular history.

To find out more about our latest releases and our monthly bargain books visit our website:
saperebooks.com

55146212R00170

Made in the USA
Middletown, DE
15 July 2019